WOLFEHOUND
A Medieval Romance

By Kathryn Le Veque

Part of the de Wolfe Pack
Generations Series

© Copyright 2025 by Kathryn Le Veque Novels, Inc.
Trade Paperback Edition

Text by Kathryn Le Veque
Cover by Kim Killion

Reproduction of any kind except where it pertains to short quotes in relation to advertising or promotion is strictly prohibited.

All Rights Reserved.

The characters and events portrayed in this book are fictitious. Any similarity to real persons, living or dead, is purely coincidental and not intended by the author.

AI Statement: No AI or ghostwriting was used in the creation of this story, or any story, authored by Kathryn Le Veque. All text, structure, content, ideas, and concept are 100% human generated solely by the author. It is prohibited to use this material, or any copyrighted material, for AI engine training.

KATHRYN LE VEQUE
NOVELS

WWW.KATHRYNLEVEQUE.COM

ARE YOU SIGNED UP FOR KATHRYN'S BLOG?

You'll get the latest news and information on exclusive giveaways, exclusive excerpts, coming releases, sales, free books, cover reveals and more.

Kathryn's blog followers get it all first. No spam, no junk.

Get the latest info from the reigning Queen of English Medieval Romance!

Sign Up Here

kathrynleveque.com

De Wolfe Motto: *Fortis in arduis*

Strength in times of trouble

The Mother of All Secrets is blown wide open in this epic Medieval Romance set in the lush, family-driven world of de Wolfe Pack.

Secret identities, age-gap romance, and alpha males abound!

Twenty years ago, during the reign of Edward I, the last Welsh prince was sentenced to death. All that remained of his bloodlines was his infant daughter, who was arrested and sent to live at Sempringham Priory. She was to become a nun, never to procreate, because should she ever marry and rise to power, she could bring about the collapse of England.

Gwenllian was the infant's name.

The English knight who took charge of her as an infant had a duty to fulfill until William de Wolfe, Earl of Warenton, intervened. Not only did the infant never make it to Sempringham Priory, but an entirely new life was planned for her. Not out of compassion, but out of vengeance. A decoy child was sent to Sempringham in her place. No one knew of this deception but a select few, but many years later, a deathbed confession thrust the secret out into the open.

Now, the king's men are looking for the infant once known as the Princess of Ghosts and Dragons, only she's not an infant any longer. She's a beautiful young woman from a fine Northern English family who has no idea of her true identity.

Cambria de Royans, as she's known, is about to marry Liam Herringthorpe, one of the knights who helped spirit her to safety. The pair are madly in love and looking forward to a life together. But Liam is also part of the de Wolfe family, the most powerful in Northern England, and when they realize Gwenllian's secret is out, that puts the King of England on a direct collision course for the House of de Wolfe.

A cataclysmic clash is on the horizon as it's de Wolfe versus the Crown of England in this sweeping Medieval saga.

Author's Note

Wow, did this story have a long, long road!

I don't want to give too much of it away right from the start, but suffice it to say that our heroine is a real historical figure—now with her future reimagined as part of the de Wolfe Pack. The heroine had such a tragic life (in real life) so I'm giving her something wonderful in this tale. I'll explain more in the Afterword (don't skip ahead!! Lol), but suffice it to say that she deserved better than the English gave her.

So, I'm going to give it to her.

We start off with a knight who was a secondary character in my novel *Nighthawk*. You'll see why once the story gets going. But what's so great about the kickoff of this tale is that we get to see William de Wolfe, Paris de Norville, and Kieran Hage once more in action. That's what I love about the de Wolfe Pack series! These great knights never really die. They come back, again and again, and we get to revisit with them like old friends. What a joy it was to write about them once more.

However…

This book starts off six months after the prologue in *A Wolfe Among Dragons*, the story of James de Wolfe, William's fourth son. This is the aftermath of the ambush in the prologue and the death of James, so it is an extremely difficult time for William and the de Wolfe Pack gang. William is a little darker these days, grief-stricken over James, so be prepared for that. It's not all light and fun right now. It's also only a couple of years since Kieran lost his son, Christian, in the Holy Land, so there is grief all around at this point.

Something I want to mention about this book, and my other books, is that oftentimes I'll refer to a king or queen or a famous historical figure by the name we know them as in modern times purely for ease for the reader, so you know who I'm talking about. For example, Richard the Lionheart and Edward I (Longshanks) were referred to by their nicknames during their respective reigns. However, Edward the Black Prince was not known as the "Black Prince" during his lifetime. That came later. I always try to keep the title or nicknames as historically accurate as possible.

I can't get too much more into the author's note without giving things away, so suffice it to say that this one is very political, very involved, and, at times, brutal. Old school Le Veque at its finest. There is an Afterword that explains a lot of things, but don't skip ahead. Read this one straight through and then the Afterword will make so much more sense.

The usual pronunciation guide:

Welsh is one of the most difficult, most beautifully lyrical languages ever. For native English speakers, it's a tough one because there are sounds in their language that English doesn't have.

Gwenllian—whenever you see the double L in the Welsh language, it's a sound that we don't have in the English language. The best way I can describe the sound is to put the tip of your tongue behind your front teeth and blow out either side of your tongue from the roof of your mouth. Any double L in Welsh is going to have that sound—go to YouTube and you can see the way they pronounce it. It's almost a hissing sound.

Cymraeg—pronounced like come-rye-g. And roll the "r"! That's what the Welsh call Wales and also the Welsh people.

Cambria—CAME-bree-uh

Bran—Brawn. It means "raven."

Cai—like "eye" with a hard "c" in front of it. Cai like kite (with no "t")!

And with that—on to the story, but let me once again remind you that there is nothing so complicated as England's politics when the Plantagenets were in power. And this story proves it!

Hugs,

Kathryn

PROLOGUE

Year of Our Lord 1302
Hyssington Castle, England
Demesne of the Lords of the Trilaterals, House of de Lara

THE OLD LORD was dying.

Colm de Lara had seen more than his fair share of adventure and battle over the course of his lifetime, things that often hardened men or weakened them, spiritually and mentally, things that could crush a lesser man. Colm had seen everything with the House of de Royans, battling the Welsh on the marches with great armies or the Scots or any number of enemies that allies had deemed he should fight. Allies like William de Wolfe, Earl of Warenton, and inarguably the greatest knight of his generation. He'd served de Royans and de Wolfe well until his father died a few years ago and, as the heir to the Trilateral castles of de Lara, he'd come back to the marches.

But that tenure as Lord of the Trilaterals was about to end. No sooner had he returned than a cancer had infected him. He'd suffered with it for years, but now it was overwhelming his body. He didn't have much time left. And, God help him, it couldn't end before he told what he knew.

A man sat next to his bed, smelling of wine and urine. It radiated from the filthy woolen robes he wore, clothing that proclaimed his place as a prince of the church, but robes that in reality hid the darkness of the man's soul. He called himself St. Zosimus and he came from St. Mary's church, the largest church in the nearby village of *Y Trallwng* and the source of strange and unsavory happenings for years. Women vanishing and orphans being subject to heavy labor were among some of the sins. There was even rumor that St. Zosimus had convinced a wealthy local man to give all of his money to the church in the hopes of saving his immortal soul. Then he'd spent the money on wine and food. For himself.

In short, St. Zosimus was not a man to be trusted.

And that was what Colm was counting on.

"You were saying, my lord?" St. Zosimus said after ingesting a large drink of wine from his third cup of the evening. "You have something important on your mind. That is clear. Please tell me what you have summoned me for so that you may die in a state of grace. Surely a knight with your reputation requires much forgiveness for your actions over the years."

That was true. Colm tried to speak but his throat was dry, so he ended up coughing that hacking cough that was caused by a cancer that was eating him alive. St. Zosimus could have given him a sip of wine to ease his throat, but he didn't. He didn't have that kind of compassion. Therefore, Colm coughed until the blood started coming up again, and only then was he able to stop somewhat.

Ragged breathing filled the air of the stale, dim chamber.

"I must confess something," he finally rasped. "I must speak of it because I cannot die with it on my conscience. Others will. They will die with this burden upon their breast, but I will not. I once promised I would not speak of it, but I must break that vow because I fear that God will ask me why I would not confess such a thing. I was there. It *is* my secret to tell."

Secret. That word had St. Zosimus leaning just a little closer to the bed, his angular features illuminated by the light from the bedside taper. He knew that de Lara had served with an ally of a very powerful house, one that was entrenched in the politics of England. In fact, neither England nor the Crown moved these days without the assistance of the House of de Wolfe. There were so many of them now that they'd all but taken over the north of England. Allied to the Houses of de Velt, de Royans, and de Reyne, other major northerner warlords, the four major families locked up England from Leeds to the Scots border.

Secret.

St. Zosimus was very curious what that might be.

"Speak, my lord," he said. "I am listening. God is listening."

He threw "God" into the conversation to force Colm into spilling whatever juicy mysteries he might be harboring, the unspoken threat of a deity that demanded truth from all. Perhaps the man had cheated a neighbor. Perhaps he'd even cheated a brother or his father. Or perhaps he'd stolen something that he now wanted absolution for. Whatever it was, St. Zosimus was ready.

Somewhere in the night, a dog howled. The mournful cry wafted in through the lancet window, contributing to the sense of disquiet in the chamber. Colm was breathing heavily, his eyes closed, and he let out a sound that led St. Zosimus to believe he was about to speak. But it was a false start. Colm remained silent for several long seconds before he finally began his confession.

"You must swear before God that you shall not repeat what I am about to tell you," he rasped.

St. Zosimus nodded. "Of course," he said, picking up his wine cup and taking another long drink. "Speak, my son. It will do you good."

Colm's eyes remained closed. "You know that I once served an ally of the Earl of Warenton," he said. "The first one, I mean. William de Wolfe himself."

"I know."

Colm's eyes slowly rolled open. "He was a great man," he said. "I do not criticize him, but long ago, he did something… something that could be considered treason."

That perked up St. Zosimus considerably. "Did he?" he said. "But I am certain that a man like de Wolfe has done many things in his lifetime that could be considered questionable. Men like William de Wolfe do not achieve legendary status unless they have."

"Even concealing something that could possibly bring about the destruction of England?"

St. Zosimus wasn't quite following him. "What could that possibly be?" he said. "De Wolfe was always in support of the Crown. Henry depended on him. That is well known. Surely Edward did as well, since de Wolfe served two kings."

"Edward did not know what de Wolfe had done," Colm muttered. "But I do. I was there."

"Where?"

"*There*," Colm said, raising his voice as much as he could. "I was there when de Wolfe betrayed Edward. Mayhap Warenton has been dead for a few years, but this secret did not die with him. It continues to live, and I fear it will come back to cause chaos."

"What could this terrible secret be?"

"Swear to me again that you will not tell."

"Of course I will not tell. What is it?"

Colm turned his head stiffly until his gaze fell on the priest who was pouring himself another cup of wine even as they spoke. He did not believe him when he said he would not repeat what he was about to be told, and that was how Colm would get the word out. It wouldn't be *him* divulging the news, but an idiot priest who couldn't, or wouldn't, keep his mouth shut.

That was how they would know.

And Colm could go to his grave in peace.

"How much do you know about the battles in Wales between Dafydd and Llywelyn against Henry and Edward?" he finally asked.

St. Zosimus shrugged. "As much as anyone, I suppose," he said. "Edward finally defeated them and eventually proclaimed his own son the Prince of Wales."

"He did," Colm said, his eyes taking on a distant cast. "I was involved in those wars, you know. I was there when Dafydd was killed and when his brother, Llywelyn ap Gruffudd, was ambushed whilst running from the English. If anyone tells you that he died an honorable death, it is not true. He tried to escape and the English caught him in a forest. They hacked the man to death. There is nothing noble about that."

St. Zosimus thought he knew what Colm meant. "And you need absolution from killing the last Prince of Wales?"

"Nay," Colm said, remembering that time not so long ago. A mere twenty years ago. But it seemed like a lifetime. "I did not participate in the death of Llywelyn. It was what came after that concerned me."

"What came after?"

Colm cleared his throat quietly and closed his eyes. "Llywelyn was married to Eleanor de Montfort," he muttered. "Were you aware of that? The man was married to a woman of royal blood. Simon de Montfort was her father, and the daughter of King John, also Eleanor, was her mother."

St. Zosimus took another long drink of wine, growing impatient waiting for this great confession to come forth. "I know the lineage," he said. "I've served here on the Welsh marches for thirty years, my lord. I am well aware of those you speak of."

Colm's eye peeped open, seeing that he was close to losing the man's interest because he hadn't gotten to the point yet. But there was a reason for that. He needed to make the situation clear before he hit the man with what would undoubtedly be a shocking statement.

St. Zosimus was simply going to have to be patient.

"Llywelyn and Eleanor had a child," he said. "I do not suppose you heard that, too."

St. Zosimus nodded. "A girl," he said. "She was taken to Sempringham Priory. Of course I know that. Everyone knows that. The child is the last of her line, of Welsh royal blood, but she also carries English royal blood. She is the daughter of a prince and the granddaughter of a king and now she is consigned to Sempringham. It is a Gilbertine priory, as I am a Gilbertine as well. I know all of this, my lord, so what did you wish to tell me about it?"

Colm had suffered enough of the man's dismissive attitude. All he'd done was drink his wine, belch, and wait for him to die. Then he would return to his church and plot his next scheme to gain more money and power. With a last surge of strength, Colm suddenly sat up.

"Listen to me, you idiot," he said, feeling breathless from his sudden movement. "I am trying to tell you something so important that it will shake England to her very foundation if it is discovered, but I tell you this for a reason, and it is not to give you a history lesson."

St. Zosimus was sitting straight in his chair at this point, startled by de Lara's abrupt show of strength. He was a big man and quite intimidating when he wanted to be, so St. Zosimus held up his hands to ease him.

"Be at peace, my lord," he said. "Lie back down. You needn't concern yourself so. I am listening, I swear it."

Colm let the man push him back down on the bed, mostly because he was too weak to fight him. Sitting up had taken nearly everything out of him. Sweating, and red in the face, he pushed St. Zosimus' hands away.

"The infant girl, Gwenllian, was in the guardianship of Dafydd when she was captured," he said. "I was part of that action. Dafydd was taken away and executed, but the infant and Dafydd's daughters were taken to Lincolnshire, to remote abbeys, so they could live out the rest of their lives as nuns, guarded by the Gilbertines. But that was not the original plan."

St. Zosimus' eyebrows lifted. "It wasn't?'

Colm shook his head weakly. "Nay," he said. "The Earl of Warenton was part of that action, too. He was in command of it. Now, understand that I was not privy to many of the reasons behind this action. I was a mere knight. I simply followed orders. But something was brewing with de Wolfe, something dark. I heard that his orders were to kill the Welsh offspring, but he could not bring himself to do it. The man has too much honor to murder small children, so he sent them to the priories instead. Edward was not entirely pleased with that action, but in the end, he agreed to it. It would look less than generous of him should a king be responsible for the deaths of small girls. De Wolfe understood that, but it took Edward time to realize that de Wolfe did him a favor. When he understood what de Wolfe had done for him, he took credit for sparing their lives. Or so I was told."

St. Zosimus was listening closely at this point. "And that is what you wish to confess?" he said. "That Warenton is responsible for sparing the children of Llywelyn and Dafydd?"

"Nay," Colm said, his gaze unnaturally focused on the priest. "That is not it. You do realize that if those girls had married and produced sons, the wars in Wales would never end. They would go on forever."

"I would imagine so."

"And if Gwenllian had married and borne sons, she would be the living link between Wales and England," Colm said, his voice quieting. "The woman has more royal blood in her than Edward does or Henry did. She is as rare as a unicorn. She could lay claim to both thrones, as could her sons. It would throw England and Wales into decades, if not centuries, of turmoil. There would be *no* peace."

St. Zosimus nodded. "Then it was wise of Warenton to send her to a priory," he said. "I wonder if she is aware of who she truly is?"

Colm was silent for a moment. "She is not," he said. "And she is not at Sempringham. This I do know because I saw it with my own eyes."

St. Zosimus' brow furrowed. "Was she moved? I'd not heard."

"She never made it there."

Now, St. Zosimus was starting to catch on that there was something far more to this conversation. Now, a hint of something had come into the light, and he looked at Colm most curiously.

"How do you know this?" he asked.

Colm sighed heavily. "Because I was told, by my lord, that the decision had been made to take the child to Sempringham," he muttered. "But instead of being taken to the priory, she was given over to my lord to live as his daughter while another infant was sent to Sempringham. Gwenllian of Wales is alive and well and living as an Englishwoman. She was a beautiful baby, with black hair and blue eyes, and she grew into a beautiful woman. She is twenty years of age this year and, more than likely, already married. And *if* she is married, then children are a distinct possibility. Sons, that is. Sons that, in turn, may be told of their royal blood and encouraged to embrace their unique royal heritage."

St. Zosimus' mouth was hanging open. "Did de Wolfe know about this?"

"Of course he did," Colm said. "He arranged all of it."

That was even more shocking. "He did this knowing what the cost would be if she bred sons?"

"Sons that will fight Edward and Edward's progeny for their birthright," Colm said. "We all knew what the cost would be."

St. Zosimus sat in his chair, dumbfounded by what he was hearing. "The betrayal you spoke of," he mumbled as the revelation hit him. "De Wolfe knows of the Welsh princess's identity and living arrangements. He knows what she can do to the Crown."

Colm could see that the man was understanding the situation. "De Wolfe was loyal to Henry, but Edward is another matter," he said. "Edward was always threatened by the power William de Wolfe held in the north, in particular because he had voiced his sympathy for Simon de Montfort, and the relationship between the two was tenuous at best. Worse still, de Wolfe and his family have no use for Edward's son, who will be king someday. Scott de Wolfe is the current Earl of Warenton and he is very much his father's son. He was part of the decision, too, and I'm sure the House of de Wolfe would like nothing better than for Gwenllian's sons to rebel against Edward and his offspring, destroying their reign. Mayhap they are even hoping for it."

"You think de Wolfe planned this from the start?"

"I believe he did."

"He wants a civil war?"

"I do not know his reasons other than he and Edward have never gotten on," Colm said. "I only know what happened, not the motivation behind it. But it is my guess that de Wolfe wants a stable England and does not feel that Edward, nor his son, can provide that. If I am being truthful, then I will say that I agree with him. Edward is a ruthless man and his son is a fool. Mayhap de Wolfe was hoping that nature would simply take its course."

"That may be entirely possible."

"But there is something else."

"What?"

"Two of William de Wolfe's children married into the nobility of Wales," Colm said. "He has several half-Welsh grandchildren. Once, Henry nearly destroyed his youngest daughter's husband, the hereditary King of Anglesey. It is quite possible that this is all revenge for that attempt."

St. Zosimus shook his head in disbelief. "Do you think that is true?"

"As I said, I do not know the reasons behind the action,"

Colm said. "But anything is possible."

St. Zosimus sighed heavily as he pondered it all. "My God," he muttered. "It seems fantastic."

"I know, but I assure you that it is all true."

"I believe you," St. Zosimus said. "But Gwenllian… She is living as a nobleman's daughter?"

"She is."

"Will you tell me where?"

Colm didn't say anything right away. The only sound in the chamber was of the gently crackling hearth, with the silence growing progressively more oppressive. St. Zosimus waited with increasing impatience, needing to know what more there was to this tale. And it was a wild tale at that.

"My lord?" he finally said.

Colm's eyes were closed, indicative of his exhaustion now that he'd spent so much energy speaking on something he'd never told anyone. Not even his wife. But he was one of the very few who knew the truth. He couldn't take it to his grave because if he did and Gwenllian did indeed produce sons, the deaths of those killed in the battles that would undoubtedly come would be on him because he knew everything.

And he hadn't told the truth.

He'd been wrestling with the dilemma for twenty years.

"Only a handful of us knew the truth," he finally said. "Four or five at the most. Three that knew are dead."

"Who is that?"

"William de Wolfe and his closest friends, Paris de Norville, Lord Bowmont, and Sir Kieran Hage," Colm murmured. His strength was fading. "I was the fourth. There is a fifth."

"Who is that?"

"The knight who raised Gwenllian as his daughter."

"What is his name?"

There was the question. Colm had told St. Zosimus his deepest secret for a reason, but now that the priest had asked for the last key piece of information, he was oddly hesitant. He didn't know why. Perhaps it was because he'd be betraying a man he'd once served with, a man he considered a friend. He knew St. Zosimus was going to take this revelation straight to the king. He knew that meant his friend, the one who had raised Gwenllian as his own, would be in a good deal of trouble. But the reality was that the man had done something he should not have, knowing full well the consequences.

Betray his friend?

Or betray his country?

Colm made the only choice he could.

He told him.

PART ONE
THE PRINCESS OF GHOSTS AND DRAGONS

CHAPTER ONE

Nanhysglain, Wales
Year of Our Lord 1282
Twenty Years Earlier

"WHAT DO YOU intend to do with the children?"

The question came from Paris de Norville, captain of the army from Northwood Castle in Northumberland. He had directed it to the Earl of Warenton, William de Wolfe, his best friend in the entire world but also a man who had been fueled by rage and hatred for the past six months. Ever since losing one of his sons, James, in an ambush in Llandeilo, Wales, William had been inconsolable.

The man was bent on revenge.

Unfortunately, that revenge was now focused on several small children, all offspring of the Welsh princes who had taken his son from him. The final battle had ended today, in the wilds of Wales, after chasing the scattered Welsh princes. It had no longer been a battle, but a hunt. One prince had been killed and now… now, they had the last one, cornered in a bog and brought to his knees. This was it, the moment they'd been waiting for.

The end.

But it was not without complications.

Complications that included the next generation of Welsh royalty, children of the princes. One infant, two small girls, and two small boys, all of them under the guardianship of Dafydd ap Gruffudd, brother of Llywelyn the Last, a man who had been betrayed and then executed by a gang of enraged Englishmen. Though William hadn't been part of the betrayal, he hadn't done anything to stop it. War was vicious by nature. But he had been responsible for the capture of the brother of the man responsible for his son's death. Dafydd, and the children, were all his prisoners now.

God help them.

And it was something that concerned Paris greatly. He'd known William since they had been children, closer than brothers, and he'd never seen the man so… bitter. That was the best way to describe it. And William's sons—Scott, Troy, and Patrick, his eldest boys—spoke in hushed whispers about their father these days. They'd never seen him like this, not ever. William de Wolfe was, if nothing else, a man who was consummately in control, always fair, always rational, and always with a heart of compassion.

But James' death had done something to him.

It had changed him.

Perhaps the man in the most distress about it was Sir Kieran Hage, William's second-in-command and, next to Paris, his closest friend. He was a man of great wisdom, of reason, and even he couldn't seem to snap William out of his darkness. There had been so much fighting going on with the Welsh this year, something that had only been a duty to the men sworn to

King Edward of England, until James' demise at Llandeilo in the summer.

Now, the battle had become personal.

"William," Kieran said, reining his horse alongside William's steed as the man overlooked the English encampment where they had the prisoners gathered. "Did you hear the question? I am rather curious, too. What are your intentions with the children of Dafydd and Llywelyn?"

William's gaze was hard as he watched the activity in the encampment. It was sunset at the end of a very long day and the colors brought on by the clouds looked like blood. It was ominous. It had been a productive day, perhaps even a satisfying one, but William gave no indication that he was either pleased or satisfied by it.

There was no indication of anything he was feeling.

He was stone-faced, as usual.

"I heard the question," he finally said. Then he looked over his shoulder where his sons were positioned, exhausted knights on horseback after a long day. "Scott? You will bring Dafydd to me when I settle in my tent. I want to talk to the man."

Scott de Wolfe, William's eldest, glanced at his two brothers before answering. "It has been a very long day, Papa," he said. "Dafydd is badly injured and being tended to. Whatever you have to say to him can wait until the morrow."

William's piercing gaze lingered on his son. "Are you disobeying my order?"

"Nay, my lord," Scott said, being formal with his father because the man was so volatile these days. "I am simply stating a fact. The prisoner is injured and needs tending or he will not survive. If your questions cannot wait until the morrow, then I will bring you to him. But he should not be moved."

William didn't argue with him, but it was clear that he wasn't pleased. When there was no retort to his statement, Scott silently motioned to his brothers and to Paris and Kieran's sons to vacate the area and go about their duties. In fact, that would be preferable to waiting on pins and needles for William to make more demands that no one wanted to carry out.

Scott, Troy, and Patrick headed off along with Hector and Apollo de Norville, all of them returning to the army to settle the men and complete their assigned tasks. Only Kevin Hage remained. Kieran's middle son was very much like his father, a man of great emotion and counsel. He had spent a good amount of time with his father and Paris and William, mostly supporting his father's efforts to supply William with advice and comfort. Kieran wasn't well these days and hadn't been for a while, yet he'd come to Wales with William because he would never let William fight without him, so Kevin's presence was more to support his father than anything else.

He'd promised his mother he would.

Kieran knew this, and he could see Kevin out of the corner of his eye. He eventually turned to his son, silently ordering him away, but Kevin wouldn't move. Not when William was in a mood like this. This moment wasn't merely a culmination of almost a year in battle for William, but also for Kevin because James had been his best friend. He, too, had watched him die in a horrific ambush, so Kevin was as invested in this moment as much as William was.

Invested in the end of something that had brought them such grief.

"Uncle William?" Kevin said, directing his horse in front of William's. "May I bring you some wine? Anything at all? It has been a long day. Surely you are weary."

William turned to look at the young knight. He looked a good deal like his father, but William saw beyond that. He saw Kevin and James together, friends since birth. They were essentially the same age. He saw two young boys stealing sweets, or stealing the potent wine that their fathers drank. They had been around six years of age at the time and Kieran had caught them, forcing them to drink the entire bottle, which had made them ragingly drunk. As a result, Kevin had tried to fist-fight his father while James had run out into the bailey, challenged every soldier to a sword battle, and then vomited all over the dirt before passing out in his own filth.

They never stole wine again.

The memory had always made William smile.

In fact, that was why he had a faint smile on his lips at the moment. He could still see those two little hooligans, running around making mischief.

It was such a grand memory.

"I do not know who was worse," he finally said. "You or James."

Kevin cocked his head curiously. "Who was the worst at what?"

"At troublemaking," William said, his voice sounding dull. "Out of all of my sons, James was the most… lively. Scott was mature before his time, Troy was the brooder, Patrick was simply big and frightening, and Eddie and Tommy were young and foolish. But then there was James. He was the naughty one. Paired with you, it was like taking a spark to kindling. You were both positively incandescent when you came together."

That statement had Kieran and Paris smiling, too. They well remembered the duo of James and Kevin and their tomfoolery.

Kevin smiled broadly.

"It was all his fault," he said. "I was a perfect angel, but James forced me to do his bidding."

That actually brought a chuckle from William. "Untrue," he said. "I seem to remember that you were responsible for the wine adventure, when the two of you stole wine and your father forced you to drink it all. That was *you*, Kevin."

Kevin laughed softly. "I will admit that I had a hand in it," he said. "But it was James who put straw or kindling in the boots of unsuspecting soldiers and lit it on fire. He did it to old Ranulf once and nearly burned the man's foot off."

The memory had Paris and Kieran snorting because Ranulf Kluge was an old knight they'd all served with years ago. He had been rough and gruff, but for some reason, the young de Wolfe, Hage, and de Norville sons targeted him for many of their antics. It had been great fun to see who could make the old knight roar with anger.

"Ranulf caught him and tied him to a post in the stable overnight," William said. "You have no idea how difficult it was for me to keep his mother from not only freeing her son, but from unleashing on Ranulf."

"You had to lock her in the chamber," Paris muttered, a twinkle in his eye. "I know this because you tossed the key out of the window to me."

"And she tried to climb out of that window," William reminded him, and they both laughed. "I had to sit on her most of the night. She was livid."

"'Tis never good to rile the Scots," Paris said, referring to the fact that William's wife, Jordan, was Scottish. "Their blood boils over faster than most."

"True," William said. "We would all know that, considering we all married women with Scots blood. But Kieran has it the worst—I might have been able to keep Jordan contained, but Jemma was the one who released James around midnight and then went on the hunt for Ranulf."

Kieran closed his eyes, shaking his head in resignation at his unruly wife's behavior. "You should have never told her what happened, Kevin," he said to his son. "That was your fault. You told your mother what Ranulf did to James and she made it her personal mission to release the lad. After she did so, she then lay in wait for Ranulf, and when he was unaware, she knocked him down and whacked the soles of his feet with a club. The man could not walk for a week."

Kevin chuckled at the memory of his mother, the most aggressive Scot in the bunch, going after a knight twice her size to punish him for what he'd done to her cousin's son. In fact, Paris' wife, Caladora, was also a cousin to Jordan and Jemma. That made them all kin and very protective of one another. Even one another's children. That was how Jemma saw it, anyway, when she beat the soles of Ranulf's feet and broke one of his toes in the process. But that was the beauty of family—they defended one another. They grieved for one another.

But no one grieved more deeply than a parent.

As much as the memory of James and Kevin was a much-needed moment of relief among the churning waters of war and mourning, it also brought about its own pain. When the laughter died down, the pain returned, and every time William looked at Kevin, he could feel grief anew because the man reminded him so much of James. It brought joy and it brought pain.

Grief was ironic that way.

"Jemma was the only person who ever got the upper hand with Ranulf," William said after a moment, his good mood fading. "But in answer to your question, Kevin, I *am* weary. Very weary. But you more than anyone understand that I cannot rest now. There are things I must do."

The mood abruptly went from the warmth of fond memories to the cold reality at hand. William wouldn't let the ambience veer too far away from the situation, his loss, and the brutal truths of war. They would try and he'd inevitably bring them back around again, but his latest statement had their concern. Given the wars were now essentially over, at least for the time being, the focus was shifting. They were the victors, and to the victors went the spoils of war. In this case, the prisoners.

And that was troubling.

"*What* must you do, William?" Kieran asked. "Kevin, go about your duties. I will speak with William alone."

Kevin didn't argue. He knew the situation for what it was, and when his father used that tone, it was time to clear out. Silently, he departed, heading over to the encampment, as Kieran moved his horse up on William's other side. Now, the man was flanked by Paris and Kieran and they weren't going to let him do anything he might regret. At the culmination of months of battle, this was a fragile moment for them all.

"William, I realize you have a good many conflicting feelings at this moment, but I hope you know that you can share those with us," Kieran said quietly. "We loved James, too. Every sword stroke, every Welsh death, has had his name on it since that day at Llandeilo. Mayhap if you were to speak of this moment and what it means to you, it might make us all feel… more at peace."

William looked at him. "I will never be at peace," he said. "What peace do you speak of, Kieran? You still have your sons.

I have lost one of mine. There *is* no peace."

"I do not have all of my sons," Kieran said in a low voice. "If anyone understands your grief, I do."

That was true. Kieran had lost his second-eldest son, Christian, in the Levant only a few short years earlier. The tall, blond Hage son who had been so loved had followed his duty and set out to the king's call, but it had been a call that cost him his life. William was fully aware that Kieran hadn't yet recovered from that, only the man was more in control of himself when it came to his grief.

William simply wasn't.

"I do not mean to diminish yours, Kieran," he said in a show of compassion. "We all miss Christian. But he did not die in your arms as James died in mine. You did not hold your son as he breathed his last, helpless to do anything at all. You cannot know how that eats at me."

Kieran's jaw flexed faintly. "Nay, I did not hold him," he said. "I was not there at all. My son died alone, without me by his side, and I did not find out until almost a year later. Just because I was not there at the moment of his death does not mean I did not feel it as much as you feel James'."

William sighed sharply. "Christian did not die in a bloody Welsh ambush, but in war," he said with some passion. "He chose to be there, Kieran. He knew what the risks were."

"And James did not know what the risks were when he came to Wales with an army to do battle against the Welsh princes?"

Paris intervened before the argument could grow out of control. "William, far be it from me to tell you how to feel, because I understand and approve of your rage against the Welsh," he said. "You know I do and so does Kieran. But comparing his death to Christian's is beneath you. Your grief is no greater than Kieran's. It is simply fresher."

William knew that. Deep down, he did. As he hung his head, Paris leaned into him and lowered his voice.

"I have killed in James' name and have taken delight in it," he continued. "But we are not your enemy, and for the past six months, you have been treating us as if we are, as if we have no stake in this situation whatsoever, and that flies in the face of a friendship we have had for over fifty years. Do you think so little of us that you would discount the fact that I was James' godfather and Kieran's daughter was married to him? Do you think we do not have feelings in this matter, too?"

Paris had never treated William the way Kieran did. Kieran was usually calmer, with more patience, but Paris was brutally honest and not one to shy away from an argument—but in a delicate situation like this, sometimes his manner wasn't overly welcome. In fact, Kieran held his breath as William processed what Paris had said.

His reaction wasn't long in coming.

"I never said you do not have feelings in the matter," he said. "And your support of James, of my vengeance, has been appreciated more than you know. I am not a man given to vengeance. You know this. My motivation against an enemy has never been emotional because, as we know, emotions are deadly. My motivation against any enemy is one of quiet duty. But that Welsh ambush six months ago made my motivation in Wales personal, and I cannot help that. Christ, Paris, I've not even told James' own mother about his death. I could not do that in a missive. She is continuing her life at Castle Questing, unaware that she has lost a son. Do you have any idea how much that tears at me? That my first words to her when I return home will be of the death of one of her children? It eats me alive inside until I cannot bear the pain, so if I have shown a lack of grace or understanding when it comes to the Welsh, you will forgive me. I am grieving for two right now, and it is more than I can bear."

Paris knew all of that but it was the first time William had really spoken of it. Reaching out, he put his hand on William's shoulder, trying to give him some comfort. But on William's left side, Kieran sighed faintly.

"She knows, William."

William heard the softly uttered words, turning to look at Kieran in confusion. "What do you mean?" he said. "I have not told her."

Kieran's jaw twitched faintly. "Someone else did," he said, barely audible. He sighed again and lifted his head, looking at William. "We sent some of the heavily wounded back to Castle Questing to recover, and in spite of our instructions for them not to speak of James' death, someone did."

William's confusion turned to horror when he realized what the man was saying. "My God," he breathed. "How do you know this?"

Kieran looked at him then. "You know I received a missive from my wife last week."

"I do."

"She told me that the news of James' death reached her ears before it reached Jordan," he said with sorrow. "It was Jemma who broke the news to her. She had to. Otherwise, Jordan would have heard it through the gossip mill or from a servant, and I know that is not what you want. William, it was inevitable. Men talk. We sent men who had been at Llandeilo back to Castle Questing and it was simply inevitable that someone would talk. And someone did."

William stared at him. Long ago, he'd lost his left eye in a battle in Wales, ironically, but the gaze in his remaining eye was nothing short of fierce. William de Wolfe could do with one eye what most men couldn't do with two. He stared at Kieran until he could stare no more.

And then he simply walked away.

Kieran and Paris watched him go with heavy hearts.

"You should have told him sooner," Paris muttered. "This is going to cause problems, Kieran. It will unnerve him."

Kieran was watching William as he wandered off toward a grove of trees. "I could not tell him until the battle was over," he said firmly. "You know this, Paris, and you agreed with me when I first told you what had happened."

"I know, but—"

"If I had told him before the end of this battle, he might have very well gotten himself killed with the distraction," Kieran said, cutting him off. "His focus had to remain on Llywelyn and Dafydd. It could not be divided by the news that his wife had been told about James. He has enough grief without worrying over the fact that he was not the one to tell Jordan about her son's death."

He was right and they both knew it, but Paris waved him off irritably, unwilling to engage him in an argument. It was done and they had to deal with the aftermath.

But what aftermath there would be was anyone's guess.

"I fear we may have a larger problem," Paris said.

"What is that?"

"The news that Jordan is aware of James' death may bring on a fresh wave of grief for William," Paris said. "That may mean his rage will bloom, and it will turn toward Dafydd and those children more than it already is."

It was difficult for Kieran to acknowledge that, true though it might be. "His behavior has been so unpredictable," he said. "I had confidence in the William I have fought alongside for over fifty years. I had confidence that he would show compassion and mercy in all situations, but this William… I do not know what he'll do. I would like to think I do, but the truth is that I do not. And neither do you."

Paris was nodding his head, agreeing with him, before he'd finished speaking. "I do not," he said. "Are there plans for the children already?"

"Aye," Kieran said. "Edward has been specific. Dafydd is to face a trial and his children are to be separated. The girls will be sent to convents in Lincolnshire and his sons are to be sent to Bristol Castle. But the infant is Llywelyn's offspring. *Tywysoges yr Ysbrydion a'r Dreigiau* is what they call her."

"I know," Paris said. "The Princess of Ghosts and Dragons."

Kieran nodded. "Edward has specifically chosen Sempringham Priory for her because it is close to Carlton de Royans' properties," he said. "He wants her placed near a knight loyal to him, to ensure she remains where she is consigned."

"So de Royans draws that duty."

"He does," Kieran said. "The priory is quite remote and well fortified."

"So she can be sealed off from the world for the rest of her natural life."

"Aye."

Pondering the fate of the infant, Paris gazed off toward the grove of trees that William had disappeared into. "May I make a suggestion?"

"What?"

"Move the children now," he said quietly. "While William is

distracted, move them out. Form escorts and move those children away from this encampment and away from William. If he takes it into his mind to deal with them personally, it will cause more problems than we can fathom."

"I regret to say that I was thinking the same thing but did not wish to voice it."

"I have no such restraint," Paris said. "We must do this for William, to protect him from whatever his grief might dictate. Return to the administrative tent and I will notify the escorts and send them to you, including de Royans. He already knows this is coming, but you can give the final instructions. If we work quickly, we can accomplish this within the hour."

There was nothing more to say to that. Kieran simply nodded and reined his horse back toward the encampment. Paris, too, was in motion, heading to the end of the encampment that contained the prisoners. The last he saw, the children were gathered there, tended to by fearful nurses and guarded by Edward's royal soldiers. Henry of England had been dead a scant month and Edward, as the new king, had been able to claim the final victory over Wales. There had been much change for all of them over the past six months, but one thing neither Paris nor Kieran wanted was for William to do something to displease Edward. Historically, there had been tension between the pair because Edward had always been threatened by William's power, so it was imperative to prevent William from interfering with Edward's Welsh prisoners because of a personal vendetta.

And no one wanted to see William dishonor himself out of grief.

Therefore, they moved quickly.

Time was running out.

CHAPTER TWO

Six Days Later
Near Folkingham, England

H E'D BEEN SADDLED with the baby.
A big, stinky baby.

But he had absolutely no recourse because he'd been ordered to mind the child on the journey from Wales, and a squire did not disobey his master. Not ever. If Liam Herringthorpe wanted to become a knight himself someday, as was expected of him, he had to be obedient no matter what the circumstance.

No matter how much the baby stank.

But it was a complicated situation. His master, Sir Carlton de Royans, and another knight by the name of Colm de Lara had been given orders from Sir Paris de Norville of Northwood Castle to take the infant to Sempringham Priory in Lincolnshire. It was all very confusing but, from what Liam understood, the orders came directly from the king himself. The baby, a little girl, belonged to one of the Welsh princes who had been so recently subdued, so the king wanted the child taken to a priory and hidden away for the rest of her life, under English protection.

It had all seemed so secretive and so hurried. There were other children involved, taken by other knights, but de Norville seemed to be rushing Carlton and Colm a great deal. There was already a wet nurse for the infant, an older Welsh woman, and it was that woman who had come along with them as they hurriedly made their way out of Wales. There were twenty of them in total, including several heavily armed soldiers, with Liam and another old soldier driving the wagon containing the woman and baby while everyone else seemed to be nervously watching the landscape as if waiting for something to happen.

Nothing had.

Not yet, anyway.

But something was in the air.

As Liam sat in the wagon seat, watching the landscape just like everyone else, a scout on horseback came thundering up the column, heading for Carlton and Colm at the head of the line. As Liam watched, the scout had a spirited conversation with Carlton, gesturing toward the west. When the conversation concluded, Carlton sent the man back the way he'd come while he reined his warhorse around and came back to the wagon.

"We will be making our stop at Folkingham," he said. "It is nearly nightfall as it is."

Liam, being young and certain he knew everything there was to know, spoke quickly. "Is there trouble, my lord?" he said. "Should I retrieve my weapon?"

Carlton de Royans was a kind man. He was well liked, part of the de Royans family of Netherghyll Castle in the north. His great-uncle, Juston de Royans, had played an important role with Henry II and Richard I, so the family had prestige and wealth along with their strong political connections. Folkingham Castle was his, through his wife, a de Beaumont, and Sempringham Priory was part of his property. That was why he was in charge of the infant and her fate.

It was his job to hide her away forever.

"Nay," he said in answer to Liam's question. "There is no need for you to fight. We shall arrive at Folkingham shortly and my wife will make us all welcome. We will be safe."

"Safe from what?" Liam wanted to know, turning to look off toward the west where the scout had gone. "Are you sure there is no trouble?"

Carlton shook his head. "No trouble," he said. "We shall be home shortly."

Liam watched him ride away, frowning. "He is not telling the truth," he muttered. "He appears concerned."

The old soldier, who had served Carlton's father-in-law for many years, glanced at the young and excitable squire. "He should be," he said, chewing on a piece of dried grass that had been hanging from his lips since the morning. "It's quite possible we are being followed."

That only made Liam strain to look more than he already was. "By whom?"

"The animal who tracks with greater stealth than a man."

Liam looked at him. "What animal?"

"A wolf."

That made no sense to Liam. "A wolf is following us?" he said incredulously. "How do you know? Who has said so?"

The old soldier fixed him in the eye. "Lad, if you are to be a knight, then you must learn to open your ears," he said. "Why do you think we left Wales in such a hurry?"

Liam had no idea. "I do not know," he said. "I suppose to take this baby away."

The old soldier nodded as if Liam had just said something important. "Exactly," he said. "We are taking this baby away to keep her safe."

"Safe from whom?"

"From a man who would use her in vengeance for his own son's death," the old man said, snapping his fingers. "Just like that, the Wolfe would take her hostage and call it justice. We had to get her away before he could, and now he is following us. It is imperative that de Royans get her to that priory before the Wolfe catches up to us."

Liam understood him. Sort of. "The Wolfe?" he said. "You mean Warenton?"

The old soldier nodded. "Now you are starting to comprehend."

Liam frowned. "He would not punish a baby because he lost his son."

"Not the baby," the old soldier said, shaking his head. "Punish the Welsh as a whole. It's what she represents. Do you know who that baby is?"

"Daughter of Llywelyn?"

"She is," the old soldier said. "But she is also the granddaughter of King John. She has more royal blood in her than anyone in this country. Maybe even the world. I cannot believe that the Earl of Warenton would actually harm the child, because he is not that sort of man, but he might want to take her into his custody. He might put her in a vault and throw away the key."

Liam didn't seem to think the situation was all that critical. "What is the difference if she ends up in a vault or in a priory?"

he said. "It is all the same. She loses her freedom either way, and the Welsh lose their princess."

"True," the old soldier said. "But if she's at a priory, no one can harm her. She's safe. But thrown in a vault, she is vulnerable to anyone who enters that vault."

"Like Warenton?"

The old soldier nodded faintly. "'Tis a strange situation," he said. "The man lost a son six months ago and the babe was born six months ago. It all happened on the same day, I heard. As I said, I don't believe Warenton would harm the child, but he could hold her hostage indefinitely as punishment to the Welsh for the killing of his son. Grief makes even good men do strange things."

Liam pondered that. He'd only heard good things about William de Wolfe, a man greatly revered and respected by nearly everyone in England. Like any warlord, he had his share of enemies, but for the most part, men spoke well of him. In fact, Liam was distantly related to him because his own father, Warwick Herringthorpe, had married a cousin to William de Wolfe's wife. Because of that connection, Liam was planning on heading to Castle Questing, Warenton's seat, in a couple of years to finish his training as a knight. It was a prestigious post his father had helped him obtain and he had been looking forward to it. Therefore, the concept that William de Wolfe might be unjust with a helpless baby puzzled him.

He refused to believe it.

"It is Edward who wants this baby sealed up in a priory," he said. "Warenton is a man of war. He knows that the child is not responsible for his son's death. He is a better man than that."

"Who says so?"

"My father."

The old soldier shrugged. "'Tis true," he said. "Warenton has a fair and just reputation, but if he wants this baby, he'll get her. Mark my words."

He sounded old and suspicious and edgy. Liam wasn't sure he believed any of it, but it would explain why de Royans and de Lara seemed uneasy. He didn't like to think about William de Wolfe being a threat, but then again, the man didn't get where he was being soft. If he wanted something, he took it.

And that was what had the rest of them concerned.

It wasn't long before they came upon the road to Folkingham. Carlton took the lead and urged the escort to move more quickly, along a muddy road that had big holes in it. The landscape was winter-gray all around them, cold and dead, and in the wagon, the babe had started to cry. That thin, piercing sound filled the air as they traveled and Liam glanced behind him, into the wagon bed, to see that the wet nurse was trying to feed the infant. It was almost impossible given how much the wagon was lurching. A hungry baby with the inability to latch on to the nipple made for a frustrating effort.

There wasn't anything Liam could do about it. They had to make it to the castle, which had appeared in the distance. Lincolnshire was flat, as flat as a plate, and this particular area seemed to be devoid of trees. There was nothing for a mile in any direction, a dark line in the distance the only indication of growth other than the dead grass upon the ground. A cold wind began to pick up and Liam didn't think he much liked Lincolnshire. He was from the north, on the sea, in fact, and he missed the smell of salt in his nostrils and the cry of gulls overhead. He'd spent nearly the past year in Wales with the English armies, with de Royans, and now they were finally returning to a castle he didn't much like.

It didn't remind him of home.
But here they were.
Little did he know what they were in for.

CHAPTER THREE

"Y OU SHOULD TAKE the child straight to the priory. Why bring her to the castle?"

The question came from Colm de Lara. He was riding point for the escort, now joined by Carlton, as they slogged toward the castle along the impossibly muddy road. Both knights had pale-colored warhorses, animals that were now brown from the neck down because of all of the muck. It was flying everywhere because they were moving quickly. Carlton heard the question, his gaze on the gray-stoned walls in the distance.

"Because the priory is still about five miles to the east," he said. "The sun is setting and a storm is approaching. If we do not get this child to warmth and safety, there will be no child to deliver to the priory, and that will not bode well for you or for me."

Colm looked off toward the east, instinctively, as if to see the priory that was their ultimate destination. "Tomorrow, then," he said. "She will not be completely safe until she is within those old walls."

"Agreed."

A pause. "Do you truly think Warenton is following us?"

Colm asked.

Carlton's gaze was fixed on his home, as if he could look at nothing else. "I do not know," he said. "We were not part of the ambush at Llandeilo, but the stories I heard… tragic at best. Men lose sons all the time, but the men who witnessed the death of Warenton's son said that he took it very hard. He tried to carry his son out of the fighting, but he could not. They were swarmed with Welsh, and Warenton's surviving sons had to pull the old man free or risk his own death. They had to leave their brother behind."

Colm didn't seem particularly sympathetic. "The man acts as if he has been the only father in history to have lost a son in battle," he said, lifting a hand in surrender when he saw the frown on Carlton's face. "I do not mean to be cruel. And I like Warenton enough. He is a decent man. But he will have to come to terms with this, and taking his grief out on children is beneath him."

"He will not take it out on the children," Carlton said. "But de Norville seemed to think that quickly removing them from Warenton's reach might remove any temptation."

Colm shook his head. "This may not have anything to do with vengeance for his son and instead be more of a swipe at the king," he muttered. "You know that Edward and Warenton have never seen eye to eye. It's Edward's fault, I will admit, but Warenton could be threatening to take the Welsh children hostage himself in order to take control away from Edward. It would be a volatile political move."

Carlton couldn't disagree. "Mayhap," he said. "But Edward knows how much support Warenton has. All the man has to do is lift a hand and half of England will rush to his side. The Scots, too, because his wife is Scots. And the Welsh would more than happily rush to Warenton's side because of his ties to them also. As I said, taking the babe to the priory tomorrow will be safer for us all."

Colm simply shook his head because the entire situation was delicate. Delicate and dangerous. The sooner they delivered the child to Sempringham, the better.

The last half-mile to Folkingham seemed to take forever. The rain had begun to fall by the time they reached the gatehouse, which was strangely open. Both portcullises were lifted. Assuming it was because the gate guards had seen their party approaching, Carlton and Colm didn't have any hesitation in entering.

The entire party charged into the rather large bailey of Folkingham, which was a motte and bailey fortress. That meant that walls surrounded a big ward with a hall and outbuildings and stables, and then toward the northern side of it was a manmade mound with a large, square keep built atop it. There was a small moat around the mound, more like a mud puddle, and a wall with a barbican that protected the stairs into the keep. Folkingham was a complicated structure and a crowded bailey in places as a result, but to Carlton, he'd never seen anything so beautiful.

He was home.

But there was someone else at his home, too.

Behind them, the portcullis slammed shut.

They all heard it, a squeaking sound followed by a loud boom as the wood and iron grate fell into place behind the last men from Carlton's escort. In fact, the men bringing up the rear had barely come through. Frowning, Carlton thought it was just a bit of clumsiness from the gate guards, so he didn't really give it much thought beyond that. He dismounted his horse, wiping rain from his eyes, when he heard Colm's quiet voice.

"Carlton," the man muttered. "Look ahead of you."

Carlton had to blink his eyes again to clear them of rain. He finally pulled his helm off because it was dripping from the crown. It took him a moment to realize he was looking at a familiar knight heading in his direction, a man he thought he'd left behind in Wales.

The tallest man he'd ever seen in his life.

Patrick de Wolfe was coming for him.

"Christ," he breathed. "What is he doing here?"

Colm couldn't even answer him. They were all afraid of Patrick de Wolfe, a mountain of a man with a long arm and an even longer sword. No Welshman had ever survived against Patrick de Wolfe's long reach, and skill, and Carlton dared to glance around to see if there were any other de Wolfe knights around. A casual glance behind him showed that there were a few at the gatehouse. That was why the gate had slammed shut so abruptly.

They were trapping him inside his own bailey.

The realization roused his anger. By the time Carlton turned around, Patrick was almost upon him.

"Before you chastise me, know that I am acting under orders," he said before Patrick could speak. "My orders come from Edward and you know it."

Patrick came to a halt. "I do," he said. "How does the child fare?"

"Well enough," Carlton said. "But we must get her out of this rain."

Patrick motioned toward the hall. "Bring her," he said. "My father wants to see her."

Carlton's eyes widened. "Warenton is *here*?"

Patrick nodded. "He is," he said. Seeing Carlton's shock, he elaborated. "We covered more ground than you did because we did not have the burden of a wagon, but even so, we only arrived here this morning. Your wife has been most hospitable."

The mention of Fair Lydia had Carlton's heart lurching. "My dearest," he murmured. "Where is she?"

"In the hall."

Carlton didn't say anything for a moment, his focus on the hall that had been built against the wall with a steeply pitched roof. There was smoke escaping from the chimney and warm light emitting from the windows, but the allure of it belied the fear of what was inside.

De Wolfe.

"Patrick," he said evenly, "you are welcome at my home. We are allies. But you will understand why I ask this question."

"What question?"

"You've not done anything to my wife, have you?"

Patrick's brow furrowed. "Why would we?" he said. "Carlton, we've not come to harm you or your wife, nor would we ever. I hope you know that."

Carlton let out a heavy sigh, one that conveyed his relief. "Did you tell her why you've come?"

"Nay. She knows nothing."

"Then why are you here?"

"I think you know why."

At this point, Colm had already fetched the child, who came forward in the arms of the nurse as the tall, blond squire tried to keep the rain off them both. Carlton held out a hand to keep them from going any further.

"I do know why," he said to Patrick. "But I want to hear it from you. I am under the king's orders and, as he is my liege, I intend to carry them out. If you've come to take the child, know that I will have to fight you. She is intended for Sempringham."

Patrick simply shook his head. "Get her inside," he said quietly. "No one is fighting for anything right now. But my father wants to see her. And he wants to talk to you."

Carlton rolled his eyes, but he motioned Colm and the wet nurse and the infant forward. As they started to move, with the squire still trying to keep them dry, Carlton and Patrick began to follow.

"Atty, you know I would kill or die for your father, but this situation cannot go too far," Carlton said with soft urgency, using Patrick's childhood nickname. Little Patrick de Wolfe had had a speech impediment and couldn't say his own name, so his family and friends used the name "Atty" to this day. "He cannot take the infant hostage. Paris de Norville thinks so, too, or I would not have been ordered to take the child out of Wales so swiftly."

Patrick nodded. "I know," he said quietly. "We agree with Paris, but you should know that my father nearly throttled him when he found out what Paris did. Kieran, too. Scott and I convinced him to come to Folkingham because that was where you were taking the infant. It also got him away from Paris and Kieran. There's nothing as ridiculous or dangerous as an old-man fight, and that was what we were facing. My father wanted to kill them both."

"Does he intend to take her?"

"I do not know. And that is the truth."

They'd reached the hall by this time. Carlton could see the other de Wolfe sons, Scott and Troy, right inside the door. Carlton grabbed the arm of the wet nurse before she could venture into the hall because of the precious cargo she was holding. Instead, Carlton took the baby himself.

If Warenton wanted her, then he would have to fight him for her.

Cautiously, he entered the hall.

He could see William de Wolfe as the man sat at a feasting table next to Fair Lydia, who caught sight of her husband the moment he came through the door. Fair Lydia de Royans—and Fair Lydia was indeed her birth name—was as delicate as a flower, a woman with arms like a bird's wings, tiny stature, and a crown of pale red hair. She gasped in joy and leapt up from the table when she saw her husband, leaving de Wolfe behind as she ran to him. She threw her arms around the man, and even though he was overjoyed to see her, he cautioned her about being too rough.

He had a precious bundle.

"Careful, my love," he said. "I bear fragile cargo."

Fair Lydia gasped again when she saw that he was carrying a baby, and before he could say another word to her, she was pulling the child out of his arms.

"Look at him," she said with the greatest delight. "Oh, Carlton! He is absolutely beautiful!"

Carlton watched as she pulled off the wet cap, revealing damp hair the color of coal. The baby blinked in the light of the hall, eyes of the brightest blue that anyone had ever seen. She was, in truth, a glorious child.

"It is a lass, my love," he said. "She is rather pretty, I agree."

Fair Lydia pulled the baby against her, hugging her tightly. "A girl," she said happily. "An angel. She is an angel!"

"Aye, my love, an angel," Carlton said. "Can you spare some of your affection for your returned husband now? I've not seen you in several months and should like a kiss, at least."

Fair Lydia nodded. Then she burst into tears. "A kiss cannot express the gratitude that I am feeling," she sobbed quietly. "I did not think you would remember, but you did."

"Remember what?"

"This month," she said, wiping at her nose. "I did not think I would be able to bear the weight of this month, the pain and agony that threatens to consume me, but you have brought me something wonderful to ease my pain. This gift, Carlton… it is more than I could ever hope for."

With that, she sobbed and sniffled, kissing the infant and holding her tightly. She didn't make a move toward welcoming Carlton further than she already had even though she hadn't seen her husband in almost a year. But evidently, their reunion would have to wait. She had a baby in her arms and that was all that mattered.

It was all she cared about.

And Carlton knew it. He wasn't thinking about the fact that he'd hardly had a reunion with her before she got her hands on the baby. He was only thinking about her words, what she'd said. The meaning of them began to sink in as he stood there, increasingly horrified. God's Bones, he'd forgotten all about the importance of this month until she reminded him. Perhaps he'd simply blocked it out.

But she hadn't.

"My dearest, this is not…" he stammered. "The child… I only brought her here so she could be warmed and safe."

"Of course she shall be warm and safe," Fair Lydia said, rocking the baby gently and gazing into that lovely little face. "She shall be the warmest and the safest of all children. I will make sure of it."

"Fair Lydia," Carlton said, pain in his features, "that is not what I meant by bringing the baby here. She is not ours, my love."

Fair Lydia wasn't comprehending what he was trying to tell her. "Nay, she is not ours, but I will love her as if I had given birth to her," she said. "More, even. She will be very happy with us, don't you think?"

She didn't wait around for an answer. She was already showing the child off to the servants who were in the hall as Carlton stood there, dumbfounded. He was trying to be gentle about the situation because he didn't want to crush Fair Lydia, but she wasn't listening to him. She was hearing what she wanted to hear or, more correctly, making assumptions that she wanted to be true. He could see how happy she was and hadn't seen that kind of joy on her face in ages.

That alone shot holes in his willpower to be clear with the truth.

As he stood there, William had come up beside him, watching the situation with some puzzlement.

"Carlton?" de Wolfe said. "What does your wife mean?"

Carlton was feeling sick. "A year ago this month, we lost our infant son," he said, sounding weak. "My God, I'd forgotten all about it until…"

He trailed off, unable to continue, but it was enough for William. He understood right away. "She thinks you have brought her an infant to replace the one you lost."

Carlton nodded. Then tears popped into his eyes. "Aye," he whispered tightly. "That must be what she thinks."

William didn't seem to know what to say to that. He watched Fair Lydia, a truly sweet and gracious woman, as she fawned over the infant and held her up so that more servants could get a good look at her. She was weeping and laughing, kissing the baby and hugging her all at the same time. An older woman entered from a servants' entrance and Fair Lydia crowed her delight to the woman, who nearly screamed in elation. There was so much happiness on the other side of the hall that it was palpable, and the knights watching the display had no idea what to do. The de Wolfe sons, over near the entry, looked to see how their father was reacting, but William didn't have any discernible reaction at all.

He was simply watching like the rest of them.

"What happened to your son?" he finally asked.

Carlton had to wipe the tears from his eyes. "We do not know," he said. "He was only about three months of age, perfectly healthy as far as we knew. He was a happy baby, a good baby, but Fair Lydia put him to bed one night and in the morning, he was cold and stiff."

William simply nodded, watching Fair Lydia hand the baby over to the older woman as they both wept over her. Carlton watched them, struggling not to get misty-eyed again, before turning his full attention to William.

"That woman is her mother," he said softly. "You have lost a son, my lord, but I lost my son also. His name was Auston. All of my hopes and dreams were pinned to that child because Fair Lydia cannot have another. It almost killed her to have him and the physic told us that another child will be the death of her, so Auston's death ended my legacy. I know you are here because of Llywelyn's daughter. We all know you intend to seek vengeance against the Welsh who killed your son and I do not fault you for that, but much like my son's death, I will tell you now that there is no one to blame. What happened to your son happened during the course of a battle and nothing more. He was a knight, and in battle, there is always the risk of death.

That is the nature of the vocation. The babe in my wife's arms did not cause your son's death, so if you've come to take her, I will be obliged to prevent you. I hope you know that."

It was quite a speech, delivered in a controlled but unmistakable manner. Carlton meant every word. William didn't reply immediately. He kept his gaze on the women who were still weeping over the baby, perhaps pondering what Carlton had said. It was difficult to tell because William de Wolfe never gave a hint at his emotions or what he was thinking. Like a wolf, the creature he emulated, he was emotionless and calculating. On the outside, anyway.

But inside, it was quite different.

After discovering that the baby had been taken, William, Scott, Troy, and Patrick had ridden to Lincolnshire as fast as the horses would take them. They had left Paris and Kieran behind because William was too angry to deal with them, and he was unwilling to let them be a part of this action. That was indicative of his level of anger because they had always been part of any action he'd ever undertaken since they'd been squires together, but not this time. He felt betrayed.

He wanted to do this alone.

Truth be told, William had spent the first four days of the ride absolutely furious at his closest friends. The only way he discovered what they'd done was that some of his men had seen Carlton and Colm departing the encampment and news of that departure had made its way back to William. He had expressed bewilderment to Paris as to why the men had left, considering the battle was not completely finished and there was still work to do, but it was Paris who had confessed why Carlton had taken flight.

And that was why William had remained furious for four

solid days, riding like a madman to make it to Folkingham Castle before Carlton did. He knew about the orders from Edward and he knew that Llywelyn's infant child was to be placed at Sempringham Priory, so the news that Carlton was carrying out the king's command did not come as a surprise to him. He already knew about those orders.

It was the one from Paris he had a problem with.

But Paris knew what they all knew—that Edward and William had been locked in some sort of strange power struggle since the waning days of Henry's rule. There had always been competition between them and it was always something that William had tolerated because it mostly came from Edward. Everyone knew that Edward was envious of William and his reputation. There was no man in England with a greater reputation for fairness and noble behavior, and quite frankly, the man had the respect of more people than just about anyone. William de Wolfe could always be counted on to do the right thing, something Edward had a fundamental problem with. William had the respect and love that any king would have longed for, and Edward was no exception, so the bad blood between them had been started by Edward.

And perhaps that was what this was all about.

William had never risen to Edward's level of animosity, though the death of James had forced him into a position of looking for someone to blame. Deep down, William knew that it wasn't rational to pin the blame on any individual. Carlton had been correct—James had been a knight, and inherent to that vocation, death was not only a constant risk, but it was expected. William had six sons and he cherished each and every one of them for their own virtues, and the pride he had in their accomplishments as men and as warriors was as vast as the heavens. He adored his sons. And the truth was that he had never expected one of them to die in battle, much less a disgraceful Welsh ambush. That simply had not been worthy of James and his level of talent. And perhaps that was William's biggest problem...

He was not only grieved by it, but he was also insulted by it.

If James had to die, then he deserved a better death.

But the truth was that when death came for him, it didn't take into consideration how much he was loved or the level of his talent. It didn't take into consideration his family or his future. It simply came for him in the form of a morning star, one that had hit him on the right side of the head and smashed his helm and skull so badly that they couldn't even get the helmet off him. The big English knight had been damaged by what was probably a lucky shot, but once he fell to the ground, dozens of Welsh had jumped on him and stabbed him with their dirty swords. By the time William had got to him, James was literally covered in blood.

And that was the image that was seared into William's brain.

His bloodied, battered boy.

Of course he'd gone a little mad with it. Any father would have. So he had spent the past six months swearing vengeance upon the Welsh as if the entire race was responsible for his son's death. If he'd stopped to think about it, he would have realized how foolish that was. So many people tried to tell him that. His dearest friends in the world, Paris and Kieran, had tried to tell him that, but he would not listen. He had been in a world of his own, a world where grief and rage ruled his very sanity. He had not been able to separate that level of anxiety from his normally calm and rational demeanor because he'd never had to face that kind of tragedy before.

But now, he did.

He had to face everything.

"Sit down, Carlton," he finally said. "We will speak like allies, not enemies."

Carlton wasn't sure about that in the least, but he did as he was asked. As he did so, he could see his wife and her mother taking the infant over to the hearth, which was blazing at this hour, and begin to gently remove the child's wet clothing. In the heat of the hearth, the baby was stripped and dried. Lovely, wholesome things were happening over by the hearth, and the more Carlton observed, the more he knew he had to put a stop to it.

"My lord, if you please, mayhap our conversation can wait," he said. "I must separate my wife from that child if we have any hope of taking her to Sempringham on the morrow."

William held up a hand. "Sit," he commanded softly. "Having nine offspring of my own, I know something about women and children. You are not going to get that child away from her. You know that."

Carlton sighed heavily. "The longer I let this go on, the more difficult it will be."

There was some happy squealing going on over by the hearth, and they both looked over to see Fair Lydia's mother holding the naked baby up in the air, drying her little bottom in the heat of the fire. The baby was grinning, a happy little thing.

"My youngest daughter is married to a Welshman," William said. "He is one of the finest men I have ever known."

Carlton looked at him. "Yet you fought his countrymen?"

William nodded. "I did," he said. "As you did. We were asked by our king to do so and we did. But Bhrodi remained on

Anglesey, where he lives with my daughter and their children, and he did not get involved in any battles that I was participating in. He deliberately stayed out of them, and if I knew he was part of a battle, I would have withdrew my men. You see, I like my son-in-law a great deal. I would never lift a weapon to him. And Bhrodi was allied with Llywelyn ap Gruffudd."

"Have you ever met the man?"

William nodded. "I did, on more than one occasion," he said. "Carlton, I've been fighting wars for as long as you've been alive. There aren't many great warlords that I do not know or have known. I've lost friends in battle. I've lost mentors. But I have never lost a son."

Carlton fell quiet for a moment before answering. "I was not there when James was killed, but I knew him," he said. "I knew him as a knight of skill."

"He was very skilled."

"He was also a great entertainer," Carlton continued. "Many a time I remember him singing bawdy songs for the men and keeping them happy. He brought joy."

William glanced at him. "Aye, he did," he said. "Though he would sing those bawdy songs at weddings and draw the wrath of his mother."

Carlton grinned. "I would believe that," he said. But his smile soon faded. "My lord, may I ask you a question? I do not mean to be disrespectful, but I must ask."

"You may."

"Would James expect you to seek vengeance for his death?"

William was precluded from answering as Scott, Troy, and Patrick joined them at the table. The men sat down, removing gloves, getting comfortable. There weren't enough cups for the wine that was on the table, so Scott took his father's cup and drained it before pouring a measure for Troy and handing it across the table. William frowned at the intrusion.

"If I wanted you to join this conversation, I would have summoned you," he said to his sons. "Sit elsewhere. It is a large hall."

They ignored him. In fact, Patrick turned to watch Fair Lydia and her mother as they doted over the infant, who was beginning to get fussy.

"Lady de Royans seems very excited to see the child," he said. "I confess that my wife would do the same thing."

"Atty," William said in a low voice, "you and your brothers sit elsewhere."

"Wait, please," Carlton said. "I would like to ask them the same question that I asked you, my lord. They were James' brothers, after all. They knew him well."

William didn't like that idea at all, but Troy spoke up. "What question?" he asked.

Carlton looked at him. "Would your brother, James, have approved of your father's quest for vengeance in response to his death?"

That brought all three brothers to an immediate halt. They looked at William, wide-eyed, unwilling to answer the question. But their hesitation didn't last long. Patrick and Troy looked at Scott for some reply because, as the eldest, that was his right. Also, if William was going to become enraged, Scott could be the target rather than all three of them.

So much for camaraderie.

In the face of an angry father, it was every man for himself.

"That is a question with a very personal answer," Scott finally said diplomatically. "If you are looking for us to condemn our father, we will not."

"I am not looking for condemnation," Carlton said. "As I told your father, I have also lost a son. My only son. But I do not seek to blame anyone. The truth is that your brother was a knight, and death is always a possibility when a man wields a weapon. James died in battle, as a knight, and not because the Welsh knew it was James de Wolfe and targeted him. They targeted him simply because he was English. Battle *is* risk, and if you do not want to take the risk, then become a priest or a cleric. Do not become a knight."

Across the table, Patrick sighed faintly. He didn't seem particularly eager to speak until the silence became uncomfortable.

"If our father had been targeted and murdered, then James would have been the first one to seek vengeance," he said quietly. "If I had been targeted and murdered, he would have done the same. But in this ambush, we were all targeted. James died because he happened to catch a morning star to the head. It could have been any one of us."

Carlton could see that he had some support for his opinion. He wasn't trying to shame William, but he was trying to make a point. "And if you had been killed by the morning star, would you have expected your father to seek vengeance against the children of those responsible?" he asked.

That was a low blow as far as Patrick was concerned. "Do not suggest my father is anything other than noble in action and deed," he growled. "You will not like my reaction if you do."

Carlton wouldn't be intimidated. "Then why did he come to my home?" he asked. "Why did you *all* come to my home if it was not to seek vengeance against Llywelyn by somehow targeting his infant daughter?"

He had a point. They were there because they'd followed William and there was no denying it.

Patrick's manner cooled.

"We came because we would not let our father come alone," he said honestly. "As for my expecting vengeance if I had been killed by a morning star, my answer is that I would not have expected it. It happened in battle. I would expect to be mourned and spoken fondly of, but I would not expect my father to seek vengeance using an enemy's infant."

He said what Scott and Troy were thinking. They all looked at William, who was still watching Fair Lydia and the child. The woman was positively overjoyed. He'd heard Patrick's words, but they were words he'd heard before. He knew how his sons felt about his sense of vengeance, but he'd ignored them. How he felt about James' death was his privilege and no one else's. He wasn't going to let them tell him how to feel.

But some of that defiance was beginning to wear down.

"Carlton, I am going to answer your question with one of my own," he said. "If your son had lived to adulthood and you lost him in an ambush, by men you'd been fighting for a very long time, would you not have thoughts of vengeance? Think carefully before answering."

Carlton paused, seeing his question turned against him. "I would be enraged, of course," he said. "I would be grieved. But my anger would be directed at the men themselves, not their offspring."

"You do not believe taking the life of one of their children would be a reckoning?"

"I do not."

William's jaw flexed. "This is *war*, Carlton," he said, his voice significantly more threatening. "If you are not willing to do what is necessary in order to gain victory, in order to protect those you love, then *you* should become a cleric. Better still, put on a dress and become a woman, because you are not worthy of the manhood you hold so dearly."

The words were sharp, biting, and insulting. Even William's sons were surprised at the viciousness of them, but in the same breath, they didn't disagree with him. A man had to do what he had to do in order to protect his family. But that also brought up something that could be considered sinister.

You do not believe taking the life of one of their children would be a reckoning?

Carlton hadn't missed it. In fact, he stiffened in his seat, assuming he was going to have to make good on this threat to prevent de Wolfe from taking, and possibly murdering, the infant.

"Then you intend to take the child," he said quietly.

William had fury in his eyes. "Worse than that," he said. "I intend to flush the Welsh out of her veins. I intend that she should become English, with English thoughts and hopes and dreams and loves. I intend that she should never know her Welsh heritage because that, in and of itself, is punishment enough for those who did unspeakable things to James. It is punishment for all they fought for, and killed for, because in the end, their progeny will have no knowledge of who they really are. They will be absorbed by the English and made English. And for a Welsh prince, death for his child would be preferable. But I will not give the child death. I will give them life, and in doing so, James' death was not in vain. That baby in your wife's arms will become the blood of England."

That impassioned speech had Scott, Troy, and Patrick leaning closer to their father, listening with great interest. "What do you mean, Papa?" Scott asked. "She is going to an English priory. Is that not enough?"

"Nay." William looked at his sons, the flame of vengeance in his eyes. "It is *not* enough. In a priory, she will wither away, known only to God. I intend that her blood shall mingle with English blood, that she shall become a woman who breeds many children, all of them English, and in doing so, Llywelyn's legacy is sealed. He will be the forefather to an entire army of English knights. That, dear lads, is a reckoning. They took my son. I will give them too many to count, sons with Welsh royal blood that will fight their own countrymen. And that will be my ultimate revenge."

It was one of the best plans for vengeance any of them had ever heard. More than that, it made perfect sense. Llywelyn's daughter could breed a host of English sons who would, in turn, fight against their countrymen. Fight against Llywelyn's birthright, all in the name of James de Wolfe. His death had triggered Llywelyn's ultimate fate.

To be bred out of existence, using his own daughter.

"You had planned this all along," Scott said, a glimmer of approval in his eye. "Why did you not tell us?"

"Why did you not trust me?" William countered. "You have known me your whole lives. Have you ever known me to condone the outright murder of children?"

The three of them had to shake their heads. "Nay, Papa," Patrick said quietly. "I feel ashamed that I did not trust you in this matter. Forgive me. It's simply that James' death seemed to drive you to the point of madness."

"It did," William said. "I will admit that it did, but in that madness was clarity. I knew what I had to do. And if those idiots Paris and Kieran had given it more thought, they would have figured it out, too. With friends such as those, I do not need enemies."

That drew a grin from the sons, mostly because they knew he wasn't serious. But there was a part of him that was hurt because those closest to him had thought the worst. Truthfully, he could have told them of his plans, but he hadn't. Those plans of vengeance were private, part of his grieving process. He was only willing to share them now because he had little choice.

The time had come to make those plans a reality.

"Atty, you will do something for me," he said.

"Anything, Papa."

William's expression was intense. "You will go into the countryside. Find a farmer or a servant with a child the same age and sex as Llywelyn's infant. If it is a family with many mouths to feed, mayhap they would be willing to give you the infant for a price. Assure them that the child will not be harmed or abused in any way. That is crucial because it is true. Our purpose is not nefarious, but to give the child a life of piety and devotion at Sempringham Priory as a nun. Am I making myself clear?"

Patrick nodded. "Aye," he said, but he was puzzled. "But what about Llywelyn's child? There will be two of them going to Sempringham?"

William shook his head as he looked at Carlton. "Your wife will never relinquish that child, so do not force her," he said. "Raise her as your own. Give her an English name and raise her as an English noblewoman, and when she comes of age, she will be married to a knight and give birth to his sons. And that is how Llywelyn's legacy is erased from this earth. The infant Atty secures will go to Sempringham as Gwenllian of Wales. Edward will be satisfied, but most importantly, so will I."

Carlton's eyes were wide. "You want *me* to keep the infant?" he said, incredulous. "But… but I cannot. I answer to Edward!"

"Deny me and I shall burn your castle to the ground and tell Edward you turned against him," William said in a savage move. "I will tell him that you tried to betray him and murder Llywelyn's child. Believe me, I can emerge from this situation as the man who protected a kingdom, so do as you are told. Raise the infant but never tell anyone who she really is. Not even your wife. When you die, the secret of Gwenllian dies with you. Do you understand?"

Carlton swallowed. Hard. He knew that de Wolfe meant every word. He looked at Scott and Troy and Patrick to see their reactions, realizing they very much mirrored his own. Truth be told, William's solution was brilliant in the sense that his vengeance would be everlasting. The murder of a child of royal blood would end the bloodlines immediately, a fleeting victory and nothing more. But breeding Llywelyn's bloodlines into the English, diluting them until they were no more, would make that vengeance last forever, with each successive generation.

It was far more humiliating than a single death.

"Aye, my lord," he said. "I understand."

"Good," William said, the rage in his eyes cooling now that there would be no argument about it. "Atty, get about your business. We should deliver the child to the priory tomorrow, so you must move quickly. My suggestion would be that you go into the village to the west, to the church, and ask the priest if he knows of any families with children. If he wants to know why, you'll have to give him an excuse, but make it good. We do not want the priest suspecting anything. You can proceed from there."

Patrick nodded. "I will," he said. "May I eat first?"

"Quickly."

"I will go with him," Troy said. "The fewer who know about this, the better."

As William agreed, Carlton spoke up. "Speaking of those who know about the infant, you are aware that Colm de Lara knows," he said. "So does my squire, Liam Herringthorpe. They will not speak of it, of course, but you should be aware."

William's gaze seemed to move to the far end of the hall again, where Fair Lydia and her mother were now dealing with a fussy infant and the wet nurse was being deployed. But also on that side of the room were several wet soldiers from the de Royans' escort and one sopping squire. The lad was seated next to the hearth, eating something out of a bowl.

William's focus lingered on the lad.

"Liam," he muttered thoughtfully. "He must be thirteen or fourteen years of age now."

"He is," Carlton said.

"What kind of a man is he turning out to be?"

Carlton turned to look at the young man seated on the warm stone. "A fine one," he said. "He's strong, bright, does well with his studies, and can swing a sword as well as I can. I understand he is going to Questing in a couple of years."

"He is."

"You will be getting one of the best young prospects I have ever seen, my lord," Carlton said. "Even at his young age, it is obvious."

As William sat there and pondered that assessment, Patrick summoned food and a veritable feast was brought to the table. Boiled beef and carrots, bread and butter, and other dishes were presented and the de Wolfe sons tucked into them. But William didn't—he was still watching Liam as the boy finished whatever was in his bowl and went on the hunt for more.

Watching the lad had given him an idea.

"Scott," he said softly, "the man that Llywelyn's daughter marries must come from an excellent family. We are speaking of dual royal bloodlines, after all. It would have to be a good family."

Scott, mouth full, nodded. "Indeed," he said. "Do you have someone in mind already?"

William didn't answer for a moment. "I believe I do."

"Who?"

He gestured over to the hearth, where Liam was just sitting down again. Scott and Troy and Patrick turned to look at the area, seeing the infant and women and soldiers and a squire. Colm de Lara, who was unmarried, hadn't come into the hall, but had rather remained outside on business. Therefore, other than the soldiers, the only male in that area was the squire. When Scott realized who his father meant, his eyebrows lifted in surprise.

"Herringthorpe?" he asked.

"Why not?"

Scott didn't argue. He was too surprised to do so. He looked at his brothers to see their astonishment as well. Carlton didn't miss their expressions, but he didn't think much of them.

"His father is a great knight," Carlton said. "War is one of the best in England. His lineage isn't particularly outstanding, but it is solid. However, given the fact that the infant is dual royal blood, as you have mentioned, mayhap a more prestigious husband would be appropriate."

William cast a knowing glance at his sons before answering. "Carlton, there is something you should know about Liam Herringthorpe," he said. "What I tell you will never be repeated.

Only a select few know, but since we are about to share a deeply serious secret, I will trust you with this one, as well."

Carlton listened seriously. "Of course, my lord," he said. "What is it?"

"Liam is my grandson."

That brought a distinct reaction of surprise from Carlton. "Your *grandson*?" he repeated. "But… War is not married to one of your daughters. He married your wife's cousin."

William shook his head. "War is my son," William said quietly. "A result of a liaison between myself and his mother many years ago. I was denied her hand in marriage and she, in fact, married Edmund Herringthorpe, who raised War as his own. That is why War bears the Herringthorpe name—to honor the man who raised him and also because to bear the de Wolfe name would be to announce to the world that his mother was unchaste. It is better that he not use the name for all involved, but know that Liam is unaware of my relationship to him. I wish to keep it that way."

Carlton realized he was being trusted with a very big secret. "He will not hear it from my lips," he assured William. "But it explains his skill. He has de Wolfe blood."

William grunted in agreement. "My bloodlines go back to the conquest of England," he said. "My father was the Earl of Wolverhampton, a title that has passed to my eldest brother, and I hold the Earldom of Warenton. War's mother was a de Gray, from the great northern family, so War's, and Liam's, bloodlines are old and noble. He would make a perfect match for a de Royans daughter."

Carlton took the hint. Odd how he could already see hope for the future of his family now that he had a daughter to raise, a daughter who would marry a Herringthorpe and carry on the bloodlines through sons that would be of royal Welsh blood and noble English blood.

They would be descended from England's greatest knight.

Suddenly, he began to feel optimistic about the entire situation.

The man before him was the reason. Carlton had been fearing him for the past six days and now… now, he didn't fear him at all. William de Wolfe was the reason his life was about to change. Certainly, it was a risky undertaking, but he could hear Fair Lydia as she spoke to the baby. He could hear the joy in his wife's voice. Was Warenton's suggestion worth the risk?

Hearing his wife's happiness, it was.

It truly was.

"It seems strange," he mused, his gaze distant. "Ever since leaving Wales, I have been apprehensive of your appearance. I knew I carried what you wanted. When I saw Atty in the bailey, I was certain that I was in for a battle, one I probably would not survive. I've been sitting here in conversation with you, anticipating my future or lack thereof."

William turned for the food that Fair Lydia had brought him, food that had since grown cold. "One should never anticipate one's future until the day is done and the battle over," he said as he picked up a piece of bread. "Nothing is ever certain."

Carlton's focus moved to his wife, now going through infant clothing that a servant had brought her while her mother held the child. "Until I entered this hall, I believed my bloodlines would end with me," he said. "I had grown resigned to that fate. But your appearance here has changed that. I *will* have an offspring to carry on the de Royans legacy."

William nodded. "One that will mingle with de Wolfe

bloodlines," he said quietly, putting butter on his bread. "This is a great night for us, Carlton. But promise me something."

Carlton looked at him. "What is your wish, my lord?"

William was about to take a bite of his bread but paused. "Raise the child well," he said quietly. "Do not spoil her overly. Raise her to be grateful and loving. And when she marries Liam, ask her… ask her to name her firstborn son James."

Carlton smiled faintly. "And her second shall be called Auston."

William's lips flickered with a smile. "Hopefully she will agree."

"Hopefully."

A plan was born.

Later that night, and thanks to the priest at St. Mary's church in the village of Folkingham, Patrick and Troy didn't have much trouble finding a family with a multitude of children and a female child that was about a year older than Llywelyn's daughter. As Patrick explained to the priest, and then to the parents, Edward was granting some families what amounted to a sponsorship, sending one child to a convent to be educated for a life subservient to God. Scott added that Edward was trying to show his piety to the church in doing so, which made sense because Edward had never had a good relationship with the church. The man was desperately in need of some forgiveness. Given that explanation, the family was more than willing to accept the offer.

Of course, a girl child was far less valuable than a male child, and they already had nine girls, so they relinquished their toddler without much of a discussion. She even looked a little like Llywelyn's daughter, with dark brown hair and green eyes. Patrick never mentioned where, exactly, the child was going, or even his family name, but he identified himself as a royal knight and the family was most accepting. Even more accepting when he gave them two pounds sterling for both the child and their silence. If they spoke of the transaction, he explained, it would somewhat nullify Edward's action—a man did not boast about being pious. Humility was key.

At dawn the next day, a child was delivered, as expected, to Sempringham Priory.

But it wasn't such a simple case as far as secrecy was concerned. The silence of the parents of the child they procured wasn't their only concern. The escort from Wales, and the wet nurse, knew about the child. The men from the escort didn't care about the infant now that they were home, but the wet nurse was a different story. Fair Lydia wasn't lactating, but the child was old enough for goat's milk, so they didn't need the wet nurse any longer. Short of killing the woman to keep her quiet on what she might or might not have seen with regard to the infant, they had to figure out a way to get rid of her.

That opportunity came in the form of Patrick, Troy, and Scott, who took the wet nurse into Boston, next to the sea, and purchased passage for her back to Wales. They gave her money, bought her a few lovely things, and put her on a cog that was headed for Portsmouth, Plymouth, Cardiff, and eventually Dublin. The woman would return home, to her family, and given that Scott could speak Welsh because his wife was Welsh, she returned with a warning that if she ever spoke of the infant she had been in charge of, the English would return and wipe out her entire family.

It was a harsh threat, but necessary.

In truth, as far as the wet nurse was concerned, Llywelyn's infant did indeed make it to the priory, as she'd never seen the second child. Furthermore, she had been separated from Llywelyn's infant almost the moment they reached Folkingham. For all she knew, the infant had reached her destination, but Scott couldn't be certain that she wasn't suspicious otherwise.

Therefore, he did what was needed.

In the days following the deception, Sempringham Priory discovered that the child delivered to them was healthy and strong, liked goat's milk, and went by the name of Wencilian. That was how her arrival was recorded. Back at Folkingham Castle, news got around that Lord Carlton had returned from battle with an orphaned child, a gift to his wife to ease her loss of her own infant a year prior.

Fair Lydia couldn't have been more in love with the child, who grew up spoiled and sweet, indulged by her mother and moderately disciplined by her father. Though the girl knew she had been adopted as an orphan, her father had been vague about exactly where she'd come from. *Somewhere west,* he'd said. That the fairies had brought her was another explanation. Or he'd found her in the center of a flowerbed and brought her home. Whatever the reason, it had never really mattered to her.

The infant once known as Gwenllian had a wonderful life, after all.

CHAPTER FOUR

Fourteen Years Later
Folkingham Castle

"I DO NOT like a visit from him," Colm said with hazard in his tone. "Something is amiss. I can feel it."

Things had not changed at Folkingham over the years. Colm was still complaining and Carlton was still listening. Those dynamics made it possible for those at the castle to live normal lives, productive lives, because the relationship between Carlton and his knight remained constant and that brought comfort.

Like now.

Colm was complaining and Carlton was listening.

It was the natural order of things.

The pair had been out in the bailey of Folkingham when they received a missive that Liam Herringthorpe was on the approach. The messenger was a de Wolfe soldier who had ridden ahead of Liam and the rest of the escort. Given that Liam had been stationed at Questing for the past fourteen years, the soldiers with him bore the black and dark green of the Earl of

Warenton. Every one of de Wolfe's sons had their own variation to the de Wolfe shield standard, but the one worn by the messenger was the original standard—the tri-point shield with the stylized wolf's head in the center.

But it was anyone's guess why Liam was coming.

And that had Colm worried.

"I do not know why the man is approaching, but I am certain it is nothing more than a birth or marriage announcement, or something of that nature," Carlton said, setting the yellowed missive onto the table that carried his maps and documents, everything he needed to manage his properties. "It could also be the fact that Warenton has sent him south to visit his betrothed. You know he sends the man every year or so. He wants Liam and Cambria to become comfortable with one another, since they are to marry."

Cambria.

Dearest Cambria Eudoxia Rose, to be exact. It was the name that he and Fair Lydia had selected for their daughter, the name of ancient Wales. "Dearest" had been added because every woman in Fair Lydia's family had a term of endearment preceding their Christian name. It was tradition. In any case, Warenton's intention, long ago, had been to bury Cambria's heritage under the crushing weight of an English life, and that had all come to pass. Everything had happened as it should have. The only reference to that heritage was, in fact, her name.

And it suited her beautifully.

"When was Herringthorpe last here?" Colm said, scratching his beard. "It has to be at least two years."

Carlton nodded. "Two and a half, I believe," he said. "Bria was in that awkward stage between a child and a woman, and I seem to remember her following Liam around until the man begged for mercy."

Colm grinned. "She held his hand, constantly."

"He could not even use the hand to eat."

"She adores him, you know."

"I know," Carlton said. "But the feelings were not reciprocated in the least. However, he is in for a surprise. Two and a half years can make a big difference at this age. One moment they are children, and in the next… Well, she is a woman now, but even so, she's too young for marriage."

Colm shrugged. "She may be too young of body, but her mind is not," he said. "She speaks like a wise old woman. It is frightening sometimes."

Carlton chuckled. "She gets that from her mother," he said. "Fair Lydia always spoke to Cambria as if she were a person, not a child. She reasoned with her and spoke to her as if she had a mind and could reason in return. That has made my daughter old though she is young."

Colm shook his head. "Nay, it is more than that," he said. "Your daughter has a way of looking at people as if she can see into them."

"She can."

Colm snorted softly. "I believe it," he said. Then he took a deep breath as if to steady himself. "Then we shall assume that Herringthorpe is coming simply to see to the health and well-being of his betrothed. Do you want me to tell her?"

Carlton shook his head. "I will," he said. "I'm sure she's out with her dogs, so I will find her there."

Colm headed for the solar door. "Yesterday, she had several goats with her," he said. "I think she intends to breed them."

Carlton appeared displeased. "No more animals," he said, waving his hands around. "God's Bones, she has those black dogs that she sells for a profit, and although I have nothing but pride in her business skills, we do not need any more animals in the kitchen yard. It looks like Noah's Ark out there."

Colm opened the door. "Focus on her business skills," he said, grinning. "She does not have the pets simply to have them. She sells them. She will make you rich one day."

"Rich or insane."

"Take heart," Colm said. "She'll be Herringthorpe's problem one day."

"True."

Colm glanced out into the entry beyond. "I suppose I'd better go prepare for his arrival," he said. But he paused before continuing. "Carlton… do you think Warenton ever told him the truth?"

The door was open and Carlton's head snapped up before he motioned sharply to the panel, which Colm quickly pulled shut. Given that he'd been part of the escort from Wales those years ago, and he knew the blue-eyed infant they'd brought to Folkingham, there was no way Carlton couldn't tell him what had happened. He'd been sworn to secrecy about it, but it was something he hadn't been happy about since the beginning. He thought that Edward was going to eventually discover the deception and they'd all be sent to the executioner.

Carlton was aware of the man's feelings.

He'd heard about them constantly for the past fourteen years.

"I've told you not to speak on that," he hissed. "You are well aware of the peril."

Colm put a hand up, a silent apology. "No one is around to overhear," he said. "But you are correct. I should not have. I was simply thinking aloud."

"Do not do it," Carlton said. "If it comes into your mind, bite your tongue. Cut it out if you have to. But never speak of it again."

Properly contrite, Colm simply nodded. "It was careless," he said. "I did not mean to be. It will not happen again."

"It had better not."

Colm had his head down. "I swear it," he said. "But you do know that, as with all secrets, someday this will come out, Carlton. It is inevitable."

"If it does, it will not be because of carelessness. It will be because of maliciousness."

"Or guilt."

"What do you mean by that?"

Colm shook his head. "Nothing," he said. "I simply meant... Never mind. I did not mean anything by it. I shall go about my business now. There is much to do before he arrives."

He turned to leave, but a word from Carlton stopped him. "Wait," he said quietly.

Colm stopped and looked at him. "What is it?"

Carlton sighed sharply before answering. "Liam... He knows," he murmured. "Warenton told him everything. For his own safety, he had to."

Colm's eyebrows lifted. "I thought so," he said. "Herringthorpe rode escort with us. He, more than any of us, was physically closer to the infant. He saw... Well, he saw what happened when we arrived. With Fair Lydia and the infant. How could he not know?"

"That is what Warenton thought," Carlton muttered. "And that's why he told him. I know I've jested about her being too young to wed, and she is, but the moment she reaches eighteen years of age, the marriage will happen. That union will protect her more than I ever could."

"Why do you say that?"

"Because if the truth is discovered now, Edward would have to raze Folkingham to get to her," he said. "There would be nothing to stop him, and Warenton's aid is weeks away, up in Northumberland. But when she marries Herringthorpe, she goes north, where an army of tens of thousands of men can protect her from a king who would see her sent to Sempringham, or worse. God himself could not protect her more than a Herringthorpe husband and the de Wolfe empire could."

"Are you genuinely concerned that the truth might somehow be known?"

"I am concerned that somehow, someway, it will reach Edward's ears."

Colm considered that for a moment. "Not today it won't," he said. "But you *do* realize we're in the middle of something. The middle of Warenton's struggle against Edward. We have been ever since he took another infant to Sempringham."

Carlton knew that, but there was no point in discussing it. "I cannot change it," he said. Then he gestured toward the bailey. "You'd better go. There is no knowing how soon he will arrive, and we want to be ready."

Colm departed without another word, leaving Carlton thinking on a daughter with a betrothed who knew everything about her. More than she knew about herself. He had the feelings that most fathers had, hoping the marriage would be a success, hoping Liam and Cambria would have a contented marriage. All he wanted was a good life for her.

The little lass who meant everything to him.

Thoughts of Cambria lingered as he quit the solar. He intended to tell her about Liam's approach, yet with thoughts of her leaving him in a few years when she came of age, all he could feel was longing. The longing that any father would have for a daughter. As he headed out of the keep, he could hear a couple of servants in the small dining hall speaking about the smell of dogs in the room. Given the fact that Cambria insisted on bringing her dogs into the hall at mealtime, the smell couldn't be helped. She had eleven of them these days—a big male, three adult females, and seven puppies who would soon be going to good homes. Her dogs, big and black and fearsome in adulthood, were much in demand among the nobles of Lincolnshire. In fact, she'd given Liam a puppy when he last came to visit out of the first litter she'd ever had. Carlton hoped he still had the dog because it would most definitely upset his daughter if he didn't.

She was even attached to the pets she no longer had.

She was a woman concerned for all living creatures, everywhere.

It was a busy day in the bailey of Folkingham as Carlton headed for the kitchen yard. It was located on the north side of the keep, a big area between the stables and the outdoor kitchen area. There were fences and gates to keep the livestock in their yard and away from the kitchen, and he had to pass through two of those gates to get to the yard he was looking for.

And there she was.

Her dark hair stood out anywhere she went. Black, like coal, and falling in silken curls to her buttocks. She was always pushing it out of the way, out of her eyes, over her shoulder, because her hair seemed to have some affection for her face. It always wanted to touch it. He didn't blame her hair, of course, because Cambria had the most angelic face, round and sweet, with skin the color of cream. Black, arched eyebrows and black lashes framed eyes the color of cornflowers. They were an unnaturally bright shade of blue, always warm, always kind. Cambria didn't have a nasty bone in her body unless she didn't get what she wanted, which wasn't often, or she was incensed about something. When that happened, men ran for cover. But Carlton rather liked that about her. What was it Warenton had told him? Not to spoil her?

He had disobeyed.

"Bria?" he said. Then he glanced around the yard. "Where's your mother, Dearest?"

Cambria had been bent over one of her dogs, inspecting an eye that seemed to be crusty. "With the cook," she said, standing up to face her father. "Why? Shall I fetch her?"

He shrugged. "Nay," he said. "That is not necessary. You can simply tell her that Liam Herringthorpe will be our guest today. I thought you might like to know."

As he anticipated, her blue eyes flashed. *Liam Herringthorpe*. Those were magic words as far as his fourteen-year-old daughter was concerned because the affection she'd always felt for Liam had never died. It was still there as she grew older, part of her as much as an arm or a leg. She'd known of her betrothal to Liam since she'd been a child, so she knew that whenever he showed up, it was her husband coming to call. Someday he would actually marry her.

They all knew she looked forward to that day.

But she was stubborn. Somewhere over the past year, she'd mentioned outgrowing him, being no longer interested in him. He hadn't come to see her in so long that her pride was wounded. Carlton knew any talk of disinterest was a bold-faced lie, because any mention of the man and her features would light up, like the sun bursting through the clouds. Just like now.

But she must have known her father was onto her game because Cambria stilled her reaction almost immediately. The flash in her eyes dimmed and her expression hardened.

Carlton could see the ruse coming a mile away.

"Why should I like to know?" she said, turning back to her dog. "He has not been here for over two years. I'd forgotten all about him."

Carlton had to fight off a grin. "Truly?" he said, rubbing his chin. "You've forgotten the man you are to marry?"

She bent over the dog again. "He is of no consequence to me," she said. "And clearly, I am not to him, either, or he would have come sooner."

"He has probably been busy."

"With what, pray tell?"

Carlton shrugged. "There has been a good deal of action on the borders as of late," he said. "Especially Berwick, and that is a de Wolfe property. I hear the Scots want it badly and there have been battles. Mayhap he has been busy with that. He is a knight, after all."

She grunted, disinterested. "I have nothing to say to him, Papa," she said. "If he has come to see me, tell him I am busy."

"I will do no such thing."

"Why not?"

"Because you are betrothed to the man," Carlton said, pointing out what she already knew. "If you want him to think you are too busy to see him, then *you* tell him."

She stopped fussing with the dog's eye and looked at her father, frowning. "You will not do that for me?"

"I will not because you are being foolish."

The frown on her face deepened. "How can you say such a thing to me?"

His smile broke through. "Because you adore Liam and you always have," he said. "You are lying if you say otherwise and we both know it. You should never lie to your father."

Cambria could only hold the frown for a few more seconds before she broke into a grin like her father had. "I did not lie to you," she said. "I only told you what I was feeling at that moment."

"And what do you feel in this moment?"

Cambria's smile widened and her cheeks flushed a sweet shade of pink. She didn't even have to say what she was feeling because it was written all over her face. Carlton laughed softly and kissed her on the top of her dark head.

"Since I do not know when he is arriving, mayhap you would like to go now and change into something that the dogs have not pawed over," he said. "Surely you want to look clean for the man or he'll think he's marrying one of the puppies in the pile."

Cambria snorted. "I will," she said. "It has been more than two years. He may not even recognize me."

Carlton eyed her, though he tried not to. She'd developed quite a womanly figure over the past two years, narrow of waist and big of breast. She was still a little slender in the hips, though Fair Lydia assured him that rounding out would come with time. A young woman's body was a constantly growing thing, especially at this age, but Carlton didn't like to think about her growing into a woman at all. He had only just been getting to know the little girl.

"I think he'll be surprised with how much you've grown," he assured her softly. "Your teeth are straight now. I think you were missing one or two the last time."

Cambria instinctively touched her teeth, straight and nicely shaped as they were. "But they look well enough now, don't they?"

She peeled her lips back, baring her teeth at him, and he chuckled softly. "They do, Dearest," he said. Then he pointed to the keep. "Hurry, now. Wash the dog smell off your hands and change your dress. Liam will be here any moment."

That was enough to get Cambria moving, rushing toward the keep with her long hair waving behind her like a banner. Carlton watched her go, a smile on his lips, thinking of his daughter and what the future would hold for her. He hoped she would outgrow that stubborn stance once she married Liam, because he wouldn't take any of her foolishness either. He began to head out to the bailey once more, reflecting on the future Lady Herringthorpe and thinking about what he'd told Colm. She'd be living in the north with her husband and the entire de Wolfe Pack. She would be safe then and his role in this great deception would essentially be over. That was the sad part. He wouldn't have the pleasure of seeing her grow into the role of wife and mother. He had to consider himself fortunate with the time he did spend with her.

But it could have been so different.

He couldn't imagine her living in a convent. He thought of that often, actually. That bright, lovely, brilliant creature hidden away in a convent, praying twelve times a day, married to Christ. Carlton wasn't particularly religious, but even he knew what a cold husband Jesus would be. The loneliness would surely be staggering. But instead, a farmer's daughter was living that life while *Gwenllian* was living as an English noblewoman. She didn't even know the Welsh language or anything else about Wales other than it was a country that gave England a good deal of trouble. That very trouble was why the Earl of

Warenton had wanted vengeance for his son's death, but there was the irony of it all.

James hadn't been killed after all.

It was all quite the mess, from what Carlton had heard. Five years after James' alleged death at Llandeilo, the man had turned up in the midst of a Welsh rebellion *as* a rebel. Somehow, someway, James de Wolfe had survived that horrible ambush, but at a very great price. He had been saved by a Welshman who raised him to believe that he was a Welsh rebel himself and that the English were enemies, and because the morning star had damaged his memory so much, James hadn't known any differently. It had been a very rocky time for William and his family, trying to navigate a new world where James had returned as somebody completely different. Carlton didn't know all the details, but it had been implied that they were quite emotional and difficult.

But William had never said anything more about it to Carlton in person.

In truth, it wouldn't have mattered anyway because Carlton and Fair Lydia, by that point, were completely in love with their daughter as only parents could be. The return of Warenton's son didn't affect them one way or the other. If Warenton's vengeance was satisfied with the return of his son, Carlton's life would not have changed because Cambra *was* his daughter. He would not have given her up, or returned her to the Welsh, or anything else Warenton wanted. He would have continued to raise her as his own and love her as much as he could. But Warenton had never made mention of it, thankfully, and everything went on as it should.

That meant Liam came to Folkingham every year or two and had since Cambria was a young child. The first time he came had been when Cambria was about four years of age. He'd come every year until she was ten years of age, and then he came once more when she was around eleven, nearly twelve. That was the last time they had seen him. Therefore, his coming today was to be a very special event.

Things had changed, indeed.

Crossing the bailey, Carlton was nearly to the great hall when he heard the sentries on the wall. He paused, turning an ear to the activity, quickly realizing that their anticipated visitor was approaching. There was a big bronze bell on the wall and whenever there were arrivals, the sentries rang that bell. He could hear it ringing clearly right now. That told him Herringthorpe was on his doorstep.

He was fairly certain that Cambria had heard the bell, too.

With a grin, he headed to the gatehouse.

Soldiers were racing about, already opening Folkingham's dual portcullises. As Carlton approached, he caught sight of Colm coming off the wall.

The man headed straight for him.

"It's Herringthorpe," Colm said as he drew near. "He's riding with an enormous de Wolfe escort. There have to be a couple of hundred men with him."

Carlton was just shy of the gatehouse, with a perfect view of the road beyond. "That's a rather large escort," he said. "I wonder…"

"What?"

Carlton shook his head. "I suppose I was wondering if there is any trouble," he said. "I'm curious why he would bring so large an escort."

Colm lifted his eyebrows in a gesture that suggested he was concerned, too. "We shall soon find out."

That was the truth.

Both men wait silently for the escort to arrive. It was less than a half-hour, but it seemed to take days. The head of the escort, comprising a pair of knights followed by several soldiers, entered before Herringthorpe made his way in.

Carlton and Colm recognized the knight immediately and Carlton lifted a hand in greeting. That brought Herringthorpe to him, astride a blond stallion that was sweaty and foaming. When he tossed his head, the white foam hit Colm in the arm. He grunted unhappily, smearing it away, as Herringthorpe dismounted. Carlton couldn't help but notice that the man seemed much taller and broader than he had been only a couple of years ago. It was true that he'd always been tall, and a little big for his age, but he'd filled out tremendously and not with flab, but with muscle.

Everything about him seemed to ripple with power.

"My lord," Liam said as he pulled his helm off, revealing blond hair that was sticky with sweat. "It has been a long time."

Carlton smiled at a young man he genuinely liked. "Liam, you do not have to address me so formally anymore," he said. "I am no longer your master and you are no longer my squire."

Liam grinned, revealing a straight line of white teeth and big dimples in each cheek. "I know," he said. "But it seems sinful to do anything else. I do not think I shall ever look at you as anything other than my master."

Carlton chuckled softly. "I understand," he said, glancing at Colm, who nodded in agreement. "I viewed my old mentor the same way. I think we all do."

Liam's focus shifted to Colm briefly. "De Lara," he greeted him. "It is good to see you. I did not expect to, to be honest."

Colm knew what he meant. His father, Garreg, had been in

bad health and Colm was expected to return home to take his place at his father's side. At least, that had been the situation the last time Liam visited. But the truth was that Colm and his father had never gotten on well and he'd been reluctant to go, even though that had been expected of him. He'd made the decision to return when his father passed and no sooner, which was why he was still at Folkingham. But that wasn't something he was ready to discuss at the moment, so he glossed over it.

"I've not gone home yet," he said. "Someday, but not now. But let us not discuss me—we are honored by your unexpected visit, Liam. To what do we owe the pleasure?"

Liam's smile faded a little. "I bring news," he said. "May we go somewhere to speak?"

Carlton nodded immediately. "Will the hall do?"

"I would prefer the solar. It is more private."

Carlton started to move toward the keep, casting a long glance at Colm as he did so. Perhaps Colm's paranoia had some basis now. The three of them headed toward the keep, with Carlton asking about Liam's journey, talking about the weather, and anything else inconsequential. By the time they reached the steps to the keep, he'd run out of things to say, so they continued in silence until they reached the solar and Colm quietly closed the door behind them. Then it was just the three of them and a room full of silence.

Liam was the first one to speak.

"Thank you, my lord, for welcoming me into your home once again," he said, settling his helm on the nearest table. "I realize that my visit is unexpected. I hope it is not inopportune."

Carlton shook his head. "Nay," he said. "Your visits are never inopportune, but we are understandably curious. Colm thinks you've come to bring doom and gloom upon us."

Liam smiled weakly, looking at Colm, who simply shrugged. "That is his nature," he said. "He is naturally suspicious of certain situations. Mayhap that is why he has stayed alive so long—his natural suspicion."

Colm chuckled. Even Carlton smiled. But that smile quickly faded. "I think we all have that innate suspicion that has kept us alive," he said. "That is part of a knight's training. And my innate suspicion tells me that you've not come to discuss trivial subjects. Am I correct?"

Liam nodded. "You are," he said. "I've come to deliver news."

"What news?"

Liam cleared his throat softly. "Not good news, I am afraid," he said. "There are several messengers riding through England at this time, delivering the same news. It is something that should be delivered in person."

"*What* news, Herringthorpe?" Colm demanded. "Do not make us beg for it."

Liam glanced at him, but his focus was on Carlton. "Six weeks ago, on the twentieth day of June, the Earl of Warenton, William de Wolfe, passed away. Scott de Wolfe is now the new Earl of Warenton."

Colm stared at him a moment before closing his eyes and dropping his head, a gesture of genuine sorrow. Carlton's gaze was steady as he processed what he'd been told, but that steadiness morphed into the same expression that Colm had as a sense of mourning began to fill the chamber.

"The Wolfe of the Border has finally passed into legend," Carlton said softly. "Truthfully, I am surprised to hear this. He'd lived so long that I was certain he would live forever."

Liam nodded, the strain of grief on his features. "We all did," he said. "You were not alone in that assumption."

"How did it happen?"

Liam lowered himself into the nearest chair, a weary gesture. "It was the strangest thing," he said. "According to his wife, he'd had a restless day. He seemed to be moving from one task to another, insisting things needed to be done. You know that his son, Blayth, has mostly taken over command of Castle Questing. It has been that way for about five years now, ever since Warenton fell from his horse and injured himself. His wife scolded him for a full day and a full night until, finally, he relinquished command to his son."

"Blayth," Carlton said curiously. "I do not know a son by that name."

"It is James," Liam said quietly. "You heard that he was discovered in Wales, without memory of his former life due to the head wounds he had received at Llandeilo."

Carlton nodded. "I had heard about his return," he said. "So he calls himself Blayth?"

"It means 'wolf' in Welsh."

It made a little sense, but Carlton wasn't nearly as curious about the returned son as he was about William's passing, so he continued to focus on that. "So he was restless that day," he said. "But he was in good health?"

Liam nodded. "So we all thought," he said. "He seemed normal. He ate a good meal in the evening and then retired to bed, but according to Lady Warenton, he was tired and aching. He could not sleep. She rubbed at his back, which he said pained him, but it was to no avail. He soon became short of breath and the physic was summoned. The physic gave him a potion to help him sleep, so he did. And he did not wake up. He went very quickly, in his sleep."

There it was. The moment that the greatest knight of his generation quietly passed into legend, as Carlton had put it. No great dramatics, blood, or battle. Simply sleep and peace. After a moment, Carlton nodded as if accepting what he'd been told.

"How is Lady Warenton?" he said. "I cannot imagine she has taken this well. They were married for many, many years."

"Over sixty," Liam said. "And Lady Warenton is a strong woman. She has shown great strength since that day. The entire family has. I have spent my time shadowing Blayth, as I have been appointed his right hand. If he needs something done, I am there to do it, so while Blayth has been comforting his mother, as the rest of the family has been also, the duty for securing all de Wolfe properties has fallen to me. I would have come sooner, only it was not wise to leave Castle Questing so soon after his passing."

"Why?" Carlton asked with concern. "Has something happened?"

Liam shrugged. "As I am sure you are aware, the past few years have not been without strife," he said. "The Scots are unsettled. Edward used Berwick, which belongs to Patrick de Wolfe, in order to show his support for John Balliol. This did not sit well with supporters of Robert Bruce, as you can imagine, so there has simply been a good deal of chaos and contention since then. If it is not one thing, it is another."

"I would believe it."

"Blayth and Scott wanted things to settle down before they sent out messages about their father's death," Liam said. "When they deemed it safe enough, they sent out several knights to allies. I've already been to a few. You are the last one."

"Good," Carlton said. "You may stay with us for a while and

rest. In fact, we will hunt. It has been a while since I've gone on a good hunt."

Liam smiled weakly. "I would like that," he said. "But I've also come to see Cambria. Has she been well?"

"Very well," Carlton said. "Where is the dog she gave you?"

Liam's smile grew. "Bran is well," he said. "He was riding in the wagon when we arrived because he's practically walked all the way from the north. Also, he tangled with a badger yesterday and suffered a little in the battle. The ridiculous dog must learn he cannot chase down a *brock*."

A brock was another name for a badger, a creature that most sane dogs wouldn't deliberately tussle with. But Bran the dog, named for a fearsome mythological canine, still hadn't learned that he couldn't take on the world and win.

Carlton shook his head. "The dogs that my daughter continues to raise are big and strong," he said. "No one ever said they were smart."

Liam laughed softly. "He's actually quite smart," he said. "Sometimes, anyway. But he loves me and I love him, and I must thank Lady Cambria for the gift. She has no idea how much better that ridiculous dog has made my life."

Carlton patted him on the shoulder in a gesture reminiscent of the days when Liam had been his squire. Truth be told, Carlton was a mild-tempered man and he'd never raised his voice to Liam the entire time the lad had been his squire. He'd always calmly instructed or calmly reprimanded him, but never a harsh word. Harsh words came from Colm. But Liam had always appreciated the way Carlton had treated those in his command.

Like now.

It was a gesture of comfort.

"You will tell her soon enough," Carlton said. "But you have had a long journey and I am sure you could use some rest. It cannot be easy telling men that the great William de Wolfe has passed away. He was fond of you, Liam. I know. He told me."

Liam appeared pensive for a moment before he looked up at Carlton. "I will tell you a secret," he said, eyeing Colm as he did so. "It must go no further. Will you swear this to me, both of you?"

"Of course," Carlton said seriously. "What is it?"

"William de Wolfe was my grandfather."

Colm's eyebrows lifted in surprise as Carlton sighed faintly, perhaps with some genuine sympathy for the young knight who seemed to show a crack in his composure when he'd said that. Something in his eyes flickered. The pain was there, a pain he'd had to keep hidden because few knew of his true relationship to William, but he'd felt comfortable enough with Carlton and Colm to let his guard down a little. With men he'd served with years ago, men he trusted.

That kind of trust was rare.

"I know," Carlton murmured. "Warenton confided in me on the night Cambria was brought to Folkingham. He only told me because he wished for there to be a betrothal between you and Cambria, so it was only fair that I knew why he wanted you, since I was to raise Cambria as my own."

Liam didn't seem particularly surprised to hear that Carlton had already known. As he'd said, given the fact that Liam was betrothed to his adopted daughter, it was only fair he know the extent of their relationship.

"Did he tell you why it is a secret well kept?" Liam asked after a moment.

Carlton nodded. "To protect your father's mother," he said.

"Your grandmother's reputation must be preserved."

That was the truth. With a nod, perhaps one of grief for the man he could never publicly acknowledge as his grandfather, Liam tried to stand up but realized his legs were too weary to do so. It was true that he'd traveled a great deal over the past few weeks, and this was honestly the first time he'd been able to let his guard down. It was probably the first time since the passing of Warenton, because he'd been in command and control mode since then to relieve the family of any burdens. But now… now, he could acknowledge his weariness, and it was great. When Carlton saw him struggle to rise, he simply motioned him to stay in the chair.

"Rest here," he said. "I will ensure that a room is prepared for you. Colm will make sure your men are settled. You brought quite a few with you."

Liam leaned his head back against the high back of the chair. It was carved wood, and uncomfortable, but it didn't matter. He was exhausted.

"One hundred and eighty," he muttered. "They can camp outside the walls if you wish."

"That is not necessary," Colm said, moving past Carlton as he headed for the door. "I will clear a place in the bailey for them."

"That is appreciated."

Colm headed out. Carlton followed shortly, without another word, leaving Liam sitting in that stiff chair, wondering if he would ever rise again. His legs hurt, his buttocks and back hurt, and all he wanted to do was sleep.

His task was done.

Barely another minute passed before his soft snoring filled the chamber.

CHAPTER FIVE

Z ZZZZZZZZZZZZZZzzzzzzzzzzzzzzzzzzzzz………
She could hear… something.

Like someone sawing wood.

The sound was coming from her father's solar and, as far as she knew, no one was sawing wood in there. But there was clearly something happening because Liam Herringthorpe was in the chamber, so her father had said, so he was making some kind of noise.

Quietly, she opened the door.

Liam was sitting in her father's carved chair, the one that had come from some cold country far to the east. It was beautiful to look at but not particularly comfortable. Even so, Liam was sleeping like the dead in it.

ZZZZZZZZZZZZZZZzzzzzzzzzzzzzzzzzzzz……

With a grin, she entered the solar, tiptoeing over to a chair near her father's table. She was halfway there when she stubbed her toe on the corner of his table, tripped over her own feet, and ended up falling right onto Liam's lap and lower abdomen.

He let out a grunt that God himself would have been sympathetic over.

"Jesus Christ!" he groaned, instinctively grabbing the body on his lap. "What in the bloody…?"

Cambria was in a panic. "Let me go!" she nearly howled, throwing an elbow into the man's belly. "I am terribly sorry, but let me go!"

Liam had no choice. He'd just had his lower abdomen and groin assaulted and now there was a bony elbow in his belly. He released the wildcat in his arms, and when she pushed herself off him, she used his face as leverage. He found himself rubbing his injured nose as she stumbled away from him, crashing into the table again before steadying herself.

Liam found himself looking into brilliant blue eyes.

He knew those eyes. He knew that black hair. He also knew that face, or so he thought, but he'd known those three things a few years ago on a young girl whose teeth hadn't all quite grown in. She'd been skinny and wiry and had a high-pitched giggle. That was the Cambria he knew.

But this woman before him was something quite new.

And something quite different.

In fact, he was astonished when he realized who it was. Cambria had grown into her teeth, into her figure, and before him stood a goddess. She was still petite, and slender, but she had become a woman.

He could hardly believe it.

"Bria?" he said, incredulous. "Is that truly you?"

Cambria stood on the other side of the table, frowning at him. "I'm surprised you remember me," she said. "It has been so long since you've visited."

He laughed at the sound of her peeved voice, his bright smile lighting up the room. "I was busy," he said.

"Doing what?"

"Fighting Scots," he said. "If you'll sit, I'll tell you everything I've been doing over the past two and a half years. My God, lass, 'tis good to see you again."

She eyed him. The man was full of charm when he wanted to be, big smile and all, and that was something she'd always succumbed to. It wasn't as if she could stay annoyed with him for long. But she didn't want to appear too compliant, so she scowled and stomped over to the nearest chair.

"There," she said, plopping down. "I'm sitting."

Liam continued to smile at her, his green eyes twinkling. "Thank you, my lady," he said. "May I say that it is good to see you? May I at least say that?"

In response, she turned her nose up at him and looked away. Her gesture was so exaggerated that Liam had to chuckle.

"Did I offend you by saying that?" he said, trying to make eye contact with her because she wouldn't look at him. "Did I insult you?"

Cambria was well aware that he was trying to catch her attention. She could see him out of the corner of her eye, leaning over in his chair. But she kept her head turned away, unwilling to give even a little.

"Nay," she said. "You did not."

"Good," he said, playing her game. "I would never wish to insult you."

"I said you did not."

"Then why do you not look at me?"

She kept her face turned away. "Because you have spent two and a half years away," she said. "Why should I want to look at you? You did not think enough of me to come and see me in all that time, so why should I see you?"

The smile never left Liam's lips. "It was not by choice," he said. "As I said, I have been very busy. And I was wounded at Berwick, so I had to recover."

That brought about the desired result. She looked at him, quickly, and with great concern. "Wounded?" she repeated. "What happened?"

He held up a finger to beg for her patience while he stood up and unbuckled the belt around his waist. It contained his purse and daggers, among other things. Then he untied the belt that held the broadsword, unfastening the strap from his left thigh before finally setting the sword carefully on Carlton's desk. He proceeded to lift the mail he was wearing, and the tunic, to display his taut torso. But that torso also had a big scar on it, on the left side just above his hip bone.

"That," he said, "was the result of an overeager Scotsman who wanted to take down an English knight. He nearly succeeded."

Cambria gasped. "That is terrible!" she said, jumping up and rushing to him, her fingers going right to the puckered scar. "Did it hurt? Did you bleed a good deal?"

"It hurt and I bled a good deal," he said. "So if you are truly angry that I've not come to see you in over two years, know that it has genuinely not been by choice. This wound set me back about six months because it became infected with poison. It took some time to heal completely from it. I—"

He was cut off when the door to the solar swung open. Carlton was standing there and beside him was an enormous black dog on a lead. Bran seemed quite happy to see Liam, and Carlton had been prepared to deliver the dog to his master because a soldier had turned the pup over to him out in the bailey, but when he saw Liam with his tunic up, belly exposed, and his daughter with her hands on the naked flesh, he blew his proverbial top.

"Bria!" he boomed. "What are you doing?"

The sound of his sharp voice startled her and she instantly drew back her hand, eyes wide at him. "Papa!" she boomed in return. "Why are you shouting?"

"*Why* are you touching him?" Carlton fired back, but his focus swiftly pivoted to Liam. "And what are you doing with your flesh exposed? Are you trying to seduce my daughter?"

Liam dropped the tunic, lifting both hands in surrender. He'd never heard Carlton shout in his life. "I am not, my lord, I swear it," he said quickly. "She asked why I'd not come to visit in so long and I was showing her a wound that nearly killed me."

"Killed you?" Cambria shrieked. "And you are only just telling me this?"

Liam looked at her in remorse, but Carlton wouldn't let him reply. "Take your dog and remove yourself, Liam," he said, handing the dog's lead over to him. "Go. Get out of here before I do something I regret."

Ever obedient when it came to Carlton, Liam took the dog's lead and prepared to swiftly move out, but Cambria threw out her arms and put herself in his path.

"You are not going anywhere," she said. Her ire immediately returned to her father. "And *you*. You would think such terrible things about me? Do you truly think I would allow Liam to seduce me? Have I ever allowed *anyone* to seduce me?"

Carlton was rightfully angry. "You are a very young woman who thinks she is a grown adult," he said. "You are fourteen years of age, lass. You should not be speaking of seduction or anything else where it pertains to a man. You should not even be alone with him in this chamber. Do you have any idea how improper this is?"

He'd never had a harsh word with his daughter in his life, but Cambria wasn't backing down. She matched his tone, his anger. "He is my betrothed," she pointed out. "You brokered the contract when I was born and in the eyes of the God and the law, I am already his wife. What is improper about being alone with the man who is to be my husband?"

Carlton lost his temper. Grabbing Cambria by the arm, he yanked her in the direction of the solar door. She didn't go easily, however, and when she dug her heels in, he spanked her on the bottom, his big hand to her tender behind, only once, and Cambria came to a halt, her hand on her buttocks as she looked at her father in shock. Her face turned red, but before she could lash out at him for spanking her, the tears came and she fled the chamber in abject humiliation.

Carlton was angrier than he'd ever been in his life. He turned that anger on Liam, who was standing there with a stonelike expression.

"You know better," Carlton spat. "You know better than to put her in a position like that. What were you thinking?"

Liam was shockingly cool. He didn't like what he'd just seen and was struggling with some anger of his own. Carlton was his old master and he had immense respect for the man, but at this moment, all he could feel was disappointment in the man's reaction. He could see where it had looked bad upon initial glance, but the Carlton he knew would have calmly asked what was happening. And Liam would have calmly told him.

But that hadn't happened.

"I told you the situation," he said in a low, controlled voice. "I was showing her the scar on my belly. That was it. Nothing untoward happened or was going to happen because I hope you know me better than what you just insinuated. My reputation is beyond reproach, and if you think otherwise, then we have a serious problem."

Carlton took a deep breath, struggling to calm himself. "I know you," he said. "I know your character, which is why I was so surprised when I walked in on this… this shocking display."

Liam was finished talking to the man because it was clear he had no intention of being reasonable at the moment. He was too angry for that. Better that they part ways and cool their anger before something was said that they would both regret. Collecting his belts, weapons, sword, and dog, in that order, he took a step in Carlton's direction.

"Nothing happened, nor was anything going to happen," he muttered. "But if I ever see you strike her again in anger, I will kill you."

With that, he left the solar, heading out into the entry beyond and leaving Carlton with a distinct feeling that Liam meant what he'd said.

Every word of it.

Liam the squire had grown up because, by damn, Carlton believed him.

ଓ

SHE'D NEVER BEEN so embarrassed in her entire life.

The tears were flowing as Cambria sat in the yard with her dogs. It was bad enough that her father had spanked her, but even worse that he'd done it in front of a witness. Liam, of all people. Carlton had spanked her as if she were a silly little girl, not a grown woman. Well, she *was* a grown woman, but maybe Liam wouldn't see her that way now. Why should he be proud to marry a woman who got spanked like a child?

But it was more than that.

Carlton had behaved in a way she'd never seen before. He'd raised his voice and accused her of being improper. Truthfully, there was part of her that could see his point. He'd walked in when she had her hand on Liam's naked torso, but it was only to see that awful scar he had. She didn't even know how he got it because he hadn't told her yet. He probably never would now. He'd get on his horse and head back to the north, where women weren't spanked by their fathers.

She was deeply ashamed. She'd run straight into the yard where she kept her dogs and sat down among them, dirtying the clean garment she'd changed into in honor of Liam's visit. The dogs milled around her with the big male licking her face. When she pushed him aside, gently, he simply collapsed and laid his head in her lap.

Hand on the dog, Cambria sat there and wept.

"Bria?" Liam was suddenly in the yard. "Get off the ground, sweetheart. You are going to get dirty down there."

He was holding a hand down to her, and when she shook her head, refusing his request, he gently took her wrist and pulled her, reluctantly, to her feet. He was still holding his dog on a lead with the other hand and all of Cambria's dogs were quite interested in the newcomer who wasn't so much a newcomer, as he'd been part of the pack those years ago. They sniffed at him, tails wagging, as Cambria wiped the tears off her face.

"I am sorry for my father," she said, sniffling. "I do not know what possessed him to say such terrible things. That's not like him at all."

Liam still had her by the wrist. "Do not fret over it," he said softly. "The man has a daughter to protect. I cannot say I would not have done the same thing in his position."

His words made her feel a little better. "He's never spanked me before, not ever," she said. "I do not know why he chose this moment to do it, right in front of you."

Liam smiled faintly. "It could be because you were shouting at him," he said. "Or resisting him."

She looked up at him, her eyes flashing. "He was being offensive."

"He was being a father who was concerned for his daughter."

"He did not have to spank me."

"Nay, he did not," Liam agreed. "Did he hurt you?"

She rubbed her bum, instinctively. "Not really."

He could see that she was humiliated more than anything else. "Mayhap he was right," he said. "Mayhap I should not have shown you my scar. It was bold of me. Forgive me."

Her features turned sympathetic. "I am glad you told me," she said. "But you did not tell me how it happened."

"I did," he reminded her. "An angry Scotsman tried to impale me. He did a fairly good job of it, actually."

"Did it hurt?"

"Of course not."

She frowned. "I should think it would," she said. "Getting stabbed by a sword is serious."

He smiled at her. "It was a tickle."

He wasn't going to budge on the pain issue because he genuinely didn't want her to worry about it, or him, but Cambria didn't realize that. She thought he was simply being noble.

"Are the wars still going on in the north?" she asked.

He shrugged. "The Scots are unhappy right now," he said. "They have a good deal of turmoil between the clans, but they also seemed determined to take Berwick and some other northern properties. It has kept us very busy, and with the death of the Earl of Warenton, we expect them to test the de Wolfe strength now."

She looked at him seriously. "The Earl of Warenton?" she repeated. "Isn't that William de Wolfe?"

He nodded. "Aye," he said, his expression tightening with sorrow. "He was a very great man and I shall miss him, but with his absence, the Scots may see it as an opportunity."

"To do what?"

"Try to fracture the north."

"And you will be in the middle of it if they do."

He nodded. He didn't have to say a word. His expression conveyed how serious it was, and that didn't do anything to ease her concern for it.

"Then you will be leaving soon," she said solemnly.

"Aye," he said. "I cannot stay long. I only came to deliver news of Warenton's death and to see to your health."

Gazing up at him, she pushed some stray hair out of her eyes. "When will you return?"

His green eyes glimmered. "As soon as I can," he said. "Will you miss me?"

"Nay."

She said it quickly, *too* quickly, and turned away from him so he wouldn't see the smile on her lips.

His grin was back.

"If I said I will miss you, would it matter?" he said.

"Why should it?"

He cocked an eyebrow. "You know that we are to be married in a few years," he said. "It is time you start showing me some regard. You *do* like me, don't you?"

Cambria's head was still turned away, but her cheeks were flushing madly. "I do not *dislike* you," she said.

He burst into soft laughter. "How good of you, my lady," he said. "I do not dislike you, either."

"That is good," she said. "For we cannot get rid of one another."

"Do you want to get rid of me?"

She did look at him then. "Not today," she said. "Ask me the same question tomorrow and I may have a different answer."

He continued to laugh. "You know how to make a man feel wanted."

She was gearing up for a petulant retort but was distracted because someone was licking her hand. Cambria looked down to see Bran, Liam's dog, licking at her fingers and she instantly softened, going down on a knee to pet the very big, black head.

"He looks healthy," she said. "I am glad to see that he is happy."

"He is very happy," he said. "I told your father that I wanted to thank you for giving him to me. I do not know what I would do without him."

Her pets on the dog slowed. "And I do not know what I would do without you," she said quietly. "If you must return north, to battle, then try not to be killed before we have a chance to wed."

The smile faded from Liam's face. That was as honest as he'd ever heard her. He'd known Cambria for the entirety of her life, before she was even called Cambria, and he'd always viewed the betrothal between them as a duty and nothing more. When he was younger, he'd been positively averse to it to the point of rebellion, but stern words from William had quelled any resistance. *Marry her and breed strong English sons from her,*

William had told him. He knew why, too. It was to breed away Llywelyn's bloodlines. He knew he'd been chosen for an important role.

He'd tried to focus on that.

Truthfully, until he rode through the gates of Folkingham this time, he'd simply been resigned to his future. The last he saw of Cambria, she'd been just a girl, skinny, with a pretty face and crooked teeth. He remembered that she'd followed him around, holding his hand, and he'd barely tolerated it. He'd expected that with this visit, he'd have to tolerate her again, but something strange had happened.

She'd grown up.

The woman before him suddenly wasn't such an unhappy duty. Not only had she physically matured, but her manner had matured as well. She was humorous. She was brave, as evidenced by her conversation with her father. She was growing up before him and he liked what he saw. He could only imagine how magnificent she would be in another four or five years, when it was time for them to wed. What had been a duty could become something else.

It might actually be a pleasure.

Bending over her as she crouched on the ground and petted his dog, he murmured in her ear.

"I will do my best," he whispered.

His hot breath on her ear startled her and she instinctively put her hand up, slapping him in the mouth in the process. He grunted, immediately tasting blood, as she bolted to her feet.

"Forgive me," she said apologetically. "I did not mean to do that."

He rubbed at the lip where there was a pinprick of blood from being cut by a front tooth. "Not to worry," he said. "I will heal. But I meant what I said. I will do everything possible to ensure the Scots do not take my life."

She nodded, seemingly satisfied by his declaration. "I hope so," she said. "Because I am certain there is no other man in England who could tolerate me."

His eyebrows rose dramatically. "And you think I can?"

She grinned, a lovely gesture. "You have no choice," she said. "It's either me or the Scots."

"That's my only alternative?"

"I am afraid so."

His smile was back and he winked at her. "I will take my chances with you," he said. "But you should know that I am the jealous type, so no flirting with anyone while I am away. It was charming when you were a child, but you are no longer a child. The only man you will flirt with is me and you cannot do that until you are a little older, so keep that in mind. Behave yourself while I am gone. Promise?"

She cocked her head thoughtfully. "And if I do not?"

"Then I'll spank you like your father just did."

"You'll have to catch me first."

He scowled, watching her fight off a smile. She was toying with him and he was going to let her. Loudly, he stomped a big boot in her direction and she squealed with terror, taking off on a run toward the bailey. He gave her a head start before following, grinning all the way.

The next several years were going to be a very, very long wait, indeed.

PART TWO
OF ROYAL BLOOD

CHAPTER SIX

Year of Our Lord 1302
London, England

"AND THAT IS the story, Your Grace. That is everything the Lord of the Trilaterals told me about William de Wolfe and Llywelyn's daughter."

In the damp, dank cloister of Westminster Abbey that smelled heavily of incense and mold, St. Zosimus was speaking to a white-haired man in a dark robe and scarlet cloak. He had just relayed the tale that Colm de Lara had told him, the one involving a de Wolfe betrayal and a princess under an assumed identity. De Lara had died shortly after his confession, and even though it was forbidden for a priest to speak of anything confided in him during confession, St. Zosimus knew this was different.

Very different.

Therefore, he'd ridden like a madman for London, seeking an audience with the Archbishop of Canterbury. Unfortunately, that was not a quick process. It had taken him weeks to obtain permission because there was a chain of command within the church that was rigidly adhered to. Technically, St. Zosimus should have gone to his superior, the Bishop of York, to request the audience, but he'd bypassed the man completely.

He didn't want to trust this information to anyone else but the man at the top.

That man was Robert Winchelsey. At first, he'd been quite annoyed with St. Zosimus and his persistence, but once he heard the man's story, he could understand why. Robert had been the archbishop for several years, a leader of the church who was usually at odds with the king, so when he heard the tale, he was delighted that de Wolfe and de Royans had managed to pull off such a scheme against Edward. Decades of fighting in Wales had come to one dark moment that would have seen royal Welsh bloodlines tucked away in a priory, but according to Colm de Lara, that hadn't happened.

Quite the opposite.

The news was revolutionary, but it was also quite valuable. Given Robert's history with Edward, and the years of contention between them, he immediately thought of how he could leverage the information.

All was fair in the deadly chess game that was England's politics.

Whatever he decided to do, he had to think fast because St. Zosimus wasn't going to keep the information to himself for long. Any man who would bypass protocols to go straight to the top was a man who would go to someone else with the same information if Canterbury didn't give him what he wanted.

And that was the gist of this little audience, he suspected.

St. Zosimus wanted something.

"Shocking," Canterbury finally said about the situation as it had been explained to him. "And de Lara swore to this?"

St. Zosimus nodded. "He did, Your Grace," he said. "There was no reason for him to lie. In fact, he seemed quite eager to tell me."

"Why, I wonder?"

"Guilt."

Canterbury looked at him curiously. "Why should he feel guilty?"

St. Zosimus shrugged. "For deceiving the king, I suppose," he said. "I did not ask. All I know is that he was most eager to tell me. Of course, I could not keep this information to myself. I will not be responsible for it."

Canterbury cocked an eyebrow. "So you would make *me* responsible?"

St. Zosimus smiled thinly. "With a great post comes great responsibility."

Canterbury was a man with a finely honed ability to read others, a talent that had gotten him far in life. The more he listened to St. Zosimus, the more he knew the man wanted whatever advancement this information could get him. All of this—the audience, the way he had delivered his information, and the generally helpful manner about him—was carefully orchestrated.

It was also sickening.

"Indeed, it does," Canterbury replied slowly. "You've not told anyone else?"

St. Zosimus shook his head. "Nay, Your Grace," he said. "Only you. My loyalties are to my profession, my fellow priests. I would not share this with anyone else."

"And you will not from this moment forward," Canterbury said, his gaze growing hard. "I am the only person you will tell. If you tell anyone else, it will be a violation of your covenant with God. Is that clear?"

St. Zosimus nodded. "I am obedient, Your Grace," he said. "Very obedient. But I had hoped..."

"Hoped *what*?"

St. Zosimus took a deep breath, pretending that it was for courage. "I had hoped to help you with this information, Your Grace," he said. "If you need a man to talk to about it, or have a need for me to help you in any way, I would be honored to remain by your side."

Now, St. Zosimus' ambitions were becoming apparent. He'd veiled them well under the guise of delivering a service to Canterbury in the form of important information, but he couldn't keep that kind of determination hidden for long.

Canterbury wasn't stupid.

"You mean that you wish to remain here in London," he said plainly.

St. Zosimus nodded. "That would be my dream," he said. "I have spent a good deal of time on the marches. It is a dismal, cold place. I was born in London."

"You want to come home."

"I would like to, Your Grace."

"And?"

"And... what, Your Grace? What do you mean?"

"Where would you like to be sent?"

St. Zosimus looked around the lavish solar of the Archbishop of Canterbury. In spite of the condition of the cloisters, the archbishop's apartments were well kept, warm, and appropriately luxurious. Of course he wanted to be here, in the beating heart of England's moral pendulum. He was looking right at the man who played God to kings and lords and peasants alike.

Where would you like to be sent?

His information would come at a price.

And he'd planned it all along.

"I am from the East End of London, Your Grace," he finally said. "My home was near Aldgate. St. Botolph was where my mother and I worshipped."

"You want to be sent to St. Botolph?"

"I think so, Your Grace."

Canterbury didn't say anything to that. He simply nodded as if pondering the request. After a moment, he stood up and went to a beautifully carved table, coated with a layer of wax to make it shiny, and poured himself a cup of wine from a crystal and pewter decanter. The cup was rock crystal, the ruby color of the wine showing through. He put it to his lips and took a drink, not offering anything to St. Zosimus. He didn't want to. He stood there a moment, sipping, smacking his lips, and thinking.

"Since this information would be of more interest to the king than to me, why did you tell me?" he finally asked.

St. Zosimus wasn't sure about the intent of the question. "Because... because it was given to me in confidence, Your Grace," he said. "I cannot tell the king."

"And you should not have told me," Canterbury said, finally looking at him. "You are well aware of the seal of confession."

St. Zosimus sat a little straighter, perhaps with some apprehension. "Of course I am, Your Grace," he said. "But this seemed too important... and he did not exactly tell it to me in confession, but rather upon his deathbed. It was more like a conversation."

Canterbury was hardening right before his eyes. "He told you because you are a priest and he deemed you trustworthy," he said. "But why he should tell you this information is beyond my powers of comprehension. He should have let the secret die with him, but he did not."

"Nay, he did not, Your Grace."

The whole thing seemed to be making Canterbury angry. He stood next to the carved table and drank the entire cup of wine before pouring himself another. All the while, he seemed to be considering the situation, trying to decide what to do about it.

It didn't take him long.

"Listen to me and listen well," he finally said. "You are not to repeat the story, not to anyone. If I discover you have, I will excommunicate you myself and then I will have you thrown in the vault. Do you understand me?"

St. Zosimus nodded quickly. "I do, Your Grace."

"Then get out," Canterbury said, waving a hand in the direction of the door. "Where are you lodged?"

"I've not found lodgings yet, Your Grace."

"Then go to the cloister and tell them you need a bed, on my request," Canterbury said. "You will stay there until I send for you."

"Aye, Your Grace."

Canterbury waved him off again and St. Zosimus took the hint. He bolted to his feet and quickly fled the chamber, leaving Canterbury still standing with the cup in his hand. When he was certain that the greedy priest from the marches wasn't going to return, he took another sip of his wine.

"Well?" he said. "Did you hear all of that?"

The room was surrounded with tapestries on the walls and alcoves covered by heavy curtains, dusty things that kept the chamber warm in the brutal winters of London. On the left side of the room, one of the curtains flipped back and a big man with a sword strapped to his thigh appeared. He was tall and handsome, with dark hair and hazel eyes. He fixed on Canterbury, an almost amused smile on his face.

"I did, Your Grace," he said. "I must say that is not what I was expecting."

Canterbury grunted. "Nor I," he said, moving to reclaim his chair. "I do not know what I expected, but that priest has been trying to gain an audience with me for three weeks. I assumed that whatever he wished to discuss was something of local corruption or complaining about his lodgings or profession. God only knows what I thought. But hearing what came out of his mouth… Nay, I did not expect that."

"Seems fantastic."

Canterbury looked at him. "Do you think it is true?" he said. "You knew William de Wolfe, Ronec. Your family is allied with the entire de Wolfe empire."

Sir Ronec de Nerra nodded. "There is a collection of us who have been allied with one another for centuries," he said. "A tight band of allies—de Lohr, de Wolfe, de Shera, de Lara and the like. Most of the families came over with the Duke of Normandy, ancestors who formed a band of knights called the *anges de guerre*, men who forged this nation."

"Was your ancestor with them?"

Ronec shook his head. "Nay," he said. "My ancestors came from the Carpathian region, believe it or not. Long ago, we were rulers. We were not from Normandy or Brittany and the *anges du guerre* came from that area. But our rule was taken from us in some damn bloody wars, and we migrated to Rome, where we entered into service for the church. We came to these shores because we served the pope at the time and he lent legions to support the Duke of Normandy. We stayed in service with the

Normans once they settled these lands, mostly with magistrate duties or within the army of the church. That is how I came into your service, Your Grace. I was gifted to you, if you recall, by a grateful prince of the church."

Canterbury smiled faintly. "I remember very well," he said. "You are one of the greatest gifts I have ever received—but do not let that swell your head, and if you tell anyone, I will deny it."

Ronec chuckled softly. "I will not speak of it, I promise," he said, but he quickly sobered. "So now we have something of a volatile piece of information given to us by that fool."

Canterbury snorted. "You thought him a fool, too?" he said. "The man is greedy. He only gave me the information because he wants something. I know an ambitious man when I see one."

"What are you going to do?"

Canterbury sighed heavily and set his cup down. "I am not entirely certain," he said. "A few things were crossing my mind as I heard the news."

"Like what?"

"Like using the information as leverage against Edward," he said. "You know as well as I do that he has increased the taxes on the clergy and I have little ground to stand on in protest. Edward is old, but he is cunning and he'll do what he can to exert power over me, yet if I had Gwenllian of Wales in my possession..."

He trailed off, and Ronec could see where this was going. He was the unofficial advisor to the Archbishop of Canterbury, an elite knight who was supposed to be the man's protection and nothing more, but Canterbury had discovered early on that Ronec was so much more than muscle and skill. The man had impeccable advice and wisdom. Canterbury relied on him more for his moral and ethical advice rather than the religious kind. He had an army of priests for that. But Ronec kept him grounded.

"If you have Gwenllian of Wales, I do not think it will have the effect you are looking for," he said. "We all know the story of the children of Llywelyn the Last and his brother, Dafydd. The girls were sent to a convent and the sons were taken somewhere and disappeared. But Gwenllian has the distinction of being the granddaughter of King John, so she shares that with Edward. They are related by blood. That means she is treated differently."

Canterbury nodded. "She was sent to a priory in Lincolnshire," he said. "But why do you say that taking her hostage will not have the desired effect against Edward?"

Ronec tried to phrase his advice carefully. Canterbury was a powerful man who always believed he was right, so this had to be handled delicately. "Because right now, it is simply a power struggle between the two of you, Your Grace," he said. "You have a tense relationship, but he is not out to destroy you. He tolerates you as you tolerate him. If you take Gwenllian and use her against him, however you choose, then he will see this as an assault. He will go to war with you, and I can only imagine that it will make the situation between the Crown and the church that much worse."

Canterbury pondered the advice carefully. He picked up his cup again, drinking deeply, as if that would somehow help his mind work.

"I do not want to make things worse than they are," he admitted. "But this information cannot be ignored."

"I agree, Your Grace," Ronec said. "You need not ignore it. But be strategic. Think about the gratitude the king would feel if you told him about her. He would think you were doing him a favor."

That lit a fire in Canterbury's eyes. "Of course," he said as if a tremendous idea had just occurred to him. "If I told him about her, then that would put him in my debt."

"That is precisely what I was thinking."

So was Canterbury. "Think on it, Ronec," he said excitedly. "I tell him about Gwenllian and William de Wolfe's betrayal and the next time I make a request of him, he will grant it because he is beholden to me."

Ronec nodded. "I think it is a better idea, Your Grace," he said, feeling relieved that the man was listening to him. "Tell him what you know and let him do what he will with the information. As that foolish priest told you, let the burden no longer be yours. It will be where it belongs—with Edward. Let the king decide what's to be done."

Canterbury considered the situation a few moments longer before standing up. "Very well," he said. "Go to Edward's men personally and arrange an audience with him. Tell him… tell him I have information I think he'll very much want to hear."

Ronec headed for the door. "Immediately, Your Grace."

He'd made it to the door, but Canterbury stopped him. "Wait," he said, pausing. "You never did answer me about William de Wolfe. Do you think he was capable of this kind of betrayal?"

Ronec had his hand on the door latch. "William de Wolfe possessed intelligence and support that Edward could only dream of," he said quietly. "He had a more contentious relationship with the king than you do. See how you are treating the information now, how you intend to put Edward in your debt with it. Do you think, for one moment, that if de Wolfe had the opportunity to stab Edward in the back, he would do it? Of course he would. Considering how Edward treated him over the years, I would say Edward deserves it. If you truly want to ally with someone, Your Grace, pick a de Wolfe every time. They will be your strongest supporter or your worst enemy. With Edward, unfortunately for him, it is the latter."

Canterbury accepted that explanation. "He's not made many friends, has he?" he said. "I think that with this scrap of information, he might realize just how much his warlords hate him."

"Edward? I doubt it."

Perhaps that was true, but Canterbury didn't debate it. He waved him on. "Hurry, now," he said. "I would deliver this news to Edward quickly."

Ronec lifted the latch, but he didn't go out the door. In fact, he hesitated, so much so that Canterbury looked at him curiously.

"What?" he said. "What is it?"

Ronec drew in a long, thoughtful breath. "You know that St. Zosimus will not keep silent on this," he said. "He could very well go to Edward himself and you would be left with nothing."

Canterbury eyed him. "I've thought of that," he said. "There is nothing to keep him from disobeying me and going to Edward directly."

"My thoughts exactly," Ronec said. "He is not to be trusted. Even if he does not tell Edward, he will tell others. I know the sort."

"Then what do you suggest?"

Ronec was hesitant, but only for a moment. "Will you trust me to solve the problem, Your Grace?"

"Implicitly."

"Then consider it solved."

Canterbury nodded. "I will," he said. "And I will further assume the problem solver will be Tyrus le Mon."

"It will be, Your Grace."

"Once he has finished solving that problem, send him to me. I have further need of him."

"May I ask what for?"

Canterbury fell silent a moment, pondering everything he'd been told and the direction they'd decided to take. But he was currently rethinking that.

"To confirm a rumor," he finally said. "I can go to the king with what we know, but it is simply the ramblings of a dying man. Mayhap I do not need to hold the Welsh princess hostage, but what if I were to have proof of her existence?"

Ronec cocked an eyebrow. "If you were to send someone like le Mon to discover the truth, it would do no good because it would, once again, be one man's word on the situation," he said. "The only proof you could have would be to literally have the princess in your custody."

"Then mayhap we should rethink that."

Ronec knew what the man meant. In spite of deciding to simply lay the rumors at Edward's feet, now Canterbury had changed his mind. Perhaps he needed her after all. At the very least, he needed to confirm if there was, indeed, a young woman bearing Welsh royal blood at Sempringham Priory.

Or not.

It would take a special man, indeed, to make the discovery.

All princes of the church had their faithful men, but Tyrus le Mon went beyond the usual covert operative. He was a fourth-generation assassin and spy, having once served with the Executioner Knights, a spy organization that had been formed by William Marshal, Earl of Pembroke, during the reign of King Richard the Lionheart. If the Executioner Knights were considered the beating heart of England's spy underworld, then Tyrus le Mon was part of the dark and dirty soul of it. So dark and dirty, in fact, that the Executioner Knights had exiled him from further service. And given what those men did for a living, that was saying something.

That was when Tyrus came into the service of the Archbishop of Canterbury.

Canterbury used le Mon like his own personal attack dog. In the dangerous world of England's politics, a man like le Mon was worth his weight in gold. He could end problems, create problems, or anything else that was needed. He charged his weight in gold, too, but his services were impeccable. When Canterbury said he needed the man for a task, he wasn't jesting.

It would be a most important and secretive task.

One le Mon was most suited for.

Something deadly...

As soon as Ronec left the chamber, the wheels were already in motion.

CHAPTER SEVEN

Westminster Palace

"ALTHOUGH I CANNOT tell you who gave such information because confessionals are privileged communication between God and man, I can tell you that the information came from someone who was close to Carlton de Royans for many years. He witnessed everything with his own eyes."

Canterbury finished speaking, watching the expression of the man seated across from him with great anticipation. Edward III, or Edward Longshanks as he was colloquially known, had never been one to keep his feelings or opinions hidden. He'd been king for many years and had a reputation of being shrewd, hard-hitting, and, at times, conniving. But Edward was so much more, a many-faceted man, who gazed steadily at the ecclesiastical prince across the table. Even though he and the Archbishop of Canterbury weren't on the greatest terms at the best of times, he'd never known the man to lie.

Frankly, he was trying to conceal his shock at what he'd just heard.

"Preposterous," he finally said in a tone that suggested the entire story was utterly foolish. "Who told you such nonsense?"

"A loyal priest," Canterbury said steadily. "Why? Do you know differently?"

Edward eyed him, annoyed. "I do," he said. "Years ago, I sent someone to ensure she was at the priory and in good health. I have even granted her a pension to pay her expenses at the priory. She *is* there."

"How do you know it is *the* Gwenllian of Wales?"

That gave Edward pause because he didn't know. Not for certain, really, and that seemed to annoy him further. "Because Mother Cecelia, the prioress, confirmed it," he said irritably. "She confirmed that the very child was delivered by Patrick de Wolfe, Earl of Berwick, having been brought straight from Wales."

"And if the child given over to Sempringham was a decoy, and Berwick delivered her on the instruction of his father, do you not think he could have lied to the prioress?"

Unfortunately, that was very true, but Edward didn't want to admit it. To admit that he might have been duped after all these years was to admit weakness, and that wasn't something Edward would ever acknowledge. He was the Hammer of the Scots, after all. There was no weakness.

Except when there was.

Unfortunately, the archbishop's words were beginning to cast doubt.

"It is possible he could have," Edward finally said. "Anything is possible. But Patrick de Wolfe has held Berwick for years in my name. Why should he lie about something like this?"

"Because you are not his father," Canterbury pointed out. "Who do you think he will be more loyal to in the end? You or his father?"

They both knew the answer to that one. Edward wasn't going to dignify the question with a reply. That doubt was starting to claw at him, making him feel sick and irritable. With a heavy sigh, he shifted the focus slightly.

"This priest who told you about this," he said. "How trustworthy is he?"

Canterbury shrugged. "He is ambitious, but I do not think he is a liar," he said. "Liars are discovered sooner or later, and he would not risk that. He hoped to gain a favorable position in my household by relaying this tale to me."

"And is that the same reason you relay it to me?"

It was, but Canterbury wasn't going to admit anything. He wasn't going to admit the leverage he was seeking by relaying the information or the fact that St. Zosimus wouldn't be around to confirm the tale. If le Mon did his job correctly, there *was* no more St. Zosimus.

Just the way Canterbury had planned it.

"I am telling you because Llywelyn's daughter is living incognito with de Royans and she is already betrothed," he said evenly. "Since it seems to have been orchestrated by de Wolfe, he has already selected someone, though who, exactly, was not made clear to me. De Lara evidently died before he could give a name. But my concern is that de Wolfe selected one of his own grandsons. The House of de Wolfe is already dangerously close to the Welsh princes, but imagine if they had all of Wales behind them? The dowager Countess of Warenton is Scottish and, historically, most of the Lowlands have been loyal to de Wolfe. That being the case, their power would rival yours."

"So this is about power?"

"What else could it be?"

They were playing that dangerous chess game again. Edward would move, and then Canterbury would move, and then they would spend the rest of their time counter-moving against one another until one of them came out on top. Usually, it was Edward, but today... today, it seemed that Canterbury had the upper hand.

Because nothing he said was untrue.

The smug expression on Edward's face faded.

"According to the information you have relayed, William de Wolfe betrayed me years ago," he said matter-of-factly. "But how is that possible when one of his grandsons is my Lord Protector? Does that not show the man's loyalty?"

Both Edward and Canterbury turned to look at the big, tall knight standing several feet away. He was dark-haired, hazel-eyed, and had most of the women in London begging for a glance or a smile or a lock of his hair. This particular de Wolfe male was, as most men and women would describe him, uncannily beautiful. He was also talented, strong, educated, and unwaveringly loyal to the king.

Edward crooked a finger in the knight's direction.

"Cassius, come here," he said.

Cassius de Wolfe immediately moved out of the shadows, going to stand in front of Edward.

"Your Grace?" he said smartly.

Edward looked up at the knight. "Did you hear what Canterbury told me?"

"I did, Your Grace."

"Do you know anything about this situation with de Royans and Llywelyn ap Gruffudd's infant daughter?"

"Nay, Your Grace."

"Was your grandfather disloyal to me?"

"Nay, Your Grace."

"If he had been, would you tell me?"

"If you asked me, I would tell you the truth, Your Grace."

"You would betray your grandfather?"

"Never. But I would tell you the truth, and the truth is that he was not disloyal to you, Your Grace."

Canterbury, who had been listening to the crisp replies, cast a long look at Edward. He wanted to see how he was handling the answers from a man who was in charge of the king's personal protection. Young knights from the House of de Wolfe had been historically offered the position, and that was for a reason—to keep a de Wolfe close to the Crown. It was a position of honor, but also one of political leverage. The House of de Wolfe wouldn't do anything overtly against the Crown if one of its members were so close to the king. Scott de Wolfe, the current earl, didn't have the same quarrelsome relationship with Edward that his father had, but that could change.

Edward liked to think of Cassius' position as insurance against such an occurrence.

But in this case, whatever happened had occurred twenty years ago. Whatever insurance he held today against Warenton's behavior was a moot point. The betrayal had already happened.

The more he thought about it, the more anger he began to feel.

"Cassius, how old were you when your grandfather was in Wales fighting Llywelyn the Last?" he asked.

Cassius had to think about it. "Twenty years ago I would have been fostering at Kenilworth, Your Grace," he said. "I was around ten years of age."

"Then you were not at home when your grandfather returned."

Cassius shook his dark head. "Nay, Your Grace," he said. "But I received word through my father that my uncle, James de Wolfe, had been killed in Wales."

"Killed and resurrected," Edward said. "He returned as Blayth the Strong, the product of Welsh rebels who restored his damaged memory with lies."

"He serves my grandfather flawlessly now, Your Grace."

Edward waved him off irritably. "I am aware," he said. "Though he has no love for me, so I'm told. Pity. I hear he's an excellent knight."

Cassius wasn't sure what to say to that. His Uncle James, thought killed in Wales, had in reality suffered a terrible head injury that erased most of his memory. That was what the king referred to when he mentioned his damaged memory. Cassius had been too young, and also fostering far away, to really know the extent of William's bitterness and grief when it came to James' death. And the truth was that he knew nothing about the news he'd just heard from Canterbury, but the man was insinuating that William de Wolfe had done something underhanded against Edward years ago, which had his dander up. In Cassius' eyes, his grandfather could do no wrong, and he would tell Canterbury that to his face if the man asked him a direct question.

Edward, however, was another matter.

Cassius had been serving the king for not quite a year on the recommendation of his older brother, who had originally been offered the position of Lord Protector. Markus de Wolfe had fallen for a woman in the north of England and declined the position to remain with her and start a new life. That was why he had recommended Cassius. In fact, Cassius had been quite honored by the recommendation and tried very hard to serve with distinction. Entering into the position, he wasn't exactly sure what it was going to be like as the personal protector of the king, but it had turned into something far more than anything he had anticipated.

Cassius was more than a protector, more than just a skilled sword at the disposal of the king. Edward had more than his share of advisors, nobility who constantly vied for his attention and favor. He was also dealing with the behavior of his son, also Edward, who had his share of favorites, and those favorites were a thorn in the side of the nobility. Going into the position, Cassius had known there was going to be politics in the court of England, but he hadn't realized how much it played into every single day and every breath he took. This was no easy task, and there were times when he cursed his brother for recommending him for the position. There were times when he simply wanted to walk away and return home and serve his father.

But there was something else at play here.

Though Edward had never said anything about it, Cassius thought that he wanted a de Wolfe close by either because it seemed to give him comfort or he thought Cassius knew what his grandfather was up to. That was not the case, as Cassius wasn't the first person William de Wolfe had spoken to whenever he made a decision, and it was ridiculous that the king seemed to think so. But quickly, Cassius had begun to see that his position close to the king gave him a bird's-eye view into the man's plans and politics, and on at least two occasions, he had sent word to his father on Edward's movements simply so Patrick and the rest of the de Wolfe family were aware of things that might directly affect them. Therefore, Cassius' position with Edward was as advantageous to him as it was to the king, and he had no intention of walking away from it—but at this moment, he was having a good deal of difficulty with the Archbishop of Canterbury and the message the man bore. In fact, he considered himself very fortunate that he'd been here to witness the exchange.

It was definitely something his family would need to know.

"Cassius?" Edward said, jolting him from his train of thought. "Did you hear what I said about your uncle?"

"I did, Your Grace."

"You did not comment."

"That is because I cannot confirm or deny your assertion, Your Grace," he said. "I am not close to my uncle and therefore do not know his mind."

Edward's gaze lingered on him for a few moments before he stood up from his chair and began to wander the audience chamber. There were great lancet windows that faced the River Thames and a moist breeze blew in from the water. Birds could be heard, crying overhead, as Edward meandered over to the window, clearly lost in thought. A gentle wind lifted his gray hair as his gaze beheld the city, the river, and the country he commanded.

He was a man with much on his mind.

"Cassius, I am going to ask you a question and you will answer me without hesitation," he finally said.

Cassius moved in his direction, closer, so he could hear him better. "Your Grace?"

"Do you know Carlton de Royans?"

Cassius came to a pause about ten feet away. "I've only met him once, Your Grace," he said. "That was very long ago."

"Do you know Colm de Lara?"

"I know *of* him, Your Grace, but I do not know him personally."

Edward nodded, but he still seemed to be preoccupied. "Is one of your brothers or cousins betrothed to a de Royans daughter?"

"Not that I am aware of, Your Grace."

"Do you ever recall hearing your father or grandfather discuss de Royans or Sempringham Priory?"

"Never, Your Grace."

"But Colm de Lara says they are in this together," Edward said. "That your grandfather and de Royans plotted against me when it came to the last Welsh princess. That your grandfather made the decision to have her assume the identity of a de Royans daughter while he sent another child to Sempringham, posing as the princess. If this is true, then he has deceived me."

Cassius didn't look at Canterbury, but that anger he'd managed to keep down at the mention of his grandfather's lack of loyalty to the king was beginning to surface again. He didn't like Robert Winchelsey making problems for a dead man. Since Edward and William had never really seen eye to eye, his grandfather didn't need any help when it came to raising the king's ire and suspicions.

Even from the grave.

"Your Grace, may I speak freely?" he asked.

Edward turned to him. "Of course," he said. "I wish you would."

That was when Cassius turned to look at Canterbury. "Meaning no disrespect to the archbishop, I fear I must point out the obvious," he said, returning his attention to Edward. "Your Grace, Canterbury is giving you third-hand information. Allegedly, a dying knight has told a priest, who in turn ran to Canterbury, who in turn has come to you. As I said, I do not know Colm de Lara, but he was the Lord of the Trilaterals and an ally of my father and grandfather. They do not ally with fools or liars. I do not know who this priest is who came to Canterbury, but it is quite possible he is lying for his own gain. Canterbury himself admitted that the man was ambitious. What better way to secure a coveted position for himself than by relaying a bit of scandalous gossip about a dead man who cannot defend himself? I fear you do my grandfather's history of service a great *dis*service by believing malicious rumors."

Edward's eyes crinkled with a hint of humor. After a moment, he chuckled. "God's Bones," he muttered. "I do believe I've just been reprimanded."

Cassius quickly shook his head. "Not at all, Your Grace," he said. "That was not my intent. I simply wanted to point out that an ambitious man brought this information to Canterbury. If it can be proven, then I would suggest he do so."

"I intend to do so." Canterbury stood up, furious that a mere knight had challenged him. Even if that knight was the grandson of the man in question. "I have sent for a man who has been of great service to me to discover the truth of these rumors."

Cassius turned to him again. "May I ask whom you have summoned, Your Grace?"

"Tyrus le Mon."

Even Edward looked sharply at him when he heard the name, but before he could say a word, Cassius spoke.

"Your Grace, forgive me, but everyone knows le Mon is a man of questionable tactics," he said sternly. "He used to serve with the Executioner Knights in de Lohr's circle of spies, and considering what the Executioner Knights do on a regular basis, the mere fact that they exiled le Mon should tell you what kind of man he is."

Canterbury had little patience for the king's Lord Protector. "I know what kind of man he is," he snapped. "And a knight should know his place. I do not care if your father is the Earl of Berwick, nor do I care that your grandfather was the great William de Wolfe. That does not give you the right to speak to me in such a manner."

Cassius didn't back down. He merely cocked an eyebrow. "I did not mean to offend, Your Grace," he said. "But the man you have summoned for something as important as determining if my grandfather was a liar is a man not even the Executioner Knights could trust. Why do you?"

Canterbury's face turned red. "Do you question my judgment?"

Cassius had pushed the archbishop as far as he could. He looked to Edward to see how the king wanted him to respond, only to see Edward gazing back at him with an amused expression on his face. *He's enjoying this,* Cassius thought. Unwilling to engage in fisticuffs with a prince of the church, he simply lowered his head in submission.

"I do not, Your Grace," he said. "Your reputation is without compare. It is simply that men like le Mon can ingratiate themselves to great men, and I did not want to see you fall victim to his unsavory ambitions."

He made it sound as if he were trying to look out for the archbishop, which eased the situation a little. The man's insult was doused, but not by much. Edward was still watching the interaction, taking great pride in Cassius' unwillingness to be bullied by Canterbury. As he strolled back in their direction, sending Cassius back to his post with a nod of his head, he caught sight of the other knight in the chamber. Yet another protector from another powerful family, this time of the

Norfolk House of de Winter.

Big, blond, brawny, and powerful.

Denys de Winter was that knight.

"Denys?" he said. "Have you been listening to all of this?"

Denys stepped out of the shadows.

"I have, Your Grace."

"And what do you think about Canterbury's tale?"

"I think that William de Wolfe is beyond suspicion, Your Grace."

Edward turned to Canterbury. "There," he said. "You see? Both of these men think your priest lied to you. They do not believe Warenton betrayed me."

Canterbury was feeling bullied and offended. "One is Warenton's grandson and the other is from a family who is allied with de Wolfe," he pointed out. "Let them stand on their words, because le Mon will get to the bottom of this. I've already sent my own man, Ronec de Nerra, to fetch him, and then we shall soon know if my priest lied or not."

"Or if the source lied to him," Edward reminded him. "It could be either one of them."

"Or neither," Canterbury said, glancing resentfully at the two big knights in the shadows. "The man who gave the original confession could have told the truth. There would be no reason to lie."

"We shall see."

A silence settled between the men as Edward returned to his window and Canterbury hit the wine. There was a rock-crystal decanter of it on a nearby table and he poured himself a healthy measure of the ruby liquid. As this was going on, there was a knock at the chamber door. Denys went to the door and opened it, only to find a royal courier standing outside.

"What is it?" Denys asked.

"A missive, my lord," the courier said. "For the king."

"Can it wait?"

The courier shook his head, spying Cassius back in the chamber, before returning his focus to Denys.

"It is from Castle Questing," the courier said to Denys, lowering his voice. "The messenger was most insistent it be delivered to the king immediately. It is of the utmost importance."

That set off warning bells in Denys' head. Brow furrowed, he took the missive and quietly shut the door. Cassius hadn't heard the courier's mention that it was from Castle Questing, seat of the de Wolfe empire, so he was unconcerned as he watched Denys as the man moved past him, heading for Edward. The king took the missive from Denys, inspecting the seal as Denys returned to Cassius, resuming his place beside him.

"It's from Castle Questing," Denys whispered.

Cassius looked at him, surprised. "That seems oddly coincidental," he muttered. "We've been speaking of the Earl of Warenton and suddenly there is a missive from my uncle?"

"It's probably to tell Edward that the Scots are on the move again," Dennis murmured. "Mayhap the de Wolfe army has stopped them from taking yet another castle, which puts Edward into their debt."

"One cannot suspect a man of treason when he is saving the northern lands of the country you rule."

"Exactly."

Cassius sighed faintly. "This position was much more fun when my grandfather and Edward were friendly," he said. "They had their problems in the past, but it eased up entirely when my grandfather passed away. I hope the animosity is not back again after Canterbury's lies."

Denys could only shake his head. "Edward is still madly jealous of your grandfather," he said. "That envy will always be there because William de Wolfe is a legend. Longshanks is..."

"A mere king."

They glanced at each other. There was nothing more to say to that. They both knew what the situation was and the entire conversation between Edward and Canterbury and Cassius had proved it. They returned their attention to Edward as he read the missive from Scott de Wolfe slowly before a grimace rolled across his face, which concerned Cassius because he thought that his uncle had done something that displeased the king.

In all of the years of both animosity and allyship between Edward and William, strangely, the sons had not been pulled into that situation. They supported their father, of course, but William supported Edward—such as it was—so the sons supported him, as well. That was a long-established alliance. Cassius was hoping Scott, or Troy, or even his father hadn't done anything that would cause Edward to turn against them also. Cassius wasn't sure he could hold his position any longer if someone had pulled a rogue move. As he watched, Edward read the missive once again, all the way through, before handing it over to Canterbury.

"Cassius," Edward said quietly, "come here."

Cassius obediently made his way over to the king. "How may I be of service, Your Grace?"

Edward faced him, his expression tense. Cassius had to wonder if it was because a fist was about to come flying at his face, because the king was clearly distressed, so he braced himself. The king was quite tall, but Cassius was about three inches taller. Given that his father, Patrick, was a giant among men, the height was not surprising. All of his brothers, save one, had it. Cassius was standing there, wondering what could have possibly been in that missive, when the man spoke softly.

"Cassius, you know that in spite of our history, I have nothing but the greatest respect for your grandfather and those who served with him," he said. "The days of William de Wolfe when he served at Northwood Castle with Paris de Norville and Kieran Hage are legendary. That is when the entire de Wolfe legend got started."

Cassius nodded. "I know, Your Grace," he said. "You have always made that clear. And our conversation has not offended me."

Edward eyed him for a moment. "This discussion with Canterbury," he said. "The situation with Llywelyn's child and the suggestion that your grandfather possibly disobeyed my orders when it came to her has made me… angry."

"I am aware, Your Grace."

"But it does not change my great admiration for your grandfather and the men allied with him," Edward said. "They were all great men."

Cassius smiled faintly. "Uncle Paris is the only one left," he said. "He's as mad as a box of frogs these days, and he'll kick you if you attempt to kiss him, but when I see him, I see my grandfather. William and Paris and Kieran were the greatest men I ever knew, men who helped forge a nation alongside the Crown, and they were all very proud of that service."

Edward sighed heavily. "Cassius, the message is from your uncle, Scott de Wolfe," he said quietly. "He wanted us both to know that Paris de Norville, that great and legendary knight, has passed away."

At first, Cassius didn't understand what the king was telling him. That wasn't what he had expected to hear. It took him a few moments to process the statement, and when realization dawned, his eyes widened.

"Uncle Paris?" he said, struggling to find the words. "He… he's gone?"

"I'm afraid so."

Cassius stared at him a moment, disbelief rippling through his features, before he turned to Canterbury.

"May I read the missive, too?" he asked.

Canterbury was finished with it. The mood of the chamber, so recently filled with suspicion and accusations, suddenly shifted to something else, something sorrowful and poignant because the end of an era had been announced. Everyone could feel the shift in ambience, Cassius most of all. When Canterbury extended the missive, Cassius took it with the greatest of sorrow.

Slowly, he held it up so he could read it.

"Paris de Norville was a great man, Cassius," Canterbury said, trying to be of some comfort because the situation called for it. "I will have a requiem mass said for him tonight."

Cassius almost didn't hear him. He was looking at the carefully scribed words on the vellum.

This is to inform you that on the twenty-first day of April, Year of Our Lord 1302, Paris de Norville, Lord Bowmont, peacefully passed away. Please inform my nephew, Cassius, of this family matter. He will want to know.

Scott de Wolfe
Earl of Warenton

It was short and to the point, as an informational missive would be. No sentiment, no mention of mourning or pain or sorrow. No mention of how much the man was loved or how much he would be missed.

Cassius was so grieved with the news that he didn't know what to say. It wasn't as if it was his father or even his grandfather, but Paris de Norville had been a constant in his life. He'd called him uncle, and even though he wasn't by blood, he was in heart and spirit. Paris de Norville was one of a kind, a powerful knight, a dedicated friend, and a revered father and grandfather. Cassius could only imagine what Paris' family was feeling. If it was half of what he was feeling, then it was terrible, indeed. It was the end of a generation.

Now, they were all gone.

Edward, in a surprising show of sympathy, put his hand on Cassius' arm.

"Go," he said quietly. "Go to the cathedral if you wish and pray for de Norville. I know what he meant to your family."

Cassius didn't even argue with him. He simply nodded in agreement. Somehow all of this conjecture about missing princesses and deception didn't seem all that important anymore. Not now. With the missive still in his hand, Cassius headed out of the chamber. Edward caught Denys' eye and pointed to Cassius, indicating for him to follow the man and provide any support needed. Denys did, without hesitation, following Cassius into the corridor before he caught up to him. Silently, the two of them headed out into the midmorning sunshine.

As Denys quickly discovered, all Cassius wanted to do was wander. He didn't go to the cathedral, but rather walked around aimlessly in the bailey, all the while clutching the missive in his hand. Denys finally had enough of wandering in circles and directed him out of the main gatehouse that faced north. There was a wide street out there and businesses lining the avenue, and Denys grabbed him by the arm and pulled him toward an area called White Hall where there were several businesses, including a tavern. Denys directed Cassius inside, ordered food and drink for them both, and then planted the man at a table by the window overlooking the street.

Until the food and drink came, they simply sat in silence.

"I'm sorry for your loss, Cass," Denys finally said. "The old guard has died away, one by one. It's a sad day when the last of them goes."

Cassius seemed to snap out of his trance. "Sad, indeed," he said. "I was just thinking about the last time I saw Uncle Paris."

"When was that?"

"Almost two years ago," Cassius said. "I was trying to remember the last words we had. I remember that we were celebrating the day of birth for my grandmother."

"Matha?"

Cassius smiled weakly. "Aye," he said. "Matha. That small woman who bred a host of giant sons. I think my last words with Uncle Paris were those of farewell, just normal words, but I did tell him that I loved him. Just like the last time I saw my grandfather. I told him that I loved him, too. I was just thinking that those words seem so simple, and simple words do not reflect the totality of a relationship, yet when the words speak of love, they do. I loved my grandfather my entire life, as I loved Uncle Paris, so those words defined the totality of a relationship built on love."

Denys smiled faintly. "I never met Paris de Norville, but I met William de Wolfe once," he said. "I was younger. Much younger. I remember a very large man with a patch over one eye. He came to Norwich Castle and supped with my father."

"He lost his eye in a battle in Wales," Cassius said. Then he cocked his head as if a thought had just occurred to him. "Doesn't the Bible say something about restoring a body after death?"

Denys nodded. "I think so," he said, picking up the pitcher of wine for the first time and pouring it into the cups that had been brought alongside it. "It says that God will restore the body and soul of believers."

"Then the day my grandfather died, he awoke in heaven and saw with two eyes for the first time in more than sixty years," he said. "Strange I didn't think of that until now. And on the twenty-first day of April, he saw the best friend he ever had for the first time in six years. What a reunion that must have been."

Denys pushed a cup in his direction. "That's a lovely thought," he said. "I hope that brings you comfort."

A lump formed in Cassius' throat. "It does," he said. "But I'm also jealous. Jealous that Paris is seeing my grandfather and I am not. I had to stand through that conference today and listen to Canterbury spout lies about my grandfather and there was nothing I could do to stop him. How dare that man insinuate that my grandfather somehow behaved ignobly. How dare he intimate that he betrayed the king somehow. I should have ripped that bastard's head off."

Denys could see the grief rising, the anger. "William de Wolfe was a man of honor and integrity and everyone knows it," he said firmly. "Do not be troubled by it, Cass. It's just Canterbury spouting his vitriol again."

Cassius shook his head. "But I am troubled by it," he said.

"How can I not be? To attack a dead man like that, who is not even able to defend his good name."

"But you will. Your family will."

Cassius sighed heavily. "Aye, I will," he said. "I'll defend it to the death. And now with Uncle Paris' death… it just emphasizes the fact that my grandfather is no longer here. I miss him more than I can express, Denys. It just… hurts."

Watching Cassius wrestle with his grief, Denys lifted his cup. "Then let us honor him," he said softly. "Let us remember those men who have gone before us. To Kieran Hage, to Paris de Norville, and to William de Wolfe. Long may their stories be told."

Cassius lifted his cup in return, acknowledging the tribute, before draining the contents. Then he lowered his head and let the tears fall, just a little. Like most of the de Wolfe grandchildren, Cassius had grown up with three grandfather figures in his life. Kieran Hage was one such figure, and they'd lost Kieran the same year his Uncle James had returned from the dead. Then William's death came six years ago and Cassius still hadn't recovered from that. Now… now, Paris had finally slipped away, ascending to the heavens, and Cassius felt as if a big piece of his life was gone.

Pieces of the past, all fading into memory.

Wiping the tears from his face, he suddenly stood up and faced a common room that was half full of men and women.

"My name is Cassius de Wolfe," he said loudly, lifting his empty cup. "My grandfather was William de Wolfe, Earl of Warenton, the great Wolfe of the Border. It was men like my grandfather who made England what it is today, great men who fought and sacrificed for their country. I want you to know, all of you, that he was the greatest man who has ever lived. Today, I have received word that his closest friend, Paris de Norville, has passed away. Now those men who fought and died for England are stars in the heavens, shining down upon us, and we are unworthy. I will ask you all to drink to my grandfather's memory and to the memory of those he fought with. They have earned our respect."

The tears were back on his cheeks by the time he was finished. Denys, touched by the show of grief, quickly moved to find the tavernkeep, and in little time, ale was being distributed among the tables. As soon as men had full cups, they began to stand alongside Cassius. One man, older and with a missing right ear, spoke out.

"My name is Cannock," he said in a gravelly voice. "I served at Beverley Castle for many years until my wife got ill and we moved south, to London, where her family lived. But I fought in battles with your grandfather, Cassius. It was many years ago, but I remember them like they were yesterday. I knew Hage and de Norville and they were the greatest knights I ever saw. I'll drink with you to their memory."

That made Cassius smile. What a coincidence to find someone who had fought with his grandfather and Paris and Kieran here in London—but on the other hand, the trio had been fighting for so long that surely there had to be men everywhere in England who had fought with them at one time or another. Cannock had a couple of companions and they spoke up, one after the other, announcing that they, too, had fought with William de Wolfe. They were barely finished when a man sitting at the back shouted that he'd fought with de Wolfe at Carlisle twenty-five years earlier, and proceeded to tell the entire common room that de Wolfe single-handedly subdued the enemy that day. A little lie, of course, but it didn't matter.

Today was a day for legends of greatness.

Somehow, hearing their testimonials eased Cassius' grief a

little. He wasn't the only one who loved his grandfather or acknowledged the man's prominence. Canterbury's words had cut him so much that he needed to hear that there were still those who loved his grandfather and the men who fought with him.

It did his heart good.

Wiping at his face once more, he accepted another full cup of ale from Denys before lifting it again to the room full of men.

"To my grandfather," he said as fresh tears spilled over. "The greatest knight I ever knew. May he find peace in paradise."

"Nay, lad," said a man over near the hearth. "That's not what he wants."

Cassius turned to see an old man sitting with his back up against the stone. The rocks were warm, bringing heat to his old bones. He was a big man, heavily dressed, and Cassius noticed a broadsword on the table. *A knight.* When he saw that he had Cassius' attention, he smiled weakly and lifted his cup.

"The Northmen's idea of heaven is a place called Valhalla," he said in his raspy voice. "In a great hall, they feast and fight through eternity. There is an old poem about it, and part of it is this:

> *Wine to carry,*
> *as for a king's coming,*
> *here to me I expect*
> *heroes' coming from the world,*
> *certain great ones,*
> *so glad is my heart,*
> *as they enter the halls of Valhalla."*

Cassius smiled in return. "I've heard that, from an old tutor," he said. "It is a larger poem that speaks of the Northmen's heaven."

The old knight nodded. "That's what a warrior wants, young Cassius," he said. "He wants to feast and fight. De Wolfe cannot spend eternity walking through a green field and weaving flowers in his hair like a woman. That is not peace for a man with a fighting spirit. But let him walk through a green field with a sword in his hand, facing an enemy, and then toasting his victory all night... That's heaven for him. The Northmen understood that."

The smile on Cassius' face broadened. "Then he can do that until my grandmother comes," he said. "I do not think she would like the idea of him fighting all day."

The old man snorted. "Women never do."

That brought laughter from about half the room. It made Cassius feel so much better, bringing him comfort in such a difficult moment. He nodded his thanks to the old man.

"I am grateful," he said, feeling emotional again. "You have given me a vision of my grandfather that brings me peace."

The old man stood up and came to Cassius, smiling at him, looking him over before speaking again.

"My name is Broderick de Marsh," he muttered. "I had the pleasure of serving with your grandfather many years ago, when he was in London serving Henry. When your grandmother came to visit for a time, I was part of the escort that returned her home. The escort was ambushed and I received what many thought was a mortal wound, but I survived. I remained in London, remaining in service to the king, but I never forgot your grandfather and his kindness. I learned a great deal from him. Mostly what I learned was loyalty. I've never seen a man more loyal to his friends and family. You were fortunate to have him, Cassius. He was, indeed, a great man."

Cassius nodded, touched by the knight's words, but also feeling more grief because of them. A very great man had passed into legend. With a lump in his throat, he put a hand on the old man's arm.

"Thank you for that," he said. "It is appreciated."

Le Marsh smiled, nodded his head once, and then he was gone, leaving Cassius wiping tears from his face again. As he sat down, nursing his grieved heart, the men who had told him of fighting with his grandfather or Paris or even Kieran in the past came over to the table to continue their tales of serving alongside those great men. Those words were like a salve to his grief, a balm to his soul.

The stories went on all night.

CHAPTER EIGHT

ONE THING ABOUT meetings with Edward always rubbed Canterbury the wrong way.

He always felt as if he were on the defensive.

In this case, he was. He'd brought the information to Edward about de Wolfe and Llywelyn's daughter and the whole bloody mess of it, so in a sense, he really *was* on the defensive. This was his story, gleaned from that ambitious priest, and now he had to prove it. Edward wasn't going to send anyone to confirm the claim—Canterbury had come forth with it, so it was he who needed to substantiate it.

And then Edward would never doubt him again.

In a sense, his credibility was on the line.

Having returned to his quarters at Westminster Cathedral, he'd sent his personal guard away and pushed into his chambers, knowing that Ronec would be there.

And someone else.

But Ronec met him at the door.

"Where is he?" Canterbury demanded as soon as he passed into the dimly lit vestibule. "Did you tell him why I wished to see him?"

Ronec nodded. "I did," he said, helping Canterbury remove his cloak and tossing it off to a servant. "He's already been to see St. Zosimus."

Canterbury glanced at him. "Is the deed done?"

"It is."

"What did he do with the body?"

"In the river, weighted."

That was good enough for Canterbury. "Come with me," he said. "You will want to hear this also."

Ronec followed. They passed into the next chamber, a larger chamber with chairs and a hearth that was blazing against the cold, damp night. Even so, the room was dark but for the light coming from the hearth, and it took Canterbury a moment to spy the very man he wanted to see, sitting in a corner.

Tyrus le Mon in the flesh.

No one would have ever suspected what the man did for a living. He was in his fortieth year, a fine example of a handsome man, blond and well groomed and articulate. He was from the House of le Mon, and the men of the family had a history with William Marshal and his spy ring, a profession Tyrus's father and grandfather and great-grandfather had served with distinction. There was no question that Tyrus would follow the same path, and he had, for a while. He'd performed flawlessly except for one thing.

The man had the inability to show mercy.

With Tyrus, it was all or nothing. If he was told to kill, he killed. It didn't matter who it was—man, woman, or child. He felt no guilt in snuffing out the life of an infant if that's what was asked of him. If his target was a woman, he showed no compassion against her fear. He was, to put it kindly, a killing machine, and that was something not even his fellow Executioner Knights could break him of. He also had the inability to form relationships or bonds, making camaraderie with him difficult.

Oddly enough, he was mild mannered. He smiled quite a bit. He enjoyed jokes and had the uncanny ability to appreciate and interpret art in most forms. He was highly educated and his knowledge of horses was unmatched. But there was nothing deeper or emotional about him. He was only superficial in his ability to converse or carry on a relationship. Below that surface were the gates to hell, revealing a tormented and black soul beneath. It had come to a head when a fellow Executioner Knight ran into difficulty and, rather than help him, Tyrus had gone on to accomplish their task, leaving the man alone to become severely wounded. He'd been so focused on his orders that he considered anyone else around him, including his allies, collateral damage.

That had drummed him out of the Executioner Knights.

These days, Tyrus worked on his own and had no shortage of jobs to choose from, and the Archbishop of Canterbury was his best customer. Even now, they faced each other in the shadowed room as the archbishop took a seat near the hearth. Ronec stood back against the wall, watching.

Waiting.

It wasn't long in coming.

"I need your skills, Tyrus," Canterbury said, holding out his hands to the fire because the cold night had chilled them. "Ronec told me that you took care of the priest."

Tyrus nodded. "I did, Your Grace," he said. "It was a simple task."

Canterbury grunted. "Did Ronec tell you *why* we had to be rid of him?"

Tyrus nodded. "He did," he said. "He told me that the man had valuable information that no one else needed to know and there was only one way to ensure his silence."

"And nothing else?"

"Nay, Your Grace."

Canterbury sighed sharply, rubbing his hands together quickly before sitting back in his chair and facing le Mon.

"Then listen to me and listen well," he said, his voice low and tense. "I have just come from an audience with the king. Forgive me for being abrupt, but I must explain to you the background of this situation before I tell you what I require of you. Most importantly, you must never repeat this story. I must have your word."

Tyrus nodded. "You have it, Your Grace."

Canterbury took another deep breath. "Twenty years ago, Llywelyn ap Gruffudd was killed in Wales," he said. "The man was considered the last true Welsh prince. He was murdered at the end of many years of battle by Edward's men. His brother, Dafydd, and several children were taken prisoner, including Llywelyn's only child, a daughter, named Gwenllian. Do you understand me so far?"

"Aye, Your Grace."

"Good," Canterbury said. "It is this daughter that is in question. Not only does she carry the bloodlines of the princes of Wales, but her mother was Eleanor de Montfort. That means her maternal grandfather was Simon de Montfort and her maternal great-grandfather was King John. Her bloodlines are more royal than the very man who sits upon the throne of England at this time, so naturally, she poses a tremendous threat to English rule. It was, therefore, Edward's order that she be taken to Sempringham Priory in Lincolnshire, where she would be sequestered for the rest of her life. A nun, unable to procreate, imprisoned within holy walls. Llywelyn's bloodlines will die with her."

He paused, motioning for wine, and Ronec handed him a cup from a carved sideboard. As Canterbury took a drink, letting it ease his parched throat, Tyrus leaned forward in his chair, his brow furrowed.

"And?" he said. "What about *her*?"

Canterbury took another drink before responding. "We have reason to believe she never made it to Sempringham," he said. "The man you disposed of tonight heard a confession from a knight who served under the Earl of Warenton at that time. He was in Wales during the wars and was part of the escort that brought the infant Gwenllian to Lincolnshire—only as he told the story, William de Wolfe switched babies. Gwenllian went to live as the adopted daughter of Carlton de Royans of Folkingham Castle and another child was sent in her place to Sempringham."

Tyrus was still not much clearer on why he was being told this story. "What do you want me to do, Your Grace?"

"Discover the truth," Canterbury said simply. "Go to Sempringham and meet this Gwenllian of Wales. Determine if she is the lady in question. If she is not, then go to Folkingham Castle and discover what you can about de Royans' daughter."

Tyrus understood the assignment, but pieces were missing. "How am I to know it is her?" he said. "If there is a woman at Sempringham and a woman at Folkingham, how do I know if one or the other is Gwenllian?"

"A clue that came from the priest," Canterbury said. "As I mentioned, he heard the confession of a knight who had intimate knowledge of the situation and the knight said that

Gwenllian had black hair and blue eyes. My suggestion would be to focus on the physical appearance of the woman at Sempringham. If she has black hair and blue eyes, then mayhap that is the very woman in question. If she is at Sempringham, then we know the knight lied. We know this entire story is a figment of someone's imagination. But if she does not bear that coloring, and de Royans' daughter does, then we know the story is true."

"And if it *is* true?"

Canterbury looked at Ronec, who simply shrugged his shoulders. Silent words passed between them, mostly because Ronec suspected what Canterbury wanted to do. He'd wanted to do it since the first time he heard the story.

And Canterbury always got what he wanted.

"If she is living as a de Royans, then bring her to me," he said quietly as he returned his attention to Tyrus. "Do not hurt her. Bring her to me unharmed and I will determine what is to be done with her. Do this and I shall pay you handsomely as well as gift you with a property where you can live out your days if you so choose."

Tyrus had never been offered a property before. Truthfully, he was rather surprised by that offer, and his gaze moved back and forth between Ronec and Canterbury.

"Does this situation have so much importance to you, Your Grace?" he asked, somewhat incredulous. "So much so that you would offer me property to complete it?"

Canterbury nodded. "It is bigger than all of us," he said. "If a black-haired woman is still living with de Royans, I want her. If she is not, and she is married, then track her down. Find out what you can about her and her husband and return to me with the information. But if she is still living at Folkingham… bring her to me. Is that clear?"

Tyrus nodded. "Thy will be done, Your Grace."

Canterbury simply nodded. Sensing the conversation was concluded, Tyrus rose from the chair he'd been sitting in and headed to the entry door. He was about to open the panel when he heard someone behind him.

"Le Mon," Ronec said quietly. "Wait a moment."

Tyrus paused as the tall, dark-haired knight caught up to him. "What is it?" he asked.

"Here," Ronec said, passing him a purse full of gold and silver coins. "For your journey north. More when you return. And Tyrus… do not utter a word to anyone about this."

"I told you I wouldn't."

"See that you don't," Ronec muttered. "Godspeed, lad."

Tyrus nodded once and pulled the panel open, heading out into the cold, misty complex of Westminster. Ronec shut the door behind him and bolted it, pausing a moment to think on the mission that had been laid out before him.

Bring her to me.

If Gwenllian of Wales really was somewhere other than Sempringham Priory, Ronec knew that Tyrus would find her.

Something told him that the situation was about to get very, very ugly.

CHAPTER NINE

Folkingham Castle
Three Months Later

THE TIME HAD come.
Never mind the time. The year, the week, the day had come, and he was over the moon about it. Liam had been pushing a swift pace all the way from Bamburgh Castle, where his family lived. Fortunately, the weather had been good and the roads in decent condition, so travel had been pleasant. He had half of his family with him, father and mother included.

It made quite a brigade.

Since Liam was the eldest and the heir, his marriage to a woman he'd been betrothed to for twenty years was quite an event. Off to Liam's left, riding a black-and-white charger effortlessly, was the brother closest in age to him, Kyle Herringthorpe. Kyle was a big lad with blond hair and hazel eyes, a man who adored his eldest brother. The brother next in age, Taggart, had been left behind at Bamburgh because Liam's father had wanted at least two of his sons left behind in command. The Scots weren't completely settled these days, so he wanted seasoned knights in case anything went wrong. Tag, along with brother Brody, understood.

Liam had more brothers, six in total, but the only brothers with him were Kyle and Logan. Sisters Jane and Mary were already married and in the South of England with their husbands, while the two youngest brothers, Mac and Edmund, were fostering at Warwick Castle.

It was, therefore, mostly a family affair as the House of Herringthorpe headed toward Folkingham Castle along with about a hundred soldiers. Bamburgh was a royal outpost and War Herringthorpe, Liam's father, had been the garrison commander for many years. Therefore, the troops he kept there were mostly royal troops, though he did have some of his own. Out of a thousand-man army at Bamburgh, about a quarter of them belonged to War, personally, because the majority of his men went with Liam when he assumed the garrison at Easington Castle, northwest of Bamburgh.

Easington Castle actually belonged to War, gifted to him by the king for exemplary service, and he was quite proud of the large, squat castle that looked like a crouching lion upon the moors of the north. When War had acquired the castle, it came with five rather anemic villages and herds of sheep. The former lord had been ill for many years before dying, so the land was greatly in need of help. Liam was more than willing to give it, and in the few years he'd been commander, the villages were thriving and the sheep population had nearly doubled.

As it turned out, Liam had a good head for business, but business was the last thing he was thinking about as Folkingham came into view. He was thinking about that beautiful jewel of a woman he was about to take as his wife, something he'd been greatly anticipating for the past six years. Six long, frustrating years. The last time they'd spoken about it was when Cambria was fourteen years of age and Carlton had hinted at only four more years, but in the end, he'd been reluctant to surrender his only child. At six years, it was War who finally made the demand of marriage—or there would be a problem. Reluctantly, Carlton gave consent, and within the week, Liam and his parents were heading to Folkingham.

Riding beside him, he could hear his father chuckle.

"What?" Liam looked at him. "Why are you laughing?"

Warwick Herringthorpe, who went by the name War and had all of his life, was grinning at his son. "You," he said. "You're like a stallion champing at the bit, eager to get to the female."

Liam made a face. "Bloody hell, Papa," he said. "You do not say that in front of Mama, do you?"

War snorted again, this time louder. "She says it to me," he said. "Your mother is not naïve, Liam. She knows why you are pushing this swift pace. So does the entire escort, your brothers included."

Liam's face was still puckered with displeasure as he glanced over his shoulder at the contingent of men and the small, fortified wagon that carried his mother. "I am not eager to get to her simply to bed her," he whispered loudly. "You've only met her once, Papa. She was a girl then. When you meet her today, you'll see the woman she's become. She's magnificent."

War grinned at his son, the adoring way he spoke of his betrothed. He didn't quite believe him about not simply wanting to bed the woman because he'd waited so damn long, but didn't argue with him.

"I tried to make it to Folkingham on more than one occasion," he said. "In my defense, I was simply too busy. I know that is a weak excuse, but I will see her again today and embrace her like a daughter. For certain, any woman who has you so entranced is worthy of such attention."

Liam's gaze was on the castle in the distance, rising from the landscape around it as a silent testament to its power, its longevity. But all he could see was a certain young woman in those old walls.

"I met her when she was not even one year of age," he said wistfully. "I remember thinking that she was just a stinky baby. I had no use for her, or any baby, at that age. But she kept looking at me with these eyes that are bluer than any eyes I've ever seen, and I think even back then I knew she was special. But only in the sense that I knew who she was and I respected the fact that she was the last of her line."

War was listening, his eyes crinkling with humor. "Her line will become our line," he said. "Imagine my son, married to a Welsh princess."

"We are not supposed to speak of it."

War waved him off. "I know," he said. "But there is no one around to hear us."

"Do Kyle and Logan know?"

War shook his head. "Nay," he said. "And they should not. The fewer people know about this, the better."

Liam nodded. "Agreed," he said. But he hesitated a moment. "Papa, what do you think would happen if the truth came out now? Do you think there would be trouble?"

War shrugged. "It is difficult to say," he said. "What happened was twenty years ago, and time has a way of softening situations. Nothing could happen. Or the king might view it as a shocking betrayal."

"Would he come for her?"

War's gaze was on the castle in the distance, looming closer now. "He could try, I suppose," he said, not wanting to upset his son with what he really thought, which was that Edward would more than likely try to reclaim the Welsh princess who could effectively damage his rule were her identity discovered. "But I would not worry about it. No one knows and no one will know. You will marry Lady Cambria and have a good life together."

Liam grinned at the mere mention of her name. "We will," he said confidently. "I've waited a long time for this day, Papa. I'm ready for it. And her."

War snorted, delighted that his son, his shining star, seemed so lovestruck. Liam had been an exceptionally serious child, focused and determined at even a young age, and there were times when War wondered if the lad had a heart. He had mercy, and could be generous, but sometimes he lacked emotion. Evidently, he was saving it all up for the woman he was about to marry, and that just made War laugh.

"Papa!"

Kyle and Logan had charged to the head of the escort, with Kyle pointing toward Folkingham in the distance. "May we ride ahead and announce our arrival?" he asked, struggling to control his horse. "We should be announced, you know. It is good manners."

War waved the pair on. "Go ahead," he said, watching the excited horses take off when the young men dug their spurs in. "Do not break a leg! Or a neck! Slow down!"

No one was listening to him. They were off in a cloud of dust, heading down the road. Liam shook his head unhappily.

"If one of them gets hurt and ruins this day for me, I will never forgive him," he said. "Kyle is competent enough, but Logan is an idiot."

War chuckled. "That idiot is still your brother," he said. "He's still young, Liam. Be patient with him. He loves you dearly, you know."

That softened Liam up, but before he could reply, they could both hear shouting coming from the carriage behind them. They turned to see Annaleigh Herringthorpe's beautiful red hair reflecting the noon sunlight.

"What did you say, my love?" War called back to her.

Annaleigh was Scots to the bone and a more loving, no-nonsense mother had ever existed. He pointed to two of her sons racing down the road like tempests.

"I said those two had better not break something with their foolishness," she shouted. "Ye shouldna have sent them on ahead."

War lifted a hand to ease her. "They'll be fine," he said. "Between you and Liam, the opinion of Kyle and Logan is much maligned."

Annaleigh shook her head in disapproval. "Ye know how they are," she said, ducking her head back into the carriage. "I hope de Royans admits us after meeting that pair!"

The last few words were shouted. Liam burst into soft laughter as War grinned. He loved all of his sons equally, but he had to admit that his wife had a point. Kyle was big, aggressive, and always had a smile on his face, which was very disconcerting when he was trying to kill a man. Logan, on the other hand, wasn't such a tall or broad man, but he had unearthly skills with a sword. He also had one of the greatest intellects in the entire family, his father included, but he was young and immature at times. As War reflected on that, he thought that perhaps his wife might be right. Perhaps they'd better get to the gatehouse before Kyle and Logan offended someone.

He gave Liam the sign to pick up the pace, and the escort began to run.

☙

"The Earl of Warenton is coming," Fair Lydia was saying to a pair of female servants. "I do not know how many are in his party, but we must be prepared for many family members. Do you have things well in hand?"

The servants nodded vigorously.

"Good," Fair Lydia said. "Then go about your business. And ensure, one last time, that the knights' quarters are ready for the unmarried male visitors. Go along, now."

The servants scattered. Final preparations were underway for the wedding they'd all been waiting for. It wasn't to be a big affair, but the announcements went out several weeks ago, right after Carlton had finally given his approval for the wedding after a rather sternly worded missive from War Herringthorpe about the excessive delays. It was with sadness, yet some joy, that Carlton gave the approval for the announcement to be sent out to two families, and two only—his brother's and the Earl of Warenton's.

It promised to be a small and intimate event.

The reason for inviting Warenton was obvious. It was his father who had orchestrated the entire marriage. But with Warenton would more than likely come several members of his household, and there were lodging logistics to be considered. The keep of Folkingham had ten rooms in total—three were taken up by the family, which left seven to be occupied by the groom and his parents, and the Earl of Warenton and his wife. They would sort it out at the time, but Carlton was a nervous wreck about the event while Fair Lydia was oddly composed.

She had managed all of the arrangements herself, mostly, except for the games that Carlton had arranged to follow. Games of strength and horsemanship for the male guests and family members were on the agenda, a true celebration for an event a long time in the making.

It was the moment they'd all been waiting for.

Especially the bride.

Fair Lydia made her way up to Cambria's chamber, unsurprised when she found her daughter in her wedding dress. It was a glorious confection of scarlet and gold, specifically to match the Herringthorpe standards. Most brides wore blue or pink to symbolize things like purity and chastity, but not Cambria. She'd had the seamstress build a dress of scarlet silk brocade with gold embroidery all around the bell sleeves and neckline, and at the very back, at the nape of her neck, was the head of a dog stitched in gold thread. That symbolized Bran, the puppy she'd given Liam so long ago, something that linked them together. It meant everything to her.

She hoped it meant something to him, too.

"Elegant," Fair Lydia sighed when she saw her daughter. "All I can think of when I look at you is how elegant you look. You are a queen, Dearest. An absolute queen."

Cambria turned to look at her mother, which was no mean feat given the fact that her hair was carefully coiffed and the neckline of the dress had a stiffened collar. She smiled brightly.

"That is the reaction I hope to get from Liam," she said, turning around to continue inspecting her reflection in the big bronze mirror. "I want him to take one look at me, fall to his knees, and worship the ground I walk upon."

She wasn't entirely serious, but she did want Liam to think she looked beautiful. And perhaps she *was* serious about the worship part. In any case, Fair Lydia smiled at her daughter.

"You have grown into a woman before my eyes," she said softly. "I still cannot believe it. I think I still see you as a child, looking up at me with those bright blue eyes and wanting to know all of the secrets of heaven. I always wished I could tell you everything, but alas, you have more wisdom than I do."

Cambria was gazing at herself in the mirror, gently touching the gold net on her hair, which was elaborately braided. But as she stared at herself, thoughts other than weddings started to roll through her mind.

"Mama?" she said.

Fair Lydia lowered herself down onto a cushioned chair. "What is it, my love?"

Cambria didn't say anything for a moment. She was still touching her hair, but it was clear there was something on her mind.

It wasn't long in coming.

"Did Papa know my mother?"

That seemed like a strange subject to bring up. It was unexpected and Fair Lydia looked at her curiously. "Why do you ask?" she said.

"Because I wonder if I look like her," Cambria said. "I used to not think about it at all when I was younger, but now that I am going to be married and will have children of my own, I have been thinking more and more about the woman who gave birth to me, and I wonder if I look like her. Or if I look like my father."

Fair Lydia gazed up at her daughter with an expression of adoration, the same expression she'd had the first time she ever held Cambria in her arms. "Your papa did not know your mother," she said softly. It was the truth. "Nor did he know your father. But in my mind, you look like your mother, who was surely the most beautiful woman."

Cambria turned to her. "Why would you say that?"

"Because she gave birth to you, did she not?" Fair Lydia said. "Of course she must have been beautiful to have such an exquisite creature for a daughter, and I thank her every day for risking her life for you."

Something flickered in Cambria's eyes. "Do you know something about her, then?"

"I'm not sure I know what you mean."

"You just said she risked her life for me. How do you know that?"

Fair Lydia continued to look at her daughter, resplendent in scarlet, which was striking with her coloring. It made her blue eyes bluer and her black hair blacker. But as she looked at her, the impact of Cambria's question hit home. Did she know about Cambria's mother? Of course she did. In the days following her husband's return from Wales those years ago, Carlton had told her everything about Cambria. He only told her because he needed to stress to her how important it was that she never discuss, with anyone, who or what her daughter was. As far as anyone knew, she was simply an orphan that he'd picked up at a church. Carlton had stressed the fact that Cambria was of royal blood and, because of that, was supposed to end up in a priory. Rendered inert, a life pledged to God. He furthermore told her that if King Edward were to ever discover the truth, he would come for Cambria. Fear had kept Fair Lydia silent for all of these years.

But now, her daughter was asking questions.

However, that was a rarity. Cambria had seldom asked about her origins. She didn't seem to care. She was happy and healthy and she adored her parents, so the fact that she was a foundling didn't seem to matter. All Fair Lydia had told Cambria was that her birth parents had died in a war and Carlton had saved her from going to a foundling home. That seemed to sate her curiosity for the most part, but the question that just arose was something that Fair Lydia had put down in the past. However, she knew at some point that Cambria would want to know more and the question could no longer be put off. Everyone wanted to know where they came from.

Everyone wanted to know their roots.

But Cambria's situation was different than most, and Fair Lydia had been more than willing to keep her past a secret when she was younger, but now she questioned Carlton's edict of keeping the truth from their daughter as an adult. Increasingly, Fair Lydia didn't think that was the best course of action. Her biggest fear was that Cambria would grow to resent her parents if she felt they knew more about her background than they were telling her, and if someone told her the truth before either parent did, that might cause a horrible rift.

Fair Lydia wasn't so sure she wanted to risk it.

The truth was that Cambria was bright and educated. She understood the politics of England and she understood how the world worked for the most part. It was also true that she had led a protected life, which Carlton and Fair Lydia had intended, but that didn't mean she was naïve. There were times when she would sit with her father in his solar and they would discuss history, ancient battles and ancient kings, because those were subjects that interested Cambria very much. She enjoyed reading the Bible, but not for the religious aspects of it, rather the historical. She was a woman who had grown up always wondering about people and what made them who they were.

She was friendly to everyone, from servants and soldiers to the nobility. She loved talking to them about their lives and their families and even their experiences. Carlton never let her travel outside of Folkingham, so she'd had to live vicariously through the visitors that came to her home once in a while.

She was a naturally curious young woman.

Now, Fair Lydia was once again facing a question about Cambria's past. She had never really been able to lie to her daughter, and now Cambria was of age. She wasn't a silly, flighty female. She was a young woman of breeding and education and there was something about her that had always been mature. "An old soul," was how Fair Lydia's mother had phrased it. Cambria was now facing a marriage with a man she'd loved for as long as she could remember, and after the wedding she would return to the north and Fair Lydia would hardly see her again. The idea that she would perhaps only see her daughter a few more times for the rest of her life was a horrible, empty feeling. Perhaps in these last moments, it was time to answer Cambria's question once and for all.

Did Papa know my mother?

A simple question that had an explosive answer.

"I said it because every woman risks her life when she gives birth," Fair Lydia said after a long pause. "I risked my life when I gave birth to my son, many years ago. That is what women do, Dearest. They risk their lives so their children may live."

That momentarily satisfied Cambria's curiosity and she turned back to the mirror, inspecting the fit of the scarlet bodice. "I wish he could have lived," she said. "I would have liked to have had a brother."

"You have your cousins from Netherghyll," Fair Lydia said. "They could be like brothers, I suppose."

Cambria shrugged. "They are not particularly interested in me and I am not particularly interested in them," she said. "They seem to look down on Papa because he married for his property. Not everyone has a birthright, but those two are arrogant about it. If you want to know the truth, I never liked them."

Fair Lydia fought off a grin. "Nor I," she said. "It is a pity, however. We do not have a big family like some and can ill afford to cast off relatives. Even annoying ones."

Cambria flashed her mother a smile. "Mayhap Liam and I will have a dozen children and you will have all of those little sprites running around your feet," she said. "I will give us a big family, Mama. Wait and see."

Fair Lydia snorted. "I suppose until then I shall have to content myself with puppies running around my feet," she said. "There are more puppies out there than we can handle and you have made more money for the coffers than your father has for your dowry. Truly, Liam will be a very wealthy man when he marries you."

Cambria shook her head firmly. "I intend to spend all of my money before he can have it."

"On what?"

"Jewels," she said, watching her mother laugh. "I am serious, Mama. Jewels and silks and slippers and mayhap even fine horses."

Fair Lydia shook her head at her frivolous daughter. "It is your right, of course," she said. "The money is yours to do with as you please."

Cambria was still smiling as she turned back to the mirror and pulled a gold silken scarf off a peg on the wall. She held it up to her neck, looking at the color against her skin, as she pondered what else to wear so she would look absolutely spectacular for Liam when he arrived.

"Still," she said after a moment, "it is a pity that we will not have more family here for the wedding. Papa invited his brother, but he did not respond. Nor did those two arrogant sons of his. I feel bad for Papa."

"Why?"

"Because he has a brother he never sees," she said. "He acts as if he does not care about us. I suppose Colm was more of a brother to him than his own. Do you suppose he misses Colm?"

Fair Lydia nodded. "Of course he does," she said. "But Colm's father was ill and he had to go home to assume the lordship of the Trilateral Castles. And he married that woman he'd spoken of—Maeve, I think her name was. Remember that he spoke of her?"

"I do," Cambria said. "The one he had been fond of as a young man, but she married and then was widowed. He married her when he returned home."

"I do hope he found happiness," Fair Lydia said, remembering the miserable man who had served her husband well. "Papa did not invite him to your wedding, sadly."

"Why not?"

"I do not know. I did not ask."

"Then it seems we shall have no family here. Only us."

Thoughts of the earlier part of their conversation came around again and Fair Lydia pondered, once again, bringing up the truth about Cambria's family. Cambria seemed to be speaking a great deal of it, of family and the lack thereof. As if it meant something to her.

"Is family so important to you, Bria?" Fair Lydia asked gently.

Cambria put the gold scarf aside. "I suppose," she said. "I will confess that I always wanted brothers and sisters. Mayhap that is why I raise puppies. There are so many of them, all brothers and sisters, and I envy them. They can take comfort in their siblings and parents. It is a big family."

After hearing that rather wistful statement, Fair Lydia was struck by the loneliness projecting from her daughter. Either she hadn't noticed it before or Cambria had been good at hiding it. Whatever the case, it struck a chord in her. After a moment, she sighed heavily.

It was time.

"Come and sit next to me," she said. "I must speak with you."

Cambria didn't sense anything serious. She simply did as her mother asked and went to sit on a stool, lifting up her heavy skirts so she wouldn't crease them. With her voluminous dress spread out around her, she faced her mother.

"Are you going to tell me about procreation?" she said suspiciously. "Because I raise puppies, Mama. I know what mating is. I know what effort it will take to make a big family, so you need not embarrass yourself."

Fair Lydia cocked an eyebrow at her cheeky daughter. "If you did not know how mating works, I would be very worried for you," she said. "But I was not intending to speak to you about procreation between a man and a woman. Should I?"

Cambria shook her head. "Nay," she said. "Grandmother told me."

She meant Fair Lydia's mother, because Carlton's mother had died before Cambria was born. "When did she do such a thing?" Fair Lydia gasped. "She died when you were ten years of age!"

Cambria's lips twitched as she struggled not to smile. "In the months before she passed on," she said. "I was walking with her when we saw a soldier and a kitchen servant in a corner of the kitchen yard. She had her skirts up and he was between her legs. Grandmother had to tell me what they were doing because I saw everything and was curious. She never told you?"

Fair Lydia closed her eyes tightly, slapping a hand on her forehead in disbelief. "God be merciful," she muttered. "Nay, she never told me. I am sorry she was forced to tell you at such a young age."

"I'm not," Cambria said, taking her mother's free hand and holding it. "But that is not what you wished to speak of, is it?"

"Nay," Fair Lydia said, opening her eyes to look at her daughter. "Something else. Bria, I want you to understand something. What I must speak to you about can never leave this chamber. You can never speak about it, ever. It is something for you, and only you, to know. I must swear you to secrecy, my Dearest. Do you understand me?"

Cambria grew serious. "Or course, Mama," she said. "What is so critical?"

"You."

"What about me?"

Fair Lydia grasped her daughter's fingers as she composed her thoughts. "You are a young woman now," she said. "I believe you are capable of understanding what I am about to tell you, but, as I said, it is something no one else can ever know. If they do, then your life could be in danger."

Cambria grinned, but it was a puzzled sort of gesture. "What could be so important?"

Fair Lydia kissed her hand before continuing. "Let me start at the beginning," she said. "When your father first brought you home to Folkingham, he did not intend that you should stay. I know we've always told you that you were an orphan and Papa brought you home from battle, and that was the truth, but you were never meant to remain at Folkingham. Unfortunately, when your father brought you home, I took hold of you and refused to let you go. I had just lost your brother a year earlier, you see, and I thought your father had brought you home to me to ease my broken heart."

Cambria was listening closely. "But that was not true?"

Fair Lydia shook her head. "It was not," she said. "It was the Earl of Warenton who told your father that he should allow you to remain, so we could raise you as our own child. He found another child to carry out your destiny."

"Destiny?" Cambria said, her features twisting with confusion. "What destiny? Mama, you are not making sense."

"I know," Fair Lydia said quickly. "But I am trying to explain the circumstances of what I am about to tell you. Swear to me again that you shall never repeat this."

"I swear. Of course, I swear."

"You must not even speak to your father about it."

"I won't, I promise," Cambria assured her. "But you are starting to scare me, Mama. *What* is so serious?"

Fair Lydia put a gentle hand on her daughter's cheek. "I am not trying to scare you," she said. "I simply want to stress how this information must never be spoken of."

"May I ask why?"

Fair Lydia smiled faintly. "Permit me to finish the story and then you will know," she said. "Your father and I are indeed your family, but before us, you had another family."

Cambria's brow furrowed. "I would assume so, since I know that I was orphaned," she said. But then it occurred to her what her mother was trying to say. "Do… do you mean to tell me that you *know* my family?"

Fair Lydia nodded. "I know," she said. "Your father knows, too. He does not want to tell you the truth simply to protect you, but I do not think that is fair to you. You are old enough now to understand. Everyone wants to know where they come from, what their bloodlines are. It is an inherent need to know who your family is and I do not think it is right for you to go through life thinking you were abandoned or unloved. I am certain neither is true."

"Who *is* my birth family?"

Fair Lydia gazed deeply into her eyes as she spoke. "The man who gave you life, the father of your bloodlines, is Llywelyn ap Gruffydd. Some call him Llywelyn the Last. He was the last Prince of Wales and your mother was Eleanor de Montfort. Your maternal great-grandfather is King John of England."

Cambria's eyes widened immediately. "My… my *what*?" she said. "Mama, that is not possible."

"It is very possible because it is true."

Cambria looked at Fair Lydia as if the woman was trying to pull the mother of all jests on her, but she also knew that wasn't in her mother's nature. Even if the story coming out of the woman's mouth was ridiculous.

Absolutely ridiculous.

"Oh, Mama…" she said, shock turning to disbelief. "It is not true!"

Fair Lydia nodded. "I would not lie to you," she said gently. "Bria, your mother died in childbirth with you, and when you were less than a year old, your father was captured in Wales and executed. You were a most valuable hostage because you have the blood of the last Prince of Wales running through your veins. More than that, you also have blood from the royal English house as well as the House of de Montfort. Simon de Montfort is your maternal grandfather. That makes you an extremely important figure, so important that King Edward ordered that you be sent away to Sempringham Priory to live out your natural life as a hostage, never to procreate, never to be loved. Sempringham was to be your prison."

Cambria was back to being shocked again. "Oh... Sweet Jesù," she breathed. "Is... is that even possible?"

"It is not only possible, it is probable. It is the truth."

"Truly?"

"Truly."

Cambria took a deep breath, struggling to comprehend. "*Eleanor*," she finally said, sounding dazed. "My mother was Eleanor?"

"Eleanor de Montfort."

Hearing that again was like a thunderclap to Cambria, pounding the truth into her. "I... I know this from my lessons on the history of England," she said. "Eleanor was the youngest child of Simon de Montfort."

"She was."

"But Simon de Montfort fought Henry for the crown."

"He did."

Cambria was starting to put the pieces together, the pieces of her lineage. "That means he fought his brother-in-law," she said. "Henry was Eleanor's brother."

"Aye, he was."

Cambria didn't know what to say after that. She simply shook her head in disbelief. Seeing that she was completely overcome, Fair Lydia continued softly.

"You were never going to make it to Sempringham," she said. "The moment I took you in my arms, there was no possibility that I was going to allow that to happen. So, you were given a new name and you became an adopted de Royans child. Another infant was sent to Sempringham in your place. That is why you can never speak of this, Bria. Too many men risked everything so you could have the life you lead today. If the truth were discovered, it would be deadly to them and probably to you as well. There are still men out there who would like nothing better than to kill you and erase Llywelyn's bloodlines from the earth entirely. You were always precious, as my daughter, but your past makes you precious, and dangerous, to others as well. Guard your secret with your life, my love."

Cambria stared at her mother. It was the most fantastic tale she'd ever heard. She was in the throes between shock and disbelief, both emotions fighting for prevalence.

Mama would not lie to me.

Mama would not *lie!*

Finally, she began to tear up.

"Please," she said, hand against her mouth in shock. "Is that all really true?"

It was a last plea for confirmation, for acknowledgment that this was no joke. Fair Lydia, seeing how upset her daughter was, kissed her hand again.

"I promise you that it is," she said. "You may be upset by this. It will take time for you to come to terms with it. That is why we did not tell you when you were younger. It would not have meant anything, but now that you are older, you must understand why we did what we did. Why we hid you in plain sight. You will go on and marry the man you love and have a dozen children. You will live, Cambria. That is your right. It is the right of every child born to go on and live a productive life. Your father and Warenton gave you that opportunity. Do you understand what I am telling you?"

Cambria nodded, blinking, and the tears spattered. She still held her hand over her mouth, unable to move it away because it seemed to be holding in great cries of shock.

"I understand," she whispered. "But… I cannot believe it."

Fair Lydia didn't say any more. Cambria needed time to process what she'd been told because, clearly, it was overwhelming in nature. Fair Lydia wasn't sure that Cambria would even come to terms with it anytime soon, but did not regret telling her. She did feel bad that it wasn't something her daughter had expected, or probably had even imagined in her wildest dreams.

Yet it was the truth.

A hidden princess.

The bloodlines of Wales.

"Does Liam know?" Cambria said, barely able to speak.

Fair Lydia nodded. "He knows," she said. "But I do not think you should tell him that *you* know. If he ever brings it up to you, then you can determine at that time whether or not to confess. This secret affects him also, since he will marry you."

Cambria swallowed hard, trying to swallow away her tears. She suddenly didn't feel much like wearing her wedding dress today. She didn't feel much like anything. All she could think of was a dead Welsh prince and a dead English princess, her parents, and the heritage that fate had given her. She was half Welsh, half English. Half rebel, half not. So many half-somethings.

Slowly, she stood up.

Fair Lydia watched as she made her way over to one of the

two enormous wardrobes in her chamber. Cambria had a good many clothes, all of them neatly tucked away, and she opened up one of the wardrobe doors where her fine things were hanging.

"Bria?" Fair Lydia said. "What are you thinking, Dearest? Can I help with anything?"

Cambria was just reaching for the ties on the side of the bodice, but she came to a halt. "Bria," she muttered. "*Cambria*. Is that truly my name?"

Fair Lydia stood up from the chair. "It is now," she said. "But when you came to us, you had another name."

Cambria turned to look at her. "What was it?"

"Gwenllian."

Cambria thought on that. "Gwenllian," she repeated, hearing her birth name for the first time. "I remember saying something to my tutor once, how my name was the ancient name for Wales. Cambria, Brittania, Caledonia—all ancient names for countries. But I never thought anything of it until now."

Fair Lydia came up behind her and began unfastening the ties at the back of the dress. "I selected the name," she said. "I knew it was the ancient name for Wales and, considering who you were, it seemed fitting. Mayhap you no longer carried the name of your ancestors, but I chose to honor them through that ancient name."

Cambria smiled weakly. "You were always a woman of great generosity," she said. "Mama… thank you for telling me. I am honored that you would trust me with it. But it is… a lot. I think I should like to change into something more comfortable and keep to myself for a while. Will you make sure I am undisturbed?"

Fair Lydia nodded. "Of course," she said. "I will help you remove this garment and then I will leave you to your thoughts."

"Nay," Cambria said, turning around to stop the woman from fussing with the garment ties. "Go now, if you please. I can remove this myself."

Fair Lydia's brow furrowed. "Are you certain?" she said. "There are a lot of different pieces to remove."

Cambria forced a smile. "I can manage," she said. "Thank you, Mama. For everything."

She seemed final about it, and Fair Lydia dipped her head in surrender, giving in to her daughter's wishes. The last sight she had of Cambria before she closed the bedchamber door was of her daughter looking at herself in the mirror again, perhaps this time to question who she really was.

Cambria?

Or Gwenllian?

The expression on her face left Fair Lydia wondering if she'd done the right thing by telling her the truth.

Certainly, only time would tell.

She could only pray that it didn't come back to haunt her.

CHAPTER TEN

Folkingham Castle

H E WAS ON the approach.
That was the word from the sentries at the gatehouse because they had a bird's-eye view of the countryside and could see the approach of the Herringthorpe escort. The scarlet-and-black banners were snapping in the breeze, clearly visible. Cambria was excited, of course, but given the conversation she'd had with her mother a couple of hours earlier, she was still startled. Still overwhelmed.

Very much confused.

She needed to see Liam.

Her mother had told her not to say anything to him, but if he already knew her secret, she wasn't sure why she wasn't supposed to tell him that she'd been told. She found that she was eager to discuss it with him, to know what *he* knew in case her mother had left anything out. In case he had a different perspective. All she knew was that the news wasn't anything she'd ever imagined, and certainly not what she'd ever expected, and it was having an effect on her.

Truthfully, she was terrified.

She was also in denial. There was no possibility she was who her mother said she was... *was there*? Surely the woman was mistaken. Perhaps she'd heard someone fantasize about Cambria's true identity and taken it to heart. Whatever the case, Cambria couldn't believe she was truly a lost Welsh princess. There had to be another explanation.

Perhaps Liam could provide it.

She was out of her wedding dress at this point, donning a pale blue silk with a deep neckline and a wispy white shift underneath. The color of the dress was the same color of her eyes and she'd had it made especially for this moment, for greeting her husband-to-be. They hadn't seen one another in nearly a year, and even that meeting had been brief because Liam was delivering messages from his father, whom he'd just started to serve. He'd left his position at Castle Questing and gone to serve War Herringthorpe as a garrison commander. And that had been it. A short moment in time she'd been left with.

Until now.

Now, he had come for her.

Cambria took one last look in the bronze mirror. Her hair was unbound, down to her buttocks, but a ribbon pulled it away from her face. She was wearing a silver-and-blue sapphire necklace her father had given her when she'd turned eighteen years of age, with matching earrings that dangled from her earlobes. On her lips she wore beeswax with finely crushed rose petals in it that gave it a faint red color, positively stunning with her coloring. She looked every inch the daughter of a warlord, proud and perfect and...

She also looked every inch a Welsh princess.

A surge of confusion pulsed through her again and she turned away from the mirror, heading out to the bailey, where they were preparing for the arrival of the betrothed. Liam had been to Folkingham many times, but in this instance, it was in a different capacity and everyone knew it. There were smiles all around as everyone waited for what was known to be an impatient bridegroom. Rumors traveled quickly around the castle. When Cambria appeared at the keep entry, she could see the grinning. Attention was upon her. Slightly embarrassed that everyone was thinking the same thing, which was the fact that Liam would soon be able to legally bed their young mistress, Cambria tried not to pay any attention to the smirks from soldiers and servants alike.

She tried to retain at least some of her dignity.

"There you are," Carlton said as he came up behind her. "I did not see you walk past my solar."

Cambria glanced at her father. "Aye," she said. "Here I am. Being laughed at."

Carlton had no idea what she meant until she gestured to a couple of soldiers at the base of the stairs and how they were grinning.

"They are happy for you," he said, shrugging. "They are not laughing at you."

Cambria cast him a long look. "They are laughing because you delayed this marriage as long as you could until War Herringthorpe threatened you," she said. "Now, Liam and his family are about to charge in through the gatehouse and snatch me away. They are laughing because they know what is going to happen as soon as Liam and I are married."

Carlton wasn't following her train of thought. "And what is that?"

Cambria threw a thumb in the general direction of the kitchen yard where her dogs were. "That we will behave like dogs in season."

Carlton nearly choked in response. "Hell's Fire, lass," he said, coughing. "You should not say things like that."

Cambria fought off a grin. "I could have said that he'll mount me like—"

Carlton roared, interrupting her. "Shut your lips!" he said, putting his hands to his ears. "You will not say things like that in front of your father!"

That had Cambria laughing. She looped one of her arms affectionately around his elbow. "Apologies," she said. "But had you not delayed so long, Liam would not be so eager and everyone would not be laughing."

Carlton wasn't over the fact that his daughter had used the word "mount" in front of him when describing what her betrothed intended to do once he married her, true though it might be.

"I regret nothing," he said stiffly.

"I know."

"Shall we go forth and greet Liam together?"

"Please."

With Cambria grinning at her offended, embarrassed father, the two of them came off the stairs from the keep and headed out into the dusty bailey. The gatehouse was open, both portcullises lifted, and they could see a party through the opening, approaching from a distance. As they moved for the gatehouse, a soldier approached Carlton.

"My lord," he said. "Our scouts have reported another party approaching from the north. They should be here before supper if they remain on this pace."

Carlton looked at the man, a senior soldier who had been at Folkingham since the days of Fair Lydia's father. "Who is it?" he asked.

"The Earl of Warenton, my lord," the soldier said. "The House of de Wolfe is approaching."

"Ah," Carlton said in understanding. "Excellent. But no sign of my brother from Netherghyll?"

The soldier shook his head. "Nay, my lord."

That was disappointing, but not unexpected. Hamilton de Royans, Baron Cononley, Constable of North Yorkshire and the Northern Dales, was a difficult man to get along with. Carlton had never gotten on well with his ambitious and arrogant brother, something that had bled over into both of his sons. Baron Cononley was an inherited title, as the de Royans had held it for well over one hundred years, and Hamilton wore the title like a badge but did little to actually fulfill the requirements. He was about the prestige, not about the work. Carlton had pointed that out, once, and that was nearly the last time he'd ever had a meaningful conversation with his brother.

Such were the complex dynamics of a family.

Therefore, he didn't linger on Hamilton's lack of response. Other than Warenton, he was the only other person Carlton had invited to the wedding. It was to be a very small affair, and that was bred from the fact that Carlton was still trying to protect his daughter after all of these years. The fewer people who attended and questioned the roots of an adopted woman, the better.

The less chance of someone finding out something that he wanted to keep buried.

"Send riders out to escort Warenton," he said after a moment. "Meanwhile, we shall greet Herringthorpe."

The soldier nodded and headed off. That left Carlton and Cambria at the gatehouse, waiting with anticipation for Liam's arrival.

It wasn't long in coming.

He was, literally, the first person through the gatehouse, with his father's escort about a quarter of a mile behind him. One look at Cambria standing next to her father and he bailed from his warhorse, a gigantic grin plastered all over his face. He went to Cambria as if Carlton didn't even exist, drinking in the sight of her beautiful face.

He was a man who had waited a very long time for this moment.

"My lady," he said, reaching out to take her hand and kiss it most sweetly. "I cannot believe the beauty my eyes are beholding. Is it possible that you have become more heavenly in the time we've been apart?"

As Cambria smiled and flushed a bright red, Carlton groaned.

"Christ, Liam," he muttered. "How long have you rehearsed those words?"

Liam started to laugh. "*Too* long, thanks to you, my lord," he said. "It is your own fault. I have been saving them up for this moment."

Carlton shook his head and started to move away. "I am going to become ill if I hear one more sickly-sweet platitude come out of your mouth," he said. "Can you promise me that your father will not use the same greeting on me?"

"I cannot, my lord."

"Then I will have to throttle him."

He moved off, leaving Liam and Cambria laughing. When Carlton was far enough away, Liam's expression softened as he beheld the vision he'd been dreaming of.

"I did not intend to chase him off," he said. "But I would be lying if I said I was not glad for it. And I meant every word I said to you."

Cambria smiled shyly. "He has been dreading this," she said. "I suppose most fathers are reluctant to see their daughters married."

Liam cocked an eyebrow. "Not all," he said. "I have sisters, and I am sure there are days when my father would like nothing better than to see them married off and someone else's burden."

"Is that how you look at a wife? As a burden?"

Liam shook his head. "Not me," he said. "Because my wife shall be you, and you could not be a burden if you tried. Have you been well?"

Cambria nodded. "Very well," she said. "I—"

She was cut off when something big and black appeared between her and Liam. She looked down to see the pup she'd given him, now an enormous dog with a head that was larger than hers.

"Bran," she said softly, bending over and putting both of her hands on the dog's head. "What a beautiful lad you are. Have you been good?"

The dog was quite happy to see her, wagging his tail and slobbering on her wrists. But he was threatening to dirty the blue silk, so Liam pulled him back by the big collar around his neck.

"He's the best dog in the world," he said. "But he weighs more than you do, so be careful with him. I do not want to see him knock you over."

Cambria's hand was lingering on the dog's head. "I am not concerned," she said, giving him a final pat. "But I do not want to be made untidy by this beast. When I am in more suitable clothing, he can be as messy as he pleases around me."

Liam turned around and whistled loudly between his teeth, trying to catch the attention of someone in the escort just as the wagons were coming through the gatehouse.

"I will tie him to one of the wagons," he said. "I do not necessarily want him wandering in an unfamiliar place."

"You'll do no such thing," Cambria insisted. "Bring him into the hall. There will be scraps for him there and he can nap near the hearth. That would be better for him."

Liam looked at her dubiously. "Are you certain you want him there?"

"Of course."

"He'll try to steal food off your trencher tonight."

Cambria grinned. "I will happily give it to him."

Liam chuckled, looking to the dog. "Do you hear that?" he said. "The lady of the house has given you a reprieve from your exile. Mind that you behave yourself."

The dog just wagged his tail furiously.

As this was going on, an older couple approached from the escort that was settling off to the west, away from the gatehouse. A very big man in armor and a lovely woman with glistening red hair and fair skin were heading in Liam's direction. He happened to glance up from the dog to see the couple approaching.

"My parents are coming," he said to Cambria. "You've met my father before, but I do not think you've met my mother."

Cambria spied the same pair. "Never," she said. "But your father was very kind to me."

Liam held out a hand to her, and she placed hers in his big palm. With a wink, he led her over to his parents as Bran tagged along behind them. When they got near his parents, Bran charged ahead and jumped on War, who was forced to push the dog down. Then he took hold of the collar as Liam and Cambria came to a halt.

"Liam, you are going to have to train this dog not to jump," War said. "If he jumps on your lady, he'll knock her down and probably crush her."

As Cambria snorted, Liam conceded the point. "I've tried," he said. "You know I have tried, but he is incorrigible. My lady is simply going to learn how to push harder than he does. Speaking of ladies… Mama, this is Cambria. Bria, this is my mother, Lady Herringthorpe. I've waited a long time for this moment, when the two women I love most meet."

He was smiling warmly at them both. As Cambria curtsied for the lovely woman with the vibrant red hair, Annaleigh Herringthorpe rushed forward and put her arms around her son's future wife.

"Let us not be so formal, lass," she said in a heavy Scots accent. Releasing her, she stepped back for a moment simply to look at her. "Liam told me that ye were lovely, but he dinna tell me just how beautiful ye were. Ye're a sight tae see."

Cambria blushed. "Thank you, Lady Herringthorpe," she said. "I have so longed to meet you. Liam speaks so lovingly of you."

Annaleigh looked at her son. "He'd better," she teased. "But he's a good lad. He deserves tae be happy."

"I intend to try very hard to make him so."

Annaleigh smiled, patting her on the cheek. "I can see that," she said, her voice full of emotion. "Now, will ye take me inside and give me something tae drink? The travel has me parched."

Cambria took her by the hand, and together they walked

toward the hall. They looked very companionable doing so. Liam and War watched them go.

"Your mother likes her already," War said quietly. "That's a good sign."

Liam nodded. "I hope so," he said. "Honestly, Papa, I've dreamed of this moment. There were times I never thought we'd get here, but here we are. This is truly happening."

War smiled at his son, hearing the awe and joy in his tone. "It *is* happening," he said. "But I had to threaten Carlton to get here."

"Should we go and find him?"

"I'll find him. You go after your mother and betrothed."

The pair split off, War going in search of the bride's father and Liam going in search of his bride. He could see the women up ahead, now arm in arm as they chatted amiably. He could see them both smiling at one another. Truthfully, he was content watching them because, as he'd said, he'd been waiting for this moment for a long time. His beloved mother and his beloved bride, coming together for the first time. He would let them have their conversation without interrupting. He was just so happy to see it.

The moment he'd been anticipating was finally here and nothing could spoil it.

Nothing.

God help him, he would remember that vow in the days to come.

CHAPTER ELEVEN

HE BORE THE title of the Earl of Warenton. He was only the second man ever to hold that title and even that was simply because of the luck of his birth order. He had a twin, less than ten minutes after him, but he had been the first, so to him went the entire de Wolfe empire.

Scott had made an excellent earl so far.

His brothers all thought so. He was extremely fortunate in that none of them had been aiming for his title. Greed was not something that ran in the de Wolfe bloodlines, but ambition did. All of his brothers were accomplished, ambitious men and he was proud to be related to them.

Even the one who didn't bear the de Wolfe name.

Along with the responsibility of the de Wolfe empire, he was also the keeper of its secrets. There were many. One of the biggest, however, was the fact that his father had sired a son out of wedlock, before he'd met Scott's mother, and that son was none other than War Herringthorpe. It was mostly the worst kept secret in the north because War looked like a de Wolfe brother. He looked like William. He also acted like a de Wolfe to the bone, but the decision had been made long ago, when the bloodlines were discovered, that War should keep the name of the man who raised him, the man who had knowingly married his pregnant mother, out of respect for him. War was proud to carry the Herringthorpe name, and that meant his children were also Herringthorpes even though their bloodlines were de Wolfe.

That included Liam.

Scott was attending the wedding of Liam and Cambria because of another secret. There was a certain Welsh princess living incognito at Folkingham Castle and Scott's father had put her there. That was a secret that had been entrusted to Scott by his father, and it was Scott's responsibility to keep an eye on the situation. Now, the wedding they'd been anticipating for about twenty years was on their doorstep and that Welsh princess, the one with dual bloodlines, both Welsh and English, would be marrying a man of de Wolfe blood.

It was all quite complicated, but that was the situation. Scott had been on hand those years ago when his father made the decision. At the time, he knew why and he agreed with it. That had never been in question. But the years had passed and the brother they believed to have been killed in Wales turned out to be alive after all. Although that was a joyous event, it put into question the very reason why William did what he did with the Welsh princess, but it was too late to change anything. In fact, William had never mentioned any kind of a change. He simply let things go on the way they were. Just because James had returned, although little remained of the man they had known before, that didn't ease William's sense of vengeance.

The decision had remained.

Now, the wedding was about to take place and Scott had departed Castle Questing almost immediately after receiving the announcement of the nuptials. With him, he'd brought his wife, his mother, two of his sons, and a ward of the family. Scott and his wife, Avrielle, had several children, but most of them were fostering and he didn't particularly want to bring the youngest ones on a long and exhausting journey. His wife hadn't fought him on it and even now sat in a fortified carriage that was midway back in the escort pack. Scott suspected that she might have even been enjoying the time away from her youngest children, because they could be a handful. But she wasn't alone in the carriage.

She had companions.

One such companion was Caria de Wolfe. She had been a ward of William de Wolfe since birth. Born Tacey ferch Dafydd, she was the niece of the Earl of Coventry, Bhrodi de Shera, who had married William de Wolfe's youngest daughter, Penelope. Her mother had been Bhrodi's younger sister, who had perished in childbirth, and Caria was a product of two royal Welsh bloodlines.

William had taken the child, at Bhrodi's request, to hide her from Edward, who had been tearing through the country at that time. Even though Bhrodi was the Earl of Coventry, he also held an even older title—heir to the Kingdom of Anglesey through his matriarchal line. He was Welsh to the bone. Being married to a de Wolfe gave him some protection from the king, but he didn't want to risk his sister's infant because she would suffer the same fate as Gwenllian had she been captured.

Scott had always found it ironic that his father had hidden not one, but two Welsh princesses from the king and Edward had never been the wiser. William was open about Caria's heritage being Scottish, a cousin of his wife's, so she had been raised in complete safety. Caria was fair-haired, not dark as the

Welsh could be, so it was easy to believe she was Scots. Until two years ago, she'd believed the same until William told her the truth upon her eighteenth birthday. He also told her what her official title was, something granted to her by her brother— *Tywysoges yr Ynys Dywyll.*

Princess of the Dark Isle.

It had taken about a year for Caria to become accustomed to her true origins. The hardest part was getting used to the idea that a woman she believed to be her foster sister, Penelope, was in truth her aunt, and the man she knew as Penelope's husband was, in fact, her uncle by blood. That had been quite strange to her. Given that she'd grown up as a foster daughter of William de Wolfe, she understood the history and politics of England very well. She knew what being Welsh meant to a king who had been trying to subdue them for years. She also knew what would happen to her, and her foster father, if her identity became known.

She'd been very good at keeping the secret.

The last family member of the party from Castle Questing was none other than the dowager Countess of Warenton, Jordan de Wolfe. Questing was her home, and even when Scott and Avrielle moved in upon the death of William, they still deferred to Jordan on nearly everything involving the castle or family matters. She was the great matriarch, much loved and respected by her children. She tagged along to Folkingham because Caria was going and she was never far from Caria, whom she viewed as her child. Jordan may have been quite elderly, but her mind and body was still solid, and she and Caria and Avrielle had ridden in the carriage companionably for almost a week now. Better still, they'd been working on an embroidered blanket, the three of them, for the newlyweds, which had turned out spectacularly well.

But that journey was about to come to an end.

"Papa!" came a shout. "Look! Riders!"

Scott was riding near the carriage and his sons, Jeremy and Nathaniel, were riding point. The shout came from Jeremy, twenty years of age and already knighted. He was a big lad, blond like his father and paternal grandmother, but with the big de Wolfe build. He was pointing off toward the south, and Scott pushed his horse forward, trying to get a better view of what Jeremy was seeing. When the field of men and horses cleared, he could clearly see the riders in the distance, heading in their direction.

He spurred his horse to the front of the column.

"Shall I charge them, Papa?" The younger son, Nathaniel, was gripping his excited horse. "Shall I demand to know their business?"

Scott glanced at Nathaniel, who was a great deal like Scott's youngest brother, Thomas, in that he was big and aggressive and had no idea how strong he truly was. Like wild colts, men like that were sometimes hard to rein in. They tended to have more fire in them than sense at that age.

"Nay," Scott said evenly. "Since we are so near to Folkingham Castle, I am going to assume they are from Folkingham and are, in fact, coming to ask us to identify ourselves."

That didn't seem to ease Nathaniel. "We are flying Warenton standards," he said. "They *know* who we are."

He said it so indignantly that Scott had to grin. "Aye, they do," he said. "But it is always wise to get a confirmation, is it not? What if we were outlaws who stole Warenton banners?"

Nathaniel didn't have an answer for that, mostly because it made sense and he was insulted that he hadn't thought about it himself. At this age, and he'd barely seen eighteen years, nearly everything insulted him because he was a de Wolfe, son of the Earl of Warenton, and the world bowed at his family's feet.

Well, mostly.

As Nathaniel was wrestling with his inflated ego, Scott held up a hand to the incoming riders, who responded with a similar gesture. They reined their horses close, but not too close.

"My lord," one soldier said. "You fly Warenton standards. May I address the earl?"

"You are," Scott said. "I am Scott de Wolfe."

Both riders saluted him smartly. "Lord de Royans sends his greetings," the same soldier said. "He asks that we escort you to Folkingham."

"Lead the way."

Jeremy and Nathaniel fell right in behind the riders as Scott shook his head at his eager sons. But he lifted an arm to the party behind him, indicating for them to pick up the pace. With his sons tucked in behind the escort riders, Scott ended up riding alone the rest of the way to Folkingham, but he truly didn't mind. It gave him time to think about the coming union and the culmination of the plans his father had for the daughter of Llywelyn the Last. Long ago, they'd been plans of revenge for the death of a son, but now… now they were simply plans to keep the woman from the fate Edward had planned for her. Not that it really mattered now, because once she was married to Liam, Edward couldn't touch her.

But the fact remained that he could still do damage.

If Edward were to ever find out about William's plans, and furthermore find out where Gwenllian had been hidden in plain sight, even if she were married to Liam, he more than likely wouldn't let the subject rest. He'd see it as a challenge to his rule, a de Wolfe challenge to the will of the Crown, and given both War and Liam were garrison commanders at royal outposts, it could very well mean the end of their royal appointments.

Scott had to have a backup plan if that happened. He couldn't let Liam or War take the fall for something his father did, but first, they had to get that young woman married to Liam as the final act of keeping her away from Edward.

God help them, they had to get through this day.

Then they could all breathe.

Or so he thought.

CHAPTER TWELVE

Folkingham Castle

"Well?" Liam said, planting himself on the bench beside Cambria. "What do you think of my mother?"

Annaleigh had occupied a solid hour of Cambria's time before War finally pulled her away so the lovers could have some time together. He'd just spent that hour watching Liam as Liam watched Cambria with anxious eyes, wanting so much to be with her, but his mother was preventing it. War had had all he could take and finally fetched his wife, giving Liam that window of opportunity to slip in. Now, in the great hall of Folkingham, Liam and Cambria were sitting together.

Alone.

Finally!

"I think your mother is delightful," Cambria said, sitting as close as she could to Liam without actually touching him. "She told me that she is a cousin to the Countess of Warenton and that's how she met her husband."

Liam nodded. "All true," he said. "She is a cousin to William de Wolfe's wife."

"Then that makes you kin to the House of de Wolfe."

His smile faded as he looked at her. "Bria," he said after a moment, "since you are to be my wife, there is something you should know. Something that you must never speak of to anyone else."

Her expression grew serious. "Of course, Liam," she said. "I would never speak of something you told me in confidence."

"Thank you," he said sincerely. "You should know that I am closer to the House of de Wolfe than you think. William de Wolfe is my grandfather."

Her eyebrows lifted in surprise. "He is?"

"Aye," Liam said, nodding. "My father is his son, conceived before he met and married his wife. My father is technically William's eldest son, but because he was born out of wedlock, he cannot inherit. Nor does he want to, just so you know."

Cambria looked over at War, who was now standing with his wife as they inspected an elaborate tapestry near the dais. She studied the tall, big man with the dark blond hair that was turning silver around the face, now seeing him through different eyes.

Not as a Herringthorpe, but a de Wolfe.

"I've only met the former Earl of Warenton once," she said. "He came to visit my father about ten or twelve years ago. I remember an older man with a patch over one eye. He seemed interested in talking to me, however. He was very nice."

"He was a kind man," Liam said. "I have fond memories of him."

"Did he acknowledge you as his grandson?"

Liam shook his head. "Only in private," he said. "The decision had been made long ago to keep my father's relationship to Warenton private because to publicly acknowledge anything would be to shame my grandmother, the one who conceived my father with a man she was not married to. Neither my father, nor William de Wolfe, wanted to harm her reputation. Most people still look at a pregnancy like that, as a lack of morals or a lack of restraint. They did it to protect her, so that is why we do not speak of it, but he and the other grandsons allowed me a small mercy not long ago to share that family link."

"What was that?"

Liam put his left hand on his right shoulder. "I bear a stigmata that all of the grandsons bear," he said. "A permanent mark of the House of de Wolfe. In my case, it is almost always hidden, but I wear it with pride. It makes me feel as if I am part of something bigger."

She smiled faintly. "Thank you for telling me," she said. "I'm glad you felt you could trust me with it. It seems we shall be a family of many secrets."

"What do you mean?"

"I think you know what I mean."

He looked at her, puzzled. "Nay, I do not," he said. "What is it?"

"Gwenllian."

That changed his expression in a heartbeat. His features tensed, his jaw began to flex, and his breathing changed. It grew deep and slow. It was obvious that he wasn't sure what to say at first, but he at least did her the courtesy of not pretending that he didn't know what she was talking about. But when he continued to remain silent, Cambria spoke.

"I know that you know," she said softly. "I am not trying to cause an issue, but I want you to know that I know everything."

He looked away, jaw still flexing. "You are not supposed to know."

"Why?" she said. "I am glad that someone felt I was mature enough and responsible enough to know the truth. And I will be insulted if you do not feel the same way."

He looked at her then. "It is not a matter of maturity," he said quietly. "It is a matter of safety."

"Whose safety?"

"Yours."

"What do you mean by that?"

"I mean that the fewer people know, the better. The more chance we have of keeping this… secret."

She could see his point. Sort of. But she could also see something else. "You were never going to tell me, were you?" she asked.

He sighed heavily, once again averting his gaze. "Probably not," he said. "There is no reason to."

She cocked an eyebrow. "You know where you come from, Liam," she said. "Is it fair that I should not?"

It was threatening to turn into an argument. The air was fairly crackling with tension at this point. Without a word, Liam stood up and headed out of the hall, leaving Cambria to run after him. She caught up to him in the bailey, where she grabbed him by the arm.

"Rules shall be established now, sir," she said heatedly. "You will never, ever walk away from me in anger. Not now, not ever. That is not how two people who love each other behave. If there is a problem, we discuss it. But we do not show a lack of respect to the other by simply walking away."

Liam sighed heavily, hanging his head as he considered her words. "You are correct," he said. "But in my defense, I did not walk away in anger. I walked away knowing you would follow. What you brought up in the hall cannot be discussed in a chamber like that. People hear, Bria."

That cooled her anger somewhat, but she was still unhappy. "Very well," she said. "Since we are no longer in the hall, we may discuss it out here."

He shook his head, holding up a hand. "There is no need," he said. "If you already know, there is nothing I can add to it."

She looked at him, disappointed. "Is this how our marriage is going to be?"

"What do you mean?"

"If I want to discuss something and you do not, you will simply silence me?"

He looked at her. "Of course not," he said. "But this is not a suitable subject to discuss. If you know what it is, then you know why."

She cocked her head. "Non-suitable for whom?" she said. "You? It is quite suitable for me, and before you try to silence me again, know that I feel you're being quite unfair. You've known about this since the beginning and you never thought to tell me. Someone has, someone brave, and now I find out I am not who I thought I was. I am not the person you have told me I was, all of my life. I am confused and hurt and silencing me is not helping. I should be able to trust you with all things, Liam, and now I am discovering that when I need you most, you are not willing to help me?"

That broke him down completely. "Sweetheart, that's not true," he insisted softly, reaching out to take her hand. "Of course you can trust me. You may always trust me. And I can only imagine how you feel. But from my perspective, it has been pounded into my skull that this is a subject that can never see the light of day. I have been conditioned not to mention it, under any circumstances, because your life could be in danger if

I do. And I would never do anything to put you in danger."

She understood, but it didn't quell her need to speak on it. "Please," she murmured. "I just need to speak to you about it or surely I will burst."

With great reluctance, he surrendered. "Very well," he muttered. "Speak. I will listen."

Relieved, Cambria wrapped her hands around his enormous forearm and pulled him with her as she started to walk. "Thank you," she said sincerely. "I do not want to put anyone in danger, least of all myself, but I would be grateful if you could tell me what you know."

They were heading into an open part of the bailey where no one was within thirty feet of them, all around. People were either over near the walls or back near the kitchen yard. Somewhere behind them, Bran was wandering, as the dog had followed them out of the hall, but he was sniffing at the dirt—and clearly uninterested in what they were speaking about. Once they reached a spot that was completely open, without nearby ears to overhear what was being said, Cambria came to a halt.

"As you can imagine, the revelation came as a shock to me," she said in a low voice. "I am still in disbelief, but my mother would not lie to me."

The light of realization went on in Liam's eyes and he nodded his head as if his suspicions were correct. "Your mother told you," he muttered. "I knew it would not be your father."

"Nay, it was not my father," Cambria said. "She did not lie, did she?"

"She did not lie."

"How long have you known?"

"Since I escorted you to Folkingham from Wales."

Her brow rippled with surprise. "*You* escorted me?"

He nodded. "Remember that I was your father's squire when I was young," he said. "I was with him on the Welsh campaign. I had seen fourteen summers and, suddenly, I was in charge of a stinky baby and absolutely insulted because of it."

He meant the stinky part as a jest and she smiled weakly, but it didn't diminish the seriousness of the subject. "I knew you squired for my father," she said. "I suppose it did not occur to me that you went to Wales with him or knew me as an infant."

"I did, to both," he said, his green eyes glimmering. "The battles in Wales were brutal and shocking for a young lad of my age, but they were something that helped me grow as a knight. As for the fat baby with black hair and blue eyes, she was no trouble. She was a happy baby, as I recall. And we took her from an encampment in Wales back to Folkingham."

She mulled over his words because they were bringing about more questions. "Did you know who I was even then?"

"I knew."

"Did you know my mother? My father?"

He shook his head. "Nay," he said. "Your mother died long before I met you and I was not near your father when he was killed. I did meet your uncle, however. Dafydd. And I knew your cousins."

"What cousins?"

Liam faltered, realizing she'd not been told about the others. He couldn't very well refuse to tell her now that he'd brought it up. "There were other children, Bria," he said, trying to be gentle. "Children of your Uncle Dafydd. You were the only offspring of Llywelyn, at least the only one we could find. There were rumors that you had an older sister named Catherine, but we never found evidence of her. I suspect she ended up like you."

"What do you mean?"

"Adopted by another family to keep her safe."

That revelation seemed to stun Cambria. "A sister," she breathed. "I have a sister?"

He shrugged. "Possibly, but we may never know," he said. "But your cousins—two boys and several girls—were taken away, much as you were. The girls were sent to priories and the boys sent to Bristol Castle. Before you ask, I do not know what has become of them. That was a long time ago, sweetheart."

She was greatly torn hearing that there were other family members out there. Truthfully, that had never occurred to her. "I was just lamenting to my mother over the fact that we have no other family than my father's brother, who has no use for him," she said. "Now I find out that I actually have cousins and possibly a sister? That is astonishing."

He could see something of hope in her expression and quickly sought to kill it. "I know this all comes as a great surprise to you, but know this," he said. "If you are thinking to contact these family members, do not. They are more than likely well guarded, by royal guards, and if you try to contact them, your secret will be revealed and everything we have worked so hard for will be ruined. Edward will demand your capture, and because I will not allow it, I will be forced to go to battle against the king. I will lose my position, my father will lose his position, and my entire family, more than likely including the House of de Wolfe, will be forced to go to battle to protect you. Men will die because of this and I know that is not what you wish."

She was looking at him in resentment and horror. "I did not

say I wished to contact them," she said. "You need not be so dramatic."

"I am not being dramatic, but truthful," he said. "You must never think that any contact with your cousins would be a good thing. It would bring about your downfall, so put any thoughts of familial contact out of your mind forever."

Feeling scolded, Cambria lowered her head. "You need not be so cruel," she said. "I had no intention of trying to contact anyone."

"I did not mean to be cruel, but rather stress to you the seriousness of the situation."

She nodded, though she was still looking at her feet. "Considering what was done to Llywelyn, I believe I am well aware of the seriousness," she said quietly. "Thank you for answering my questions, Liam. I appreciate it."

Liam knew he'd been somewhat harsh with her, but as he'd said, it was to stress the seriousness of the situation. She couldn't go off and contact cousins or other family members and she had to understand that. She was Cambria de Royans, and that was what she would remain. Soon, she would be Cambria, Lady de Wolfe, and hopefully thoughts of cousins and dead fathers would simply be committed to memory. But Liam was hoping a new crop of problems wouldn't spring up now that she knew the truth of her background.

He could only pray that her curiosity was at an end.

"You are welcome," he said, reaching out to take her elbow politely. "But I would not tell your father that you know. It might put your mother in a bad way with him. She was not supposed to tell you."

She looked at him then. "I'm glad someone did," she said. "I'm proud to know who I am. I think I'm even proud of my father, who fought for something he believed in. That must be the greatest battle of all—fighting for something you believe in. Not many people can say that."

Liam began to walk her back toward the hall. "That is true," he said. "But I did hear something else about him long ago, something I overheard soldiers speaking of."

"What did you hear?"

"That he and your mother, Eleanor, were a love match," he said. "That is rare, especially in political marriages. It must have destroyed him when she perished giving birth to you."

Cambria was quiet for a moment. "Would it destroy you if that happened to me?"

"I would not want to live."

He was deadly serious. Cambria was gazing at him, seeing the intensity in his expression, and it touched her. All of these years of a budding relationship, of a carefully orchestrated courtship, and all it had managed to do was solidify that which already existed.

Love.

She'd loved him from the start.

She'd love him until the end.

"Nor I," she murmured. "If anything happened to you, I could not live. You are the air I breathe, Liam. Take away my air and I am dust."

He smiled at her, putting a big hand over her small hands around his forearm, but he was prevented from replying because of some commotion near the gatehouse. Off to their right, the noise of soldiers shouting captured their attention and they turned to see another party entering through the gatehouse. The banners of the Earl of Warenton were front and center as they came in beneath the double portcullises, kicking up dirt and creating a general commotion. They could also see, quite plainly, when Carlton and War headed in the direction of the incoming party.

"More guests," Cambria said. "It must be the Earl of Warenton. Papa said he had invited him."

Liam nodded. "Aye," he said. "That is who it is."

There was a brief pause. "He knows, too, doesn't he?"

"About you?"

"Aye."

"He knows."

Cambria didn't say anything for a moment. When she finally spoke, her tone was full of awe. Perhaps even disbelief.

"The fact that such important men would go to all of this trouble just for me is bewildering," she murmured, tightening her grip on his arm. "I was only a babe, just a little girl who was the offspring of a great enemy. Why should they go to so much trouble simply to save me? I do not understand."

Liam knew the reason but wasn't sure he should tell her. However, he didn't think it would be good to withhold it. They had just spent several moments of complete honesty, the only real opportunity they'd ever had as adults, as a couple about to be married, so now wasn't the time to refrain from telling her what he knew. Perhaps it would ease her curiosity, but he was more afraid that it might do some damage. What, he didn't know, but he didn't have any choice as he saw it.

"All I know is what I heard," he muttered. "You must understand that men like your father or William de Wolfe did not confide in me. I am no one to them. But I did hear that de Wolfe sent you into hiding as revenge against Edward for sending his son into Wales to be killed."

She looked at him with surprise. "How would that be revenge?"

"Because Edward wanted you sent to a priory," he said. "You were to live out your days at Sempringham Priory, which is not far from here. The priory is in your father's demesne and that is why he was charged with your protection. There is another woman at Sempringham right now that bears your birth name and is, for all intents and purposes, Gwenllian of Wales. De Wolfe's vengeance against Edward is in letting the real Welsh princess—you—live a normal life, married to an English knight, and bearing English sons."

Cambria thought on that. "I see," she said after a moment. "Then I was a pawn."

"You were. But you are also marrying the man you love, and that does not happen to most pawns."

He had a way of putting it into perspective that made her realize her life could have been much worse. After a moment, she nodded, accepting his explanation. Truthfully, the entire day had been so momentous that she wasn't sure she could handle one more revelation, or tale, or complaint or tragedy. She'd had all she could take. When she saw her father and Liam's father speaking with Scott de Wolfe, she suddenly felt quite weary.

She needed to be alone and process everything.

"And I do love him, very much," she said. "But… but would you mind if I did not go with you to greet Warenton? I should like to rest before the feast tonight. I should like to be at my best."

Liam smiled and lifted one of her hands, kissing it. "If that is your wish," he said. "May I escort you to the keep?"

Cambria shook her head. "Nay, I can find my way," she said, forcing a smile. "You must go greet our guest."

"Are you certain?"

"I am. I will see you this evening."

He kissed her hand again. "You certainly will."

Keeping the smile plastered on her lips, Cambria let go of his arm and turned around, heading toward the keep, but with each successive step, her smile faded. What a day it had been. Her head was spinning with all of it.

You are the daughter of a Welsh prince.

You are a pawn.

You are marrying the man you love because of it.

There is a woman bearing your name, and your confinement, at Sempringham Priory.

God help her, it was all so much to take. But this wasn't the end of it.

Not even close.

CHAPTER THIRTEEN

Sempringham Priory

H E'D MADE IT.

After his unfinished business in London had taken him longer than expected, Tyrus had finally departed and headed north, but not without several stops along the way. There were two Gilbertine priories between London and Lincolnshire and he stopped at each one. Not because he was religious, but because he wanted to get a feel for what they knew about Sempringham, about the prior and the history in general. He found out a good deal more than he bargained for, all of which would help him in the days to come.

This latest task from Canterbury had the distinction of actually being interesting to him. Usually, a task was a task. He took no pleasure or distaste in it. But this one had his curiosity because he, too, wanted to know if William de Wolfe had actually hidden a Welsh princess from the king. He was a fine investigator, one of his many talents.

He was going to get to the bottom of it.

Tyrus arrived in the late afternoon, to a priory, grounds,

and cemetery that seemed to be far from any civilization. The nearest town that he rode through was miles to the south. He didn't know what was east or west or north, because he'd come up from London, but he knew that this location was remote.

Desolate, even.

It wasn't as if those pledged to the church didn't already have hermit tendencies, but this place seemed to emphasize that. It sat on a grassy plain, with no hills or landmarks nearby. The cold wind blew in from the east, moving the grass in waves as it went. Overhead, clouds had rolled in and the threat of rain was prevalent in the air. Ahead of him, he could see a gray-stoned structure rising out of the flatlands, with a pitched roof and a steeple that reached for the sky.

This particular location was the Gilbertine monastic house that had the distinction of having both nuns and canons. In speaking to the other priories on his way north, Tyrus had learned that. He'd also learned it had a history of changing hands, of attacks by Northmen, and other unsavory actions. Upon visual inspection, the church itself was nothing unusual and he'd seen more spectacular buildings, but it was large and there were clusters of structures to the north of it as well as smaller structures to the southeast.

As he drew closer, he could see the livestock area as well as the garden, which was extensive. The entire thing was encircled by stone walls and wooden fences, designed to keep the livestock in and any predators out. But it had an unwelcome feel about it and he was fairly certain that a lone rider would be viewed with suspicion, especially since he wasn't a priest. However, he was a knight and his vocation was sworn to the church, and he also bore a missive from the Archbishop of Canterbury explaining to the prior that he must be allowed to interview the nun who bore the name of Gwenllian of Wales. His presence there was simply an inquiry into the health and welfare of the royal hostage and he didn't anticipate any refusal.

Still, he proceeded carefully. People of the church, and particularly those who lived in isolated areas like this, tended to be skittish and he didn't want to frighten anybody because, in the end, it would only be more difficult for him to complete his task. As he wound his way through a couple of garden gates, he could see people working a large vegetable garden. There were several of them. They all stopped when they saw him pass through, staring at him as if he were an object of fascination. But Tyrus ignored them, heading for the church itself because that was the most public space in the entire complex. A visitor would be expected to go there first.

He had a man to find.

After tethering his horse outside the church, he entered the dark, cool structure that smelled heavily of animal habitation. It smelled like a barn. As he walked slowly into the bowels of the place, he could see that straw was strewn all over the dirt floor. The ceiling overhead was arched, with big wooden beams, strangely elaborate in so remote a place. His boots thumped on the ground as he made his way to the front, all the while looking for someone to speak to. The church had been empty so far. Once he reached the altar, he continued around it and ended up at a door that led out into the cloister. He wasn't sure if it was the male or female cloister, so he took a timid step out into the dirt only to be met by a woman in worn woolen robes.

"Stop," she said firmly. "Who are you? What is your business here?"

Tyrus came to a halt, turning to see the older woman as she came around the corner of the church. "My name is le Mon," he said. "I am looking for the prior. I come with a message from the Archbishop of Canterbury."

That seemed to bring the woman pause. She was older, with plump, unusually smooth skin and no eyebrows. She eyed Tyrus suspiciously.

"Canterbury?" she repeated. "What use does he have for us?"

"A great deal," Tyrus said. "I am instructed to find the prior or the prioress and deliver the missive."

The woman looked him up and down a few times. She visually inspected the tunic he wore, the scarlet of Canterbury, and she inspected the sword at his side, the boots at his feet.

"Why send a knight?" she finally asked. "Why not simply a messenger?"

"Because this missive is important."

"Why?"

"Take me to the prioress so that she may discover that for herself."

The woman didn't reply right away. She was still looking him over, trying to determine if he was telling her the truth.

"Show me the missive," she finally said. "Show me the seal."

He had it in his left hand, the one under his cloak that she couldn't see. He tossed his cloak back and lifted his hand, holding the seal out so she could see it. She took a couple of suspicious steps in his direction, peering at the seal. It took her several moments before her suspicion turned to concern.

"Come with me," she said.

She was motioning for him to follow, and he did. They headed toward the collection of buildings to the north, long dormitory buildings and a few smaller ones. They were all connected by stone walkways, one to the other. Tyrus followed the woman into one of the smaller buildings where there was what seemed to be a common room of sorts and two smaller chambers. She went into the common room, where there were neatly scrubbed tables, and indicated for him to sit. She sat opposite him and extended her hand.

"I am Mother Cecelia," she said quietly. "Give me my missive."

He wasn't going to take her word for it. "Send for another nun."

"Why?"

"Do it or no missive."

She frowned, peeved, and got up from the table. He watched her walk to a door facing east, with sunlight streaming in through it, and stick her head out, shouting to someone nearby. In little time, a woman entered, wiping her dirty hands off on her apron as Mother Cecelia pulled her over to the table to face Tyrus.

"There," Mother Cecelia said. "Here is another one. What do you want with her?"

Tyrus looked at the woman. She was young, with light brown hair peeking out from underneath her wimpled head, a sweaty face, and dark hazel eyes.

"What is your name, woman?" he asked.

The woman looked at Mother Cecelia fearfully before answering. "Wentliane, my lord."

Tyrus pointed at Mother Cecelia. "Who is this woman?"

Confused, the young nun looked at the older woman. "She… she is the mother prioress, my lord."

Tyrus nodded. "Good enough," he said. "Return to your duties."

As the young woman fled, Mother Cecelia resumed her seat

and extended her hand once more.

"May I have my missive now?" she asked.

He handed it over. "You must understand that I had to make certain," he said. "I meant no disrespect."

She grunted, a doubtful expression, as she broke the seal. Knowing what the missive contained, Tyrus simply sat there peacefully until she'd read it twice. Slowly, in fact. It took the woman at least ten minutes to read it twice, and by the time she was finished, she simply set the missive down and nodded her head.

"You have already met her," she said. "Wentliane is that woman. The one you asked to verify my identity."

Brown hair, brown eyes, fair-faced. That wasn't the description Canterbury had given him about Llywelyn's daughter. That was the very first thing he was to look for—her physical description—and the woman he'd seen certainly didn't fit it. That brought him to a bit of a quandary.

"Mother Cecelia, may I ask you a question about her?" he said.

The prioress nodded. "Proceed."

"Were you here when she arrived?"

"I was."

"Did you see who brought her?"

"I did."

"Was it Berwick?"

The woman nodded her head. "He identified himself as Patrick de Wolfe," she said. "I may live at the ends of the earth, my lord, but I do know a de Wolfe banner. I had seen it before."

"How?"

She shrugged. "We've had armies move through here before," she said. "I have seen de Wolfe and de Winter and du

Reims and others. There is also the fact that I did not become a nun until I was a grown woman. Before that, I lived at home, in Derbyshire. My father was a warlord. I knew the men he associated with."

"Who is your father?"

"He is a de Lohr."

That came as a distinct shock to Tyrus, a man who was, by nature, unshockable. The House of de Lohr was in charge of the Executioner Knights, and there were many family members spread out on the Welsh marches as well as Kent and Yorkshire. Clearly, she came from one of those extended branches. Tyrus was on a first-name basis with the Hereford and Worcester de Lohrs but not necessarily on good terms, so he didn't acknowledge that he knew anything about the House of de Lohr.

He wasn't here about that, anyway.

"So the man who brought her was a de Wolfe," he said. "Patrick de Wolfe?"

She nodded. "Aye," she said. "His brother was with him, but he did not introduce himself. It was I who took young Wentliane from them, on the king's order. The child was in distress, cold and hungry, and I took her straight away and fed her. She has been here ever since."

"Do you know who she is?"

Again, the woman nodded. "I do," she said quietly. "She is the daughter of Llywelyn ap Gruffudd. She is a prisoner of war."

"She is a princess," Tyrus muttered. "Does she know who she is?"

"She does. She has been told."

"Then why does she call herself Wentliane? Her name is Gwenllian."

Mother Cecelia shrugged. "Because she has always called herself Wentliane," she said. "When she was first brought here, she could speak a little and called herself Wentliane. However, she is aware of her real name. She simply does not use it. I do not know why."

It all seemed quite odd to Tyrus. He'd been told that Gwenllian had been brought as an infant to the priory. There was no mention of her being able to speak.

"You mentioned that she could speak a little," he said. "Was it Welsh?"

"It was not."

Tyrus looked at the woman as if she'd just said something quite puzzling, because to him, she had. A Welsh child speaking, but not speaking in her native tongue?

The mystery deepened.

"Bring her to me," he said quietly. "Let me assess her condition for myself."

That wasn't an unusual request when it came to Wentliane. There had been men sent from the king in the past to see to her welfare because of who she was, but this was the first time the Archbishop of Canterbury had sent someone. The mother prioress stood up from the table and went to the door again, the one she'd used before. After a few moments, she called to someone outside and waved them over.

Wentliane returned.

She came back in again, both concerned and reluctant, once again wiping her hands on her dirty apron. It was covered with dirt, clear evidence that the woman had been working in the gardens, and she sat down across from Tyrus when the mother prioress told her to.

Anxiously, she faced him.

"I am Sir Tyrus," he began calmly. "I have been sent by the Archbishop of Canterbury. His grace wishes to ensure you are in good health and require nothing to make your stay here more comfortable."

Wentliane was confused, uncomfortable. She looked to the mother prioress as if unwilling to answer a simple question. The mother prioress had to encourage her with a nod of the head, and even then, Wentliane didn't seem to quite understand what was required of her, as if the mere presence of the knight, a *man*, was turning her world on its end. It was clear that she'd not been educated in the art of social graces, of any kind, because she looked like a cornered animal.

"Why… why should the archbishop ask about me?" she said, her voice trembling. "I do not know him."

Tyrus sat forward, his forearms on the tabletop. "Because of your heritage," he said. "You are the Welsh princess and he is concerned for your well-being."

That seemed to startle her. She looked at the mother prioress again, distressed, but the old woman put a hand on her shoulder to ease her.

"All is well, Wentliane," she said quietly. "You may answer his questions."

Wentliane's breathing began to grow more rapid as fear set in. "I am well," she said. "I work and I pray and I do as God wishes."

Tyrus nodded. "That is good," he said. "But you do know that you are different from the other nuns because of your background."

Wentliane blinked at him. That was her response. She was so frightened that she could hardly do anything else. Tyrus could see that, but rather than show compassion, which he could not, he had to try a tactic to calm the woman down purely because he would get nothing out of her if she didn't.

And he had questions.

"Wentliane," he said, softening his speech. "May I call you Wentliane? Or should I address you as sister?"

"Wentliane will do," the mother prioress said.

Tyrus nodded his thanks and continued. "You *do* understand where you were born, do you not?"

Wentliane just sat there, looking at him fearfully. "May I return to my duties, please?" she said, the trembling in her voice worsening. "I am preparing vegetables for tonight's meal. I must return."

"And you shall," Tyrus said. "But there are questions I must ask you before I go. The sooner you answer them, the sooner you may return. Crying and distress will not force me to relent, so you would do better to obey me. Do you understand?"

That only made her more afraid, but she nodded quickly, her eyes wide. "I… I understand," she said, wiping her nose with the back of her hand and smearing dirt on her cheek. "But I do not understand why you are here."

"I am here to see to your welfare," Tyrus said, although he'd already told her that. "You are a woman of royal blood, a cousin to the king, and there is concern for your health."

Wentliane took a couple of deep breaths, struggling to calm herself. If she answered his questions, she could go. He'd said so.

"What do you want to know?" she asked. "I am well. I have been well."

"Good," Tyrus said. "Tell me what you remember from the time when you came to Sempringham. What is your earliest memory?"

He shifted the subject, but he'd done it for a reason. This woman didn't match the description he'd been given, so he wanted to know what she remembered, if she could even possibly remember, given how young she was. Realizing that, he shifted his attention to the mother prioress.

"You remember when she came here," he said. "You said she was brought by someone bearing a de Wolfe standard."

The mother prioress nodded. "Indeed," she said. "I remember it well."

"You said she spoke when she came here," he said. "How old do you think she was?"

The mother prioress and Wentliane looked at one another as if they could help each other remember. "She was speaking words, so she had seen at least two years," the mother prioress said. "She could say words like 'milk' and 'mama.'"

Tyrus looked at the young nun. "Do you remember your mama?"

For the first time since sitting down, Wentliane didn't look so frightened. Having the mother prioress next to her helped, but Tyrus's question had her thinking, going back in the mists of her memory to her very earliest recollections.

"I think so," she said, barely above a whisper. "I remember an apron. A woman with an apron. When you are small, things like aprons are right in front of your face because you are short, so aprons and knees… they are right in front of your eyes. I also remember other children. Many other children."

"Who were they?" Tyrus asked.

Wentliane shook her head. "I do not know," she said. "In truth, I do not know if I dreamed them or if I remember them. It was so long ago. I think they were brothers and sisters."

"What else do you remember about them?"

Wentliane shrugged. "I am not certain," she said. "A big table. Many people around it. I remember sitting in dirt and I think I was pulling on carrots. As I said, I do not know if I dreamed the memories or if they are actual recollections. But I feel as if my mother loved me. And then I came here. I have memories of a fishpond here, and I liked to watch the fish."

The mother prioress smiled, displaying her yellowed teeth. "We do have a fishpond and I fished you out of it many times," she said, watching Wentliane grin. "You liked to get into the pond with the fish."

As the two of them shared a humorous memory, Tyrus found himself fixing on what the young woman had said. *I feel as if my mother loved me.* According to Canterbury, Gwenllian of Wales never knew her mother. The woman had died in childbirth. So many things weren't making sense. Tyrus had come to investigate whether or not Gwenllian was actually at Sempringham Priory, and he could now say, with a strong degree of certainty, that the woman before him wasn't the Welsh princess. Too many things were off.

"One more question," he said, looking at the mother prioress. "This may sound like an odd question, but I am serious when I ask it. When Wentliane came to Sempringham, did she have black hair?"

The mother prioress immediately shook her head. "Nay," she said. "It was dark brown, but it lightened over the years. It has red in it now also."

"You can confirm that it was never black."

"Nay, never. Why?"

Tyrus shook his head. "No particular reason," he said. "Something I'd heard once, but I must have been mistaken. I will not take up any more of your time. I am satisfied that the princess is healthy and content."

"She is," the mother prioress said. "You will report back to the archbishop?"

Tyrus stood up from the table, nodding his head. "I will," he said. "I believe he will want to send more money to help support Wentliane, but I will tell him that you have done a fine job of it."

The mother prioress stood up, Wentliane next to her. "I am grateful," she said. "May I send Wentliane back to her duties now?"

"Aye."

The young woman fled, out into the garden where the vegetables weren't nearly as frightening as a big knight. When she was gone and Tyrus was turning for the door, the mother prioress caught up with him.

"Is something amiss?" she said seriously. "You asked her many questions about her early memories. Has something happened?"

Tyrus shook his head. "Nay," he said. "It was conversation and nothing more. And also to confirm that she was the child brought here by the de Wolfe men."

"She is," the mother prioress confirmed. "I assure you, she is."

"And I shall inform the archbishop," Tyrus said. "Thank you for your cooperation."

The mother prioress simply nodded. She walked with him in silence back into the church, pausing at the door as he continued on, heading outside to collect his horse. The last vision Tyrus had of the old woman was of her lifting a hand to him in farewell.

He lifted a hand in return.

But, as sure as he knew that he was alive and breathing, he knew she'd been duped. The entire priory had been duped, and the king included, into thinking the woman known as Wentliane was, in fact, Gwenllian of Wales. Tyrus was willing to stake his life on the fact that she was not. That meant his next stop was Folkingham Castle.

He had a feeling the truth was waiting for him there.

God help de Wolfe if that was the case.

God help them all.

PART THREE
WOLFEHOUND

CHAPTER FOURTEEN

Folkingham Castle

CASSIUS HAD NEVER been to Folkingham before. Fortunately, it was fairly easy to find, but getting here had been something of a tribulation.

It had all started the day he was informed of Paris de Norville's death and the night he'd spent at the tavern where men had told war stories into the wee morning hours. It had been a night of nights, something he would always remember, but when dawn broke over London and the heavy smoke from morning cooking fires filled the air, he'd struggled past his grief to realize he was faced with a hell of a situation.

The events discussed between Edward and the Archbishop of Canterbury involving Llywelyn ap Gruffudd's infant daughter and Sempringham Priory was something that wasn't going to go away. As morning came, Cassius realized that something very serious was facing the entire House of de Wolfe. If William had orchestrated a covert operation to fool Edward, or punish him, or whatever the case may have been, then Cassius needed to at least see if there was any truth to it before

Tyrus le Mon did. The fact that Canterbury already had le Mon in motion was a horrific thing, indeed, but Cassius had to discover the truth first.

He had to get to Folkingham.

He wasn't a spy or an operative, but he was a knight with a good head on his shoulders. He could figure this out. But the problem was that he was emotionally invested in the situation, whereas le Mon wasn't. Emotion could cloud his judgment and he was well aware of that, but the truth was that he didn't like what had been said about his grandfather. William de Wolfe had always served the king, faithfully and honorably, but it was no secret that Edward had never treated him the same way Henry had. Henry of England had been respectful of William, a man who had taken pride in William's achievements, but Edward had only seen William as competition.

However, Edward had never said a negative word about William in Cassius' presence and that was by design, because Cassius happened to know that the same restraint didn't hold true in front of others. If these rumors were correct and William truly had fooled Edward when it came to Gwenllian of Wales, then Cassius could only imagine how Edward would react. He could only imagine how that was going to reflect on the entire de Wolfe empire, him included.

Therefore, he had to get to the truth before le Mon did.

It had been a simple thing to request time away from London, to go home and mourn the loss of an important family member. Edward had been surprisingly understanding about that and encouraged him to take all the time he needed. Denys de Winter stepped into his role at Edward's side, so the king had a big, strapping knight beside him even as Cassius departed London and headed to Lincolnshire. A stop in Peterborough for directions to Folkingham and two days later, he was on its doorstep. A big, gray structure dominating the landscape around it. But the moment he arrived, he ran straight into his cousins, Jeremy and Nathaniel de Wolfe.

The Earl of Warenton, Scott de Wolfe, was at Folkingham also.

Talk about coincidences.

More puzzled than ever, Cassius left his horse with a stable servant and had to fight off Jeremy and Nathaniel all the way to the great hall. They were at the gatehouse when he arrived and all they wanted to do was hug him, or steal his sword, and he had to punch Nathaniel in the chest to keep him from cutting his purse from his belt. In days and years past, that had been a running joke with most of the de Wolfe male cousins. They loved one another dearly, but they were always trying to steal from each other or gamble with one another. The list of foolery went on and on. But Cassius wasn't in the mood for foolery this time around.

He needed to see his uncle.

Scott, Carlton, and War were in the cold, smoky great hall, sitting at one end of the dais with a pitcher of some manner of drink between them. It was dim on that end of the hall so Cassius didn't see Liam until he was halfway to the table. Scott happened to look up and see Cassius approaching, astonished to see his nephew at Folkingham. Puzzled, but pleased, he came away from the table and put his arms around his nephew, hugging him tightly.

"Cass," he said with satisfaction. "My God, lad. What a surprise to see you here. I did not know that you were invited to the wedding also."

Cassius genuinely loved his Uncle Scott. He smiled in return, letting the man pat his cheek and even pinch it like he used to do when Cassius was young.

"It is a surprise to see you here, too," he admitted. "But I am not here for a wedding. Who is getting married?"

"Me," Liam said, grinning at Cassius as he came off the dais and hugged the man so hard that he nearly cracked his ribs. "I know it must come as a shock to you that a young lady would actually consent to marry me, but it is true. I am to be honored with the most beautiful bride in the world."

Cassius had to rub his chest where Liam had hugged too hard. "Then congratulations are in order," he said. "I had no idea, Liam. If I am welcome to attend, then I shall, but a wedding is not why I have come."

"Why did you come?" Scott asked. "Are you passing through on your way back to Berwick?"

Cassius shook his head. "Nay," he said. His gaze moved from Scott to Liam to War and to Carlton de Royans, a man he'd not seen in many years. "I've actually come to speak to Lord de Royans."

Carlton, who recognized the tall, dark, and handsome son of Patrick de Wolfe, stood up from his seat. "Of course you are welcome here, Cassius," he said. "I think the last time I saw you was at Castle Questing, many years ago. You were not yet knighted."

Cassius smiled weakly. "I was just trying to remember when we last met, my lord," he said. "I hope you have enjoyed good health and prosperity since then."

Carlton nodded. "Verily," he said. Then he indicated the table, the benches. "Please, sit. The last I heard, you were serving Edward, were you not?"

It was Scott who answered as they all took their seats again.

"As Lord Protector," he said proudly. "Cassius has assumed a very important post."

"Impressive," Carlton said. "Then I am honored to have you at my table. Have you come as a royal messenger, then? I cannot imagine what Edward would ask of me, but I shall do my best to comply."

Cassius sat down between Liam and Scott. "It is not a royal message I bring," he said. "My lord, I come with… questions. Involving your family. If you would prefer we discuss this in private, we can retreat to a location of your choosing."

Carlton's brow furrowed slightly. "Questions?" he repeated. "From Edward?"

"In a sense."

Cassius didn't elaborate, so Carlton simply shrugged his shoulders. "That sounds mysterious," he said. "And you are sitting amongst men who are trustworthy. I do not mind if they hear the king's business with me."

Cassius wasn't sure he should say anything at all, because what he was about to say would sound, on the surface, like gossip. He hesitated, looking at his uncle, at Liam, at War across the table, and finally at Carlton, all of them looking at him with interest. But then he looked to Scott and figured that he had better hear this, also, considering he was now the Earl of Warenton. These rumors would concern him.

He fixed on the man for a moment.

"The missive you sent to Edward about Uncle Paris was received," he said quietly. "Edward was distressed at the news. The Archbishop of Canterbury had a requiem mass said in Uncle Paris' honor."

Scott nodded. "That was kind," he said. "But what does Uncle Paris' passing have to do with your visit to de Royans?"

Cassius looked around to make sure there wasn't anyone else within earshot before continuing.

"There is no simple way to put this, so I will come out with it," he said. "I fear something dark is on the horizon. You've not seen a strange knight in Folkingham, have you? No visits of single knights, traveling?"

Carlton shook his head. "Nay," he said. "No one at all. Now you most definitely have my attention, Cassius. What is this all about?"

Cassius lowered his voice. "The Archbishop of Canterbury heard a confession from another priest who had come from the marches," he said. "The priest had come from Colm de Lara, to be exact. But what de Lara told the priest was something so explosive that the man came straight to Canterbury and told him what he'd heard. Colm did serve with you, did he not, my lord?"

Carlton looked at Cassius, startled. "He did," he said. "For many years. Why? What did he say?"

"He said that twenty years ago, in Wales, you were charged with bringing the daughter of Llywelyn ap Gruffudd to Sempringham Priory on the orders of Edward," Cassius said. "Colm told the priest that the infant never made it there and that another child was sent in her place, assuming her identity, because the real Gwenllian of Wales has been living under a false identity as your daughter. De Lara further went on to say that my grandfather, William de Wolfe, orchestrated everything. If any of this is true, my lord, you had better tell me."

Carlton had gone ashen. All of the color left his face as he looked at Scott, who appeared nearly as stricken. Even War, across the table, appeared shocked to the bone, but that was nothing compared to Liam. The man looked as if he were about to explode. His entire body was tense, brittle, as if a mere whisper would break him, but his focus was on Carlton.

"My God," Liam finally breathed. "He told. That ridiculous bastard actually told!"

Scott held up a hand to silence Liam as he addressed Cassius. "What is happening, Cass?" he said. "You've come here to warn de Royans?"

Cassius nodded. "Aye," he said honestly. "Canterbury is sending one of his spies to Sempringham to discover the truth, and I did not want you to be caught off guard if he came here. This knight… He is the worst of the worst. A man with no conscience."

"Who is it?"

"Tyrus le Mon."

Scott closed his eyes for a brief moment, his jaw flexing dangerously. "Damnation," he said. "I've heard that name. And what I've heard is not pleasant."

"Nay, le Mon is not a pleasant man," Cassius said. "He is an emotionless ghoul. He'll get to the bottom of this situation any way he can, and that means… Christ, are you telling me this is all true? That Poppy really *did* orchestrate the fate of Gwenllian of Wales?"

Scott didn't hesitate. He nodded, glancing at Carlton as he did so. "He did," he muttered. "It is true. I was part of it, as was your father. In fact, it was your father who found the infant sent to Sempringham in Gwenllian's place. We're all involved."

It was Cassius' turn to close his eyes for a moment as the impact of the truth hit him. "Bloody hell," he murmured. "And I defended Poppy to the king. Right to Edward's face, I told him that my grandfather would never do such a thing. But he did."

"Aye, he did."

"Why?" Cassius said. "In God's name, *why*?"

Scott faced his confused, angry nephew. "Because Uncle James had just been killed in Wales," he said quietly. "You *know* Poppy, Cass. You know that he would have killed, or died, for any of us. He could not let James' death go unanswered, so it was answered in a way that would haunt those responsible forever."

Cassius frowned. "How?"

"To send a decoy child to Sempringham was to punish Edward for sending James to Wales in the first place," Scott murmured, his gaze intense. "But for the Welsh, who actually killed James, he had something more planned. By marrying the Welsh princess to an English knight, it would guarantee that for generations to come, Welsh blood would be part of English knights who would fight, and kill, more Welsh. By breeding the princess to a man from England, Poppy could continue to punish the Welsh for decades. And that was his vengeance for James' death. But it could have been for me, or your father, or even you. He would have done the same thing. No one takes the life of a de Wolfe without penalty. And Poppy had determined this penalty."

That made tremendous sense to Cassius. He knew how devoted his grandfather was to his family, and Scott was right— William would have done the same thing had any one of his children or grandchildren been killed. William's plan had farreaching implications, so much more than Canterbury or Edward or even the priest that heard de Lara's confession would ever know. It wasn't some petty act of rebellion.

It was a legacy of punishment.

"So his plan has come to fruition," Cassius finally said. "I understand what he did and why. But when Uncle James returned from the dead, why not call a stop to it? Why not send the princess to Sempringham as planned?"

Scott shrugged. "Because by that time, she had become the daughter of Carlton and his wife," he said. "You do not have children yet so you do not understand, but relinquishing their adopted daughter was out of the question. By that time, she was a de Royans and she was English. Sometimes it is better to simply let things lie."

Cassius could comprehend the logic. It made sense. But something else also made sense to him, and he turned to Liam, on his right side.

"You are going to marry her, aren't you?" he asked. "That is the wedding we have been speaking of."

Subdued, Liam nodded. "Aye," he said. "But there is so much more to it, Cass. I love Cambria. She has become my sun and my moon, my stars and my sky. She is all to me and I am all to her. It is true that our children will have Welsh and English blood and I am sure it is true that, if we have sons, they will end up fighting the Welsh. But that is not why I am marrying her. I am marrying her because I love her and nothing more. I do not have the same feelings for this marriage that your grandfather did."

Cassius could see that. He could hear it in the man's voice as he spoke. With a faint smile at Liam, suggesting that he was happy for the man's good fortune when it came to love, he returned his attention to his uncle.

"I understand everything," he said. "And I do not condemn you or Poppy or anyone else for seeing these plans to completion, but the fact remains that we have a very big problem on our hands. Tyrus le Mon is on his way to Sempringham and I am certain that if he does not receive the answers he seeks there, he will be coming here. I do not know what orders he has from Canterbury, but I would say that de Royans' daughter is in a great deal of danger. You must get her out of here and let le Mon return to London empty-handed."

Scott could feel the urgency in Cassius' manner. "Now that we know he is coming, you are absolutely right," he said, looking to Carlton. "We must have the wedding now and let Liam take her north. She needs to be far away from Folkingham when Canterbury's man comes."

The attention shifted to Carlton, as the father of the woman in question, and the truth was that he was shaken. He'd just listened to the entire exchange between Cassius and Scott and it was his worst nightmare come to life. He had a wife and daughter he loved and he only wanted them to be safe and happy. He'd been very happy living in a fantasy world for the past nineteen years, a world where Cambria was truly his daughter and there was no danger to be had. Now, finding out that he'd been betrayed by a man who had served him for years brought him back to reality. Cambria was someone very special, and his greatest fear was that he couldn't protect her from those seeking to do a Welsh princess harm. He didn't know Colm's reasons for divulging something that should never have been spoken of, but he was furious. Furious and terrified.

Damn the man!

He looked at Scott.

"When your father came up with this idea, I was not wholly comfortable with it," he said, struggling with his composure. "But the truth is that it was a very complex situation at that time. We all believed your father wanted to kill Cambria in vengeance for his son's death, but when he spoke of allowing Fair Lydia and I to raise her under a different name, as our daughter, I could hardly refuse. Fair Lydia was already in love with the infant we had brought from Wales and I knew there was no separating her from the babe. Warenton could see that, too. He saw an opportunity and he took it, and for nearly twenty years, we have lived in peace. It has been the happiest time of my life. But I will be honest when I tell you that Colm was never comfortable with the situation. I knew he did not agree with it, but I never believed he would betray us. That comes as a great disappointment."

"He is dead, my lord," Cassius said. "It is my understanding that he told the story as a deathbed confession, so the man is gone and you will never know her reasons. But I know Tyrus le Mon, and if Canterbury had sent the devil himself after your daughter, a more fearsome man could not be in pursuit of her. Believe me when I tell you that the time for questions and conversation is over. Le Mon and I left London around the same time, so if he is not here today, he will be very soon. It is only a matter of time."

They were all waiting for Carlton to make a move. Everything hinged on him and what he wanted to do at this point, but they could see the sorrow in his features. He had been reluctant to allow the marriage between his daughter and Liam simply because he had wanted more time with her, but now her safety was at risk. He couldn't delay any longer.

She had to get out of there.

"War," Carlton finally said, "will you send for a priest? And do not send for one at Sempringham. There is a church in the village to the east, so go there. Bring him back here and we shall have his blessing in the great hall. And then you must be prepared to take Liam and Cambria away tonight."

"I will fetch the priest, but I brought a contingent of men

with me," War said. "It will take too much time to assemble all of them. Liam and Bria can leave on their own, just the two of them. They'll travel faster that way. I will follow with the escort once they are assembled."

"I'll send Jeremy and Nathaniel with them," Scott said. "Those two may be immature, but they are excellent knights. If Liam runs into trouble, he will want assistance."

"I can send Kyle and Logan with them, too," War said. "Much like the de Wolfe brothers, they can be young and excitable, but they both have excellent swords. They may be needed."

"And I'll go," Cassius said. When everyone looked at him, he shrugged. "I am supposed to be going home anyway. Besides… someone needs to keep all of those young knights in line. I fear what will happen if we allow Jeremy and Nate and Kyle and Logan to run wild. But I agree that their skills will be most useful to protect the lady and get her safely to Bamburgh."

"I was going to take her to my garrison of Easington," Liam said quietly, looking at the men around the table. "It is a big garrison and quite defensible, but should I not even do that? Should I take her straight to Bamburgh? God himself could not breach Bamburgh."

War glanced at Scott, who shrugged faintly. "I would say Bamburgh would be safer, at least for now," War said. "At least while we know that Edward is on her scent. But it might be even safer to take her to Castle Questing. I doubt anyone would look there."

Scott nodded. "Quite honestly, I'd send her to Northwood Castle or Pelinom Castle," he said. "Theodis de Velt commands Pelinom and you know how wary Edward is of the House of de Velt. He would not risk their anger. And Northwood Castle is commanded by Hector de Norville, my brother-in-law. I do not think anyone would think to look for her there."

Liam looked to his father. "What do I do, Papa?" he asked. "Where do we go?"

War considered the question carefully before answering. "Your betrothal to Bria is no secret," he said. "If Edward, or le Mon, is truly looking for her, anyone they ask can tell them that Carlton's daughter married you. That will lead them to either Bamburgh or Easington. Warenton is correct—Castle Questing or another allied castle might be better for now. At least until Edward realizes that whatever tale de Lara spun is simply untrue."

"Will he?" Liam asked, sounding doubtful. "Give up the search for her, I mean. Will he eventually forget about it or are Bria and I going to be looking over our shoulders for the rest of our lives?"

War grew serious. "Edward is old," he muttered. "His health is not good, though I suppose Cassius can tell us better than anyone."

The attention shifted to Cassius, who nodded in agreement. "His health is not the best," he said. "But he is still strong, still lucid. However, he has so many problems with the Scots that I'm surprised he's spared this matter any attention at all. It is Canterbury who seems to be pushing it, and I am certain it is because he hates Edward and wishes to see the man weakened even further. Liam, I do not think you and your wife will be looking over your shoulders forever, but for now, you will be. At least until the Scots surge against Edward again and he forgets about rumors of a hidden Welsh princess entirely. But it is le Mon that we must first deal with. He's here for Canterbury, not Edward."

There was both hope and caution in that statement. If anyone knew what was going on with Edward, it was Cassius. But there was someone else beyond the king and Canterbury who might pose an issue, and Scott was the first to speak of it.

"Does young Edward know about any of this?" he asked his nephew.

Cassius shook his head. "Young Edward only cares for his favorites and his wine," he said. "Even if he did know, he will not care about the rumor of a Welsh princess. Why should he? The Scots are the most important problem now and probably will be for years to come. So are the warlords who wish to keep his favorites away from him."

"Young Edward has bigger worries than a lost Welsh princess," War said, watching the attention turn to him. "You will not be running for the rest of your life, Liam. But for now, I believe we will have to depend on the kindness of our allies to help until that time comes."

He meant Scott, and the man gave Liam a half-grin. "Do not fear," he said. "I will put you to work. I've a pele tower on the Scots border that is in need of a commander. It is desolate and smells of Scots, but no one will find you there, I promise."

Liam smiled weakly. "Sounds perfect for a newlywed couple," he said, watching Scott chuckle. But his humor quickly faded. "And I will be grateful for it. For anything you can do to help me protect Bria, I am forever grateful."

He meant it. Scott reached around Cassius and patted Liam affectionately on the head. "Then we have a plan," he said. "I suggest we get on with it. Quickly."

No one needed any encouragement.

Liam, first and foremost, was on the move.

He had a woman to see.

CHAPTER FIFTEEN

ALL OF THE women were in the chamber.
As well as one very big, very black dog snoring on the bed.

Seated on a comfortable chair next to the hearth in the chamber of Lady Cambria de Royans, the dowager Countess of Warenton, Jordan de Wolfe, was trying hard not to pay heed to the farting, snoring dog, but it was impossible not to. He was on his back, his legs in the air, a very big set of hairy testicles on full display as women stood in front of an enormous wardrobe and discussed the best garments for the weather in the north.

It was all Jordan could do not to roll her eyes at the ridiculous dog.

Cambria had admitted the animal because he belonged to her betrothed, and she evidently had a fondness for dogs because, as Jordan had learned, she raised puppies of the same type of dog. She had a love for animals, which was commendable and sweet, but Jordan didn't think the dirty dog had any place in a young lady's room.

Cambria didn't seem to notice. Or care.

She was too busy enjoying her new friends.

Jordan had traveled all the way from Castle Questing with Caria and Avrielle, who were in front of the wardrobe with Cambria's mother, a woman with the strange name of Fair Lydia, and Liam's mother, Annaleigh. Scott was at Folkingham representing his father, the late William de Wolfe, at the marriage of Liam Herringthorpe and Cambria de Royans, a betrothal that William had brokered.

And Jordan knew why.

She may have been old, but she wasn't so old that she didn't have all of her faculties. She remembered everything, including the secret her husband had divulged to her about Cambria's origins. There were a few people in life that William had trusted as much as his wife, because she could keep a secret with the best of them.

She was a woman of honor.

Back when William had told her about the death of their son in Wales and the subsequent scheme to punish everyone from Edward to the Welsh who'd had a hand in his death, Jordan hadn't cared much for his sense of vengeance. As she had told him, it didn't bring their son back, but William wouldn't listen. He was a man of action, and as a man of action, he felt that he had to do something. He hadn't been able to save their son, as much as he had tried, so in a sense, cheating Edward out of a royal captive was taking action in the only way he could.

In truth, Jordan hadn't given much thought to the betrothal in the nineteen years since she'd been told about it. For her, life went on, and for several years after the events in Wales, it had gone on without one of her sons. Parents lost children all the time, but somehow, James' death seemed to hit her and William harder than most. She mourned for her boy every day, with every breath she took, but she kept the pain to herself. Not even William knew how much his death had affected her, and she wanted to keep it that way because he was dealing with grief of his own. The years passed and the grief faded, but it never went away completely. Then, when their son had returned from Wales—a different man, but he returned nonetheless—all she focused on was the son she had to get to know all over again. The betrothal made it in vengeance over his death was a memory that had simply slipped away.

Until now.

Her eldest son, Scott, was now the Earl of Warrenton and had been for the past six years. He was the keeper of not only his father's title but his father's secrets. When they received the announcement that the marriage between Liam and Cambria was going to take place, Jordan had been surprised. She thought that, perhaps, the whole thing had been dissolved at some point. But evidently not. Within days, they'd found themselves bundled up and on the road south to Lincolnshire.

Now, she watched her daughter-in-law and her adopted daughter as they helped Cambria and her mother pack her trousseau. The plan was for Cambria to travel north with her husband, where they would begin their life together. There was no mention of vengeance or death, or of kings or the Welsh, and to Jordan it seemed as if Cambria were just a normal young lady excited for her wedding. There was no hint that this betrothal had been started by a man grieving his son. No hint that the betrothal had been started by a death.

And that was a good thing.

What was even more interesting was watching Cambria interact with Caria. Jordan was probably the only person, other than Scott, that knew she was looking at two Welsh princesses.

Her husband had seemed to have a penchant for finding these young women who needed protection. Caria had come to them as a newborn in need of being hidden from King Edward, and Cambria was much in the same situation. They were even nearly the same age. But in appearance, they were quite different.

While Caria had bronze-brown hair and hazel eyes nearly the same color of her hair, Cambria had dramatically black hair and bright blue eyes. She also had a dusting of freckles over her nose, which Jordan found utterly charming. She was a strikingly beautiful woman. She was also the heiress to the principality of Wales, and while Caria was not the heiress to the Kingdom of Anglesey, she was the niece of the hereditary king. Jordan found herself watching two young women with more royal blood in them than perhaps anyone in the entire country.

But a casual observer would have never guessed.

They looked like ordinary, normal young women.

As she sat and reflected on that very thing, Cambria and Caria were getting along famously. No sooner were they introduced than they began to feel comfortable with one another. Now, they were inspecting a silk garment that had silver thread embroidered on it and a thick lining underneath, trying to determine if it would survive snow and cold weather. Over at the other wardrobe, Avrielle and Fair Lydia had the wedding dress hung up, with Annaleigh looking at part of the hem on the bottom.

"Jordan?" she said, looking up from the material. "Will ye come and look at this? I see a tear in the silk that needs tae be fixed, I think."

Since Annaleigh was Jordan's cousin, they were on a first-name basis. Wearily, Jordan stood up from the chair, leaning on a cane she used from time to time, and made her way over to the dress. Annaleigh held up the end for all to see, and Jordan, as well as Avrielle and Fair Lydia, noted the small tear.

"I have red silk thread that can be used to repair that," Fair Lydia said. "I swear that Bria has tried this dress on twice daily for the past month, ever since the seamstress finished with it. I am not surprised there is a bit of damage."

"She is excited," Avrielle said, smiling. "I understand that completely."

"I can *hear* you, Mama," Cambria said from her position in front of the wardrobe. "Do not talk about me as if I am not here."

Fair Lydia didn't look at her daughter, but she did fight off a grin. "Not only has she tried this dress on twice daily, but she has spent the rest of the time writing a love sonnet to read during the wedding feast," she said. "She is learning to play the harp, too."

"Mama!" Cambria gasped. "You are not supposed to tell anyone!"

Fair Lydia's smile broke through. "Why not?" she said. "I think it is very endearing. Liam will be thrilled."

"But I am not any good," Cambria lamented. "Please do not tell him any of that!"

She was pleading to the women in the chamber, all of whom were grinning to varying degrees. It was Jordan who broke away from the other women and went over to where Cambria and Caria were sitting on the floor, a pile of clothing between them.

"Not tae worry, lass," she said. "He'll love anything ye do. Why do ye worry so?"

Cambria looked up at the woman, so elderly, but somehow so timeless. Her hair was pale silver on the top, with shades of darker blonde at the nape of her neck so that when she twisted her hair into a bun, it had many colors to it. Her skin had aged somewhat, but not too terribly. Not enough to hide the beauty that she had. Cambria had heard from her father how devoted William de Wolfe had been to his wife, and she could see that the woman had an ethereal quality to her. She seemed gentle and kind, but there was still fire behind those pale green eyes.

Almost as much as her husband, she was a legend.

"I suppose I do not want to be embarrassed," Cambria said. "I want him to think I am perfect, and my harp playing is definitely *not* perfect."

Jordan smiled faintly, pulling the old shawl around her shoulders just a bit tighter because she was always cold. Even in a room with a blazing hearth. She lowered herself onto the end of the bed.

"But ye'll always be perfect in his eyes, lass," she said softly. "He'll be touched by any gesture ye make at yer wedding because it shows yer love for him. That's all a man wants—tae know he's loved."

"Believe her," Caria said, looking up from the scarf she had in her hand. "Matha knows everything there is to know about men and women and love. She and Poppy had the greatest love of all for many years. If she could keep William de Wolfe from straying, she's worth listening to."

Cambria giggled as Jordan frowned. "Dunna say such things about Poppy," she scolded. "The man never strayed a day in his life when he was with me."

"He was scared of you," Caria quipped.

The girls burst into laughter as Jordan shook her head reproachfully. "That was probably true," she said, her eyes twinkling with mirth. "But in the end, love and respect are the only things that'll make a man stay. Always treat Liam with love and respect, and if he's any kind of a man at all, he'll give it in return."

"He's like his father," Annaleigh said, still over by the dress. "He's a good man."

Cambria looked over her shoulder at her future mother-in-law. "Are you saying he's never even looked at another woman all of these years?" she said. "There are many years between us. When I was a child, he was already a man. What about then?"

Annaleigh passed a glance to Jordan. Because Liam had spent years at Castle Questing, Jordan's home, they both knew that he'd had his share of women when he was a young and virile man, mostly because for the first several years of his betrothal to Cambria, he was just coming into manhood. One young woman in particular had been the daughter of a de Wolfe ally that Liam had met at a feast, so Jordan knew of at least one encounter, because nineteen-year-old Liam had a tryst in the loft over the stables. He was only discovered when part of the wooden floor of the loft collapsed under their weight and he ended up, naked from the waist down, in a stall. He'd broken a wrist in the fall, and shattered his pride, but William had covered for him to the woman's father. Being the father of many sons, William understood randy young men better than most.

But neither Annaleigh nor Jordan were going to mention that to Cambria. She had only been five years of age at the time of the event, but still, she wouldn't want to hear of her betrothed cavorting with another woman. Not today.

It wasn't their business, anyway.

"I dunna know much about that time," Annaleigh finally said. "He was fostering at Castle Questing."

Cambria looked at Jordan, who put up a hand to silence her question before she asked it. "I was not in charge of the squires or the pages," she said. "That was my husband, so I canna tell ye any tales. Ye'll have tae ask yer husband someday."

Before Cambria could answer, the dog suddenly rolled over and sneezed, loudly. Jordan was the closest, trying to dodge the flying dog mucus.

"'Tis a big dog, lass," she said, gingerly brushing off her arm. "He must be good protection if ye allow him inside."

Cambria was smiling at the mutt. "He's very sweet," she said. "He is Liam's shadow. I love having him near me because it is almost like having Liam with me."

"Are ye calling my son a dog?" Annaleigh said, eyebrow cocked.

The women burst into laughter, Cambria included. Annaleigh had meant it in jest and they took it that way. Before Cambria could reply, there was a knock at the door. Caria was the closest and she stood up, opening the panel to see a serving wench standing there.

"What is it?" Caria asked.

The serving woman was young, the daughter of the cook. She caught sight of Cambria and spoke directly to her.

"Sir Liam has sent for you, m'lady," she said. "He asks that you meet him down in your father's solar."

Cambria didn't even hesitate. He leapt up from the floor, calling for the dog as she went. Bran went from dozing to wide awake in an instant, leaping off the bed and stepping on Jordan's feet in the process. As she lifted her stinging toes, the dog charged past Cambria, nearly bowling her over, as they both rushed for the stairs.

Down they went to the man they loved best.

Cambria burst into the solar with the dog on her heels. Liam was already there, and he opened his arms for Cambria but the dog beat her to it. He jumped up on Liam, his long tongue licking at his face, as Liam briefly petted the dog's big head before pushing him down. Cambria had to shove the dog aside to get to Liam.

"I am not sure who is more excited to see you," she said, grinning, as he took her in his arms. "Bran seems to compete with me in that regard."

He chuckled. "That is the *only* regard," he assured her, but his smile soon faded. "How are you, my love? I've not seen you in a couple of hours and I am desolate because of it."

Her smile broadened as she gave in to his strong arms. "I am overwhelmed with female attention," she said. "Your mother, my mother, Lady Warenton, and Caria de Wolfe. Do not misunderstand—it is lovely to have them here, but I am unused to such companionship."

He pulled her close. "Caria is a sweet girl," he said. "I knew her when I served at Castle Questing. She is very friendly and I'm glad that Warenton brought her. I should like for you to become friends with her."

"Why?"

"Because you do not have any female friends that I know of," he said. "You never went to foster, and when you go to church, your mother never leaves your side, so I know it has been difficult for you to make friends."

Cambria shrugged. "It used to bother me," she conceded. "But as the years went on, I had my puppies and that took up a good deal of my time. I did not have much time for friends or feasts. But I will admit that as a young girl, I used to grow very frustrated that we did not seek the company of allies or friends on a regular basis."

"But you understand why now," he said. "It was to keep you hidden as much as possible without actually putting you in a vault and keeping you there, simply for your own safety."

She nodded. "I know," she said. "That is the problem with a secret like that. You are never sure if anyone else knows because people cannot be trusted. Someone always sees something."

He nodded. "And that is what we must discuss," he said. "It seems that we have a problem."

"What problem?"

He released her from his embrace and led her over to a pair of chairs that were placed next to the hearth. They were carved oak, with big cushions on them made out of blue silk. He sat her in one while he took the other, facing her.

"You remember Colm de Lara, don't you?" he said. "The man who served your father?"

Cambria nodded. "Of course I do," she said. "What about him?"

Liam took a deep breath, seemingly thoughtful for a moment before continuing. "The only way to explain this to you is to get straight to the point," he said. "Colm de Lara knew your secret. He was here when everything was planned and executed. The man evidently passed away recently, but before he did, he told a priest about you and what your father and William de Wolfe did. This priest told the Archbishop of Canterbury, who in turn told the king, and now we must be married immediately because I must take you to safety somewhere far away from Folkingham. They must not find you, Bria. You understand that."

Cambria was horrified. "Colm?" she gasped. "He did not do that!"

"I am afraid that he did," Liam said calmly. "We have confirmation. Therefore, you and I are to be married today, probably within the hour, and then we are heading north to Castle Questing. The Earl of Warenton is going to hide us for a while until this all fades away."

Tears were starting to pool in her eyes. "Oh, Liam," she wept. "This morning, I was simply an orphan with no past, but since then, I've become a fugitive from a king who wants to shove me in a priory and let me rot."

She was wiping at her eyes furiously as he tried to comfort her. "I know it is overwhelming," he said. "But you have been so brave, sweetheart. You only have to be brave a little longer."

She was crying softly. "I'll have to be brave for the rest of my life," she said. "The king is going to know you married me. He is going to know and he is going to punish you and your father for this. This will never end!"

She was starting to ramble, and he left his chair, going down on his knees in front of her with the intention of taking her in his arms, but the moment he did so, the dog suddenly appeared and licked his face, licked Cambria's face, and tried to insert himself between them. Cambria had to cover her face with her hands because of the dog's tongue as Liam pushed the animal away.

"He loves you," he said gently. "As do I. We do not like to see you so sad."

Cambria pulled her hands away from her face, though she was wiping tears from her cheeks. "Mayhap you should simply take me to the priory," she said. "The king cannot get to me there and you would not be in trouble with him."

"I am not in trouble with him," Liam said. "Nor is my father. And if there is a woman at Sempringham Priory who bears your name, you *are* there. There will be no trouble at all."

"Then why must we flee north, to Questing?"

This was the second part of the news he had to break to her. She was already frightened and he was loath to exacerbate that fear, but it couldn't be helped. She had to know, and if he didn't tell her now, she would find out sooner or later.

"Because Canterbury has sent a man north to check on the rumors," he said. "This man is a spy, so he is used to investigating things. The fear is that he might not be satisfied with the woman at the priory and come to Folkingham because he will know of the rumor that your father raised the true Welsh princess. When he comes, you must not be here."

"Then why not simply hide me?" she said. "Why must we run?"

"Because it would be better if you were not here at all," he said. "If there is a man hunting for you, I do not want him anywhere near you. More than that, you and I are to start our life together, and we may as well start it now."

"But we are not married yet."

"We will be before the day is out."

Her tears were fading as she realized the very thing she'd been waiting for her entire life was here. It was finally going to happen, even if it was under duress.

She smiled timidly.

"And I shall be Lady Herringthorpe," she said. "Do you know that I have practiced writing that name?"

He smiled in return, glad to see that she was no longer weeping and frightened. "I have been calling you that in my mind for a few years now," he said. "Whenever I speak of you to my friends, I always refer to you as Lady Herringthorpe. And that reminds me that I brought something for you."

"You did?" she said, excited. "What? Where is it?"

Bran came around again, with more licking and tail wagging, and Liam stood up so he'd be out of the line of doggy fire. "In my bags," he said. "Those are in the wagons."

"Where are the wagons?"

He shook his head. "I am not certain," he said. "But I can find them and retrieve the gift forthwith."

She stood up. "Let me come with you."

Liam shook his head. "Nay," he said. "You remain here. I do not want you out of this keep until we can be married and depart for the north."

She frowned. "You would keep me like a prisoner?"

"I would keep you safe," he said, pinching her chin gently and depositing a kiss on her forehead. "Remain here and I will return shortly."

He turned away, but her soft voice stopped him. "Is that all you intend to do when you leave me?"

He looked at her. "What do you mean?"

She pointed to her forehead. "You only intend to kiss me here?"

A wolfish grin creased his lips. "Where do you want me to kiss you, lass?"

He said it seductively and she flushed a bright pink, but she was grinning. "There are better places to kiss the woman you love."

He laughed low in his throat, but he didn't have to be told twice. He went to her, wrapped her up in his big arms, and kissed her squarely on the lips. He'd only kissed her this way a couple of times because someone was always around and he was terrified they'd be caught, so his kisses had been to hands or foreheads. But now... now, they were alone and he would take advantage of it.

He kissed her long and hard and hot, feeling her body against his. She was breathing as if she'd just run twenty miles. But he wasn't content simply kissing her lips, so he flicked his tongue out of his mouth, licking her lips, carefully inserting it in between her lips and licking her teeth. Cambria gasped, opening her mouth to him, and that was all the invitation he needed to taste her deeply. She felt so warm and wonderful against him and any measure of control he'd ever had was blown to pieces. As his lips kissed her furiously and one arm held her close, the other arm, and hand, began to wander down her backside. He could feel her rounded buttocks through the garment she wore.

That was enough to bring on an erection.

Groaning, he forced himself to stop because he didn't want to have to explain a full-blown erection to her or to anyone else. He was going to marry her today and, God willing, consummate the marriage immediately, so he could wait.

Barely.

Christ, she felt good.

"My apologies," he murmured, kissing her in between the words. "If I keep going, I am afraid I will not be able to control myself, so let me go and retrieve that gift. It will give me time to cool my burning blood because, lady, you set me on fire."

He kissed her again, twice, and she put her hands on his face, trying to hold him against her. "We are to be married," she said as he suckled her lower lip. "If we want to kiss, who is to stop us?"

"Me," he insisted weakly, finally pulling away completely. "If I do not, we will end up on the floor, or on your father's table, doing something we should not be doing right now."

She cocked her head curiously. "Mating, you mean?"

He cast her a long look before breaking down into soft laughter. "Aye, mating," he said. "Sit yourself down and stop being so naughty. I will return shortly."

He was pointing to the chair and, with a smirk, she lowered herself down. He winked at her and turned for the door, reaching out to grasp it when it suddenly flew open and his brother was standing in the opening.

Kyle was breathless, but his gaze moved to Cambria, sitting over by the hearth. "Papa says to keep her here and away from the windows," he said. "He says you must go to the hall immediately."

Liam frowned. "Go to the hall?" he repeated. "Why?"

Kyle shook his head. "I do not know," he said. "All I know is that a rider arrived a few moments ago and now Papa and Warenton and Lord de Royans are looking as if they've seen a ghost. Cassius has run off to hide. I am to find Mama and guard her."

Liam felt as if a bucket of cold water had been thrown on him. Everything in him ran cold—his blood, his heart, and even his soul.

That was cold, too.

"*Who?*" he managed to ask. "Who has come?"

"I do not know. A royal knight, I think."

That was all Liam needed to hear. He knew exactly who it was.

God help him, he knew.

CHAPTER SIXTEEN

"WHAT A COINCIDENCE that I should find not only Lord de Royans here, but the Earl of Warenton and the legendary commander of Bamburgh Castle, Lord Herringthorpe."

The words came from a handsome, well-dressed man who looked like any other noble knight. But he wasn't. Carlton, War, and Scott were in the hall as Tyrus le Mon introduced himself. For a man with such a terrible reputation, having been drummed out of the Executioner Knights, one would have expected him to appear with horns and cloven hooves, but he didn't. He appeared quite proper and normal.

That threw Carlton, War, and Scott off guard.

"You know me?" Scott said, peering at the man. "That is strange. I do not believe I know you."

"Forgive me, my lord," Tyrus said. "When I came through the gatehouse, I saw the Warenton banners. I also saw royal standards flying alongside Herringthorpe, so I knew who was here. Quite an occasion, I must say."

"What do you mean?"

"One of your gate guards told me that you were here for a

wedding."

It was difficult for the men not to react to that. The very thing they didn't want him to know had already been divulged by a loose-lipped gatehouse sentry who didn't know any better. It wasn't as if they had been hiding the wedding.

"And so there shall be," Carlton said stiffly. "Since I do not know you, tell me your business. Or are you simply looking for lodgings for the night?"

"I am not seeking lodgings, my lord, though they would be appreciated if you can spare the space," Tyrus said. "I have come on other business and am hoping you can give me a few moments of your time to discuss it. If not now, then I can wait."

"What do you want to discuss?" Carlton asked.

"I come on behalf of the Archbishop of Canterbury."

"That does not tell me what you want to discuss," Carlton said. "What does the Archbishop of Canterbury want with me?"

"He is hoping that you can clarify a mystery that has come to his attention," Tyrus said. "And also to the attention of the king."

Carlton grunted. "That sounds strange," he said. "But I do not understand why you've come here. You *do* understand that we are quite busy. Your visit is unsolicited."

"I realize that, my lord," Tyrus said. "As I said, I can wait until such a time as you are ready to answer a few questions."

I can wait. That probably meant he had all the time in the world and Carlton wouldn't be able to dodge him indefinitely. Also, he wanted the man out of Folkingham and away from his daughter.

Better to face this now rather than later, but Carlton was prepared. He had to be because if he didn't keep his composure, the entire situation fell apart. He had been in the hall with Scott and War and Cassius, waiting for Liam to return to them, when both of Scott's younger sons had appeared to tell them that a knight by the name of le Mon had just ridden in through the gates and was asking to speak with Carlton.

That had set off a storm of activity.

Though they'd known le Mon would probably be coming to Folkingham, no one had expected his arrival immediately. Maybe in a day or a week or even a month, but not now. Yet here he was, and the gatehouse guards had let him through, so he was inside the castle walls. Greatly concerned with being seen by a man who would know him on sight, Cassius fled, but Scott had grabbed both young men and told one of them to fetch Liam while he told the other one to spread the word not to speak of the wedding from this moment on, not to anyone.

Unfortunately, the second edict had evidently been too late.

Le Mon already knew.

Now, they could only do their best with this, guarding the secret they'd been protecting for almost twenty years. Carlton was honestly thinking of simply killing le Mon because if the man was dead, he couldn't report back to Canterbury and they could say that he'd left Folkingham and they never saw him again. Men were killed on the road all the time. The only thing holding Carlton back was the fact that le Mon had been an Executioner Knight, and those were no ordinary knights. He was fearful that the man would dispatch him, if attacked, and then try to carve through Scott and War, which would prove more difficult. In any case, Carlton fought down thoughts of murder.

He had a man to get rid of.

"Speak, then," Carlton said after a moment. "I am not sure I can clarify anything, but I will try. What is it?"

Le Mon, who was still standing, indicated the nearest bench, which was at the opposite end of the table. "May I sit, my lord?" he said. "It has been a long day already."

Carlton nodded, watching the man remove his broadsword and place it on the tabletop before sitting wearily on the bench. When he was comfortable, he continued.

"May I ask if all of you were involved in the wars in Wales about twenty years ago?" he said, looking at the men around the table. "Specifically, the capture of Dafydd ap Gruffudd and the death of his brother, Llywelyn. I know the House of de Wolfe was involved, but I would like to know if all of you were there."

"Not me," War said, shaking his head. "We were having trouble with the Scots at the time, so I remained at Bamburgh, reinforcing the border."

"I was there and so was Carlton," Scott said evenly. "My father was also there. I assume you know who he is."

Tyrus nodded. "How could I not?" he said. "Everyone knows the great William de Wolfe."

Scott nodded back. "Indeed," he said. "My father was in command of several battles in the Welsh campaign. Why do you ask?"

Tyrus fixed on him. "Because the archbishop has learned of a rumor involving your father, Lord de Royans, and Llywelyn ap Gruffudd's infant daughter, Gwenllian," he said. "Edward ordered the infant to be taken to Sempringham Priory, as a royal hostage, but it seems that she did not make it there."

No one said anything right away until Scott finally shrugged. "Have you gone to the priory to confirm this?" he asked.

Tyrus nodded. "I did, my lord," he said. "Based on the physical description I was given of the princess, the woman who bears her name and has been told she is Gwenllian is, in fact, not the princess. I would stake my reputation on it."

Scott's eyes narrowed. "What makes you think so?"

Tyrus looked at the three men at the table, clearly thinking that they were either being defensive or that they really didn't know anything. His expression said everything.

"Because the mystery of the princess's whereabouts was relayed by someone who knew her," he said, lowering his voice. "We are told that she has black hair and blue eyes, and the woman I saw at Sempringham has hair of an indistinct brown and eyes that are not blue. She was also old enough to be speaking when she was brought to Sempringham, and we know that the Welsh princess was not quite a year old when taken from Wales. Too young to be speaking. Consequently, there are many things that do not make sense and I am trying to clarify them for the archbishop, who is concerned for the princess's safety. She is a woman of the English royal family as well as Welsh royal bloodlines. We are greatly concerned that she has come to harm, so my question to you, Lord de Royans, is this—do you have a daughter?"

That was a question Carlton couldn't lie about. Everyone at Folkingham knew he had a daughter. That was established. But his palms were starting to sweat as he faced down the man at the other end of the table.

"I do," he said. "Bria is her name."

"Was she born of your wife? And are you her father?"

"That is an insulting question," War growled. "Be careful how you address a man when it comes to his children."

Tyrus looked at him. "It was not meant to be offensive, my lord," he said. "It is a simple question. Either his wife gave birth to his daughter or she did not. Mayhap the child is adopted."

War glanced at Carlton, wondering how in the hell the man was going to face this line of questioning, and Scott couldn't even look at him. His focus remained on Tyrus, unmoving, unwavering.

Like a wolf staring down its prey.

It was time to take charge.

"Le Mon, if you have something to say, then come out with it," Scott said. "This is not a tribunal. We do not have to answer your questions, nor do we have the time. De Royans does not have to discuss his family with you, in any way. If there is something on your mind, then say it and let us be done with this foolishness. We are too busy for whatever it is you're trying to accomplish, so get on with it."

He was pushing le Mon, but that was by design. The man was trying to eke out answers by cornering Carlton with his questions. The hope was that Carlton would say something that would give the entire situation away if, in fact, there was anything to give away.

But Scott wasn't going to let him.

Sensing that his tactics weren't working, Tyrus focused on Scott.

"My apologies," he said. "As I said, I was not attempting to be offensive, merely direct. The point of my questions is this—we were told by a priest who took the confession of a dying knight, a knight who served under your father and Lord de Royans during the final battle against Llywelyn ap Gruffudd, that your father, the Earl of Warenton, disobeyed Edward's orders and did not deliver Llywelyn's daughter to Sempringham Priory as commanded. Instead, he gave the child over to Lord de Royans to raise as his own while sending a decoy to Sempringham. Since I have been to Sempringham and interviewed the woman in question, I have come to the conclusion that she is not Gwenllian of Wales. That means I would like to see Lord de Royans' daughter. The archbishop demands it."

The air was full of tension. It bled from the walls, the table, the floor after that pointed and determined speech. Everything le Mon was repeating was nearly exactly what had happened, which could have only come from someone who had been part of it.

The reality of this situation was becoming clear.

Colm de Lara had stabbed his old allies in the back with his deathbed confession. He'd started something in motion that could not be easily stopped. Scott thought that if the man wasn't already dead, then he would have surely killed him because of the trouble he had caused. A young woman's life hung in the balance, not to mention all of the collateral relationships and people involved. As he struggled to come up with a steady reply, he heard a voice come from behind.

"If you would like to see Lord de Royans' daughter, then I shall fetch her for you," Liam said as he crossed the floor of the great hall, having come from the direction of the servants' entrance. "We have nothing to hide and you will tell the archbishop that. No one has done anything wrong except you, coming into a noble home and throwing around gossip and rumors."

Seeing a very big knight coming in his direction with an enormous dog at his side, le Mon stood up. He also collected his sword, though he didn't unsheathe it. He simply watched, tensed, as Liam came to stand between Scott and Carlton.

"I do not know you," Tyrus said evenly. "Please identify yourself."

Liam looked the man up and down as if sizing up the competition. "The man soon to marry Lord de Royans' daughter," he said. "I could hear what you were saying when I entered the hall. You have come to see my wife, so you will deal with me."

"You still have not told me your name."

"Liam Herringthorpe, garrison commander of Easington Castle. A royal property, in case you did not know."

That seemed to bring some clarification to Tyrus, but he was still on his feet, ready for a fight. "Then you are Lord Herringthorpe's son," he said.

"Brilliant deduction," Liam said sarcastically. "In fact, I stood at that doorway over there and heard nearly everything you said. That is one of the most outlandish stories I have ever heard. Are you mad? Or just ridiculous?"

"Liam," War snapped softly. "Still your tongue, lad."

"Or what?" Liam said, looking at his father. "Or that man at the end of the table is going to fight me? It seems to me that he's come to insult Lord de Royans, demean you, and call Lord Warenton's father a traitor. Someone has to stand up to him, and since he seems to be focused on the woman I am to marry, it is going to be me."

Tyrus remained standing, remained poised. He also remained calm. "It is a simple question with a simple answer," he said. "All I am asking for is to meet de Royans' daughter. Given the situation, I have been tasked with determining whether or not the rumors are true."

Liam sighed sharply. "Did it ever occur to anyone that the ramblings of a dying man were just that—ramblings?" he said. "Pure fantasies? You may not realize this, le Mon, but there is more than just one woman in this world with black hair and blue eyes, or indistinct brown hair and brown eyes, or however you put it. You cannot base your judgment solely on a physical description. And what you are doing now is accusing William de Wolfe, a man who is infallible, of treason. A dead man who cannot defend himself. I find that astonishingly cowardly."

More harsh words. This time, War didn't silence his son. He agreed with him. Everyone was looking at Tyrus now because the burden of proof was on him.

"No one is accusing de Wolfe of anything," Tyrus said, maintaining his composure. "But I have been tasked with a job. If you show me de Royans' daughter, we can just as easily be finished with this."

Liam snorted, but it wasn't a pleasant sound. "Very well," he said. "I will bring her. But when you see that she is not the woman you are looking for, you will return to Canterbury and tell him. Let this nonsense be finished for good."

Tyrus simply nodded, a gesture that suggested he understood and agreed. At least, that was how Liam took it. He pointed to the chair behind Tyrus.

"Sit down and wait," he said. "I will fetch her now. This will only take a moment."

As Tyrus slowly lowered himself onto the bench, Liam marched out of the hall with a purpose.

And what a purpose.

He was going to end this.

The idea had occurred to him as he stood in the shadows and listened to Tyrus explain why he had come. The man had all of the facts straight, which was horrifying, and it seemed to underscore the fact that Colm de Lara was behind everything. He'd confessed something, for an unknown reason, that should have never seen the light of day. That meant they had to outsmart de Lara, which wasn't going to be difficult. Liam knew exactly what he needed to do.

He headed right for the keep.

The door to the entry was bolted, but he banged on it and demanded entry. Nathaniel opened the door for him and he pushed inside, slamming the door behind him and throwing the bolt again.

"Where is Cambria?" he asked quietly.

Nathaniel pointed to the closed solar door. "In there," he said. "She's locked in."

"Good," Liam said. "But you must find Cassius. The man has run off and no one knows where he is, so find him and stay with him. Keep him out of sight and far away from the hall."

Nathaniel's brow furrowed. "*What* is happening, Liam?"

Liam shook his head. "No time to go through it now," he said. "Just do as you're told. I'll explain later."

Frowning, Nathaniel slipped from the entry door as Liam closed it, and locked it, behind him. Then he headed up the stairs to the upper floor, where he knew his mother was along with a few other women.

There was one in particular he needed.

Making his way to the top level, he went to Cambria's chamber door. He knew the women had been in her chamber, helping her prepare for her coming wedding, so he assumed they were all still in there. They'd been ordered to remain there but, knowing his mother, anything was possible. Annaleigh didn't like being told what to do. Rapping softly on the door, he could hear a familiar voice on the other side.

"Who is it?"

"'Tis me, Mama. Open the door."

The panel lurched open and Liam found himself looking at his mother, Fair Lydia, Lady Warenton, and Caria.

He crooked a finger at Caria.

"Cari," he said softly. "Come here."

Caria had been on the floor with a pile of clothing in front of her, but she leapt up at the sight of Liam and rushed to him. They'd known each other for years since he'd fostered at Castle Questing, so she trusted him. He was like a brother to her. Liam took her by the hand as she reached the door, pulling her out as he looked to his mother.

"Close this door and bolt it again," he said. "I'll explain more later, but please do it."

Annaleigh didn't argue with him. Once Caria was free of the chamber, she shut the door. He heard the bolt thrown. Then he looked at Caria.

"I need a great, great favor from you, lass," he said quietly. "It is literally a matter of life or death, so will you help me?"

Caria's eyes were wide on him. "Aye, I will," she said. "What is happening, Liam? Why are we locked up in a chamber?"

He sighed heavily. "I will tell you, but I must do it quickly," he said. "We must get over to the hall. What I am about to tell you must never leave your lips, Caria. I know you are good at keeping secrets because I know yours. I always have, and in all of the years I have known you, you have never once mentioned it to me, so that is how I know you can keep a secret. Now, you must keep another secret that is just as volatile as your own. I know it is a lot to ask, but I must. Can you do it?"

She was looking at him with trepidation.

Caria was a woman with strength. It was innate, but she had also been raised by William and Jordan, so she was no shrinking violet. They had raised her to be brave, to stand for truth and honor, and to be loyal to family. She was also taught to trust, and she had known Liam, and had known his character, long enough to trust the man with her life. To his question, she nodded.

"I can," she said. "Tell me what you need from me and I shall do it."

He did.

CHAPTER SEVENTEEN

TYRUS WAS COMING to think that he might have a serious situation on his hands.

His orders from Canterbury were to bring him the Welsh princess if she was located, and if young Herringthorpe produced a black-haired, blue-eyed woman, he was going to have to think quickly.

And then there was the trio at the other end of the table.

Liam's appearance had them surprised, but when he offered to fetch his bride, that brought serious reactions. Carlton almost grabbed him, while Scott and War had looked at each other with expressions that were bordering on concern. Not quite, but almost. They were skilled knights, trained to keep their emotions under control, and perhaps to the casual observer their expressions would have meant nothing. But to a trained observer like Tyrus, the twitch in Scott's cheek and the slight lift of War's eyebrow meant they were concerned with what Liam was doing. To Tyrus, that meant there must be some truth about the Welsh princess as de Royans' daughter.

Why else would they show concern?

So, he waited. He waited and he watched, wishing he had

something to drink but understanding why he would not be provided with refreshments. He was also suspecting he wouldn't be provided with a place to sleep, and more than likely asked to leave when this was all over, so he started thinking about where he would stay for the night in order to remain close to Folkingham. There was a village to the west of the castle, as he'd seen from the road, and he reasoned that he'd be able to find lodgings there. But most importantly, he was thinking about what to tell the archbishop.

There is some truth to the rumor, Your Grace.

That was the only thing he could tell him at this point.

Fortunately for him, the wait wasn't excessive. Liam had told him that he would return shortly and he did. There had been very little delay. When they heard the footfalls coming from the hall entry and caught a glimpse of figures in the darkness, Tyrus was the first one to his feet. He was prepared to meet the real Gwenllian of Wales because Liam had been so aggressive, so blunt in their conversation that he wouldn't put it past the man to present the woman he sought and then dare Tyrus to do anything about it. That was what he was fully expecting.

But that wasn't what he got.

Liam appeared with a petite woman, with chestnut hair and hazel eyes.

"This is Bria de Royans, who is to be my bride," Liam said, having lost none of his aggression in the short time he'd been away. "Bria, this is Tyrus le Mon. The Archbishop of Canterbury sent him because he has heard a foolish rumor that you are the daughter of Llywelyn the Last. Sit down and answer his questions, sweetheart. This should not take long."

The woman introduced as Bria took a seat on a bench a few

feet away from Tyrus, who was looking at her with some astonishment. As if expecting something, or someone, else. But he sat down and faced her, gazing at what was inarguably a very lovely young woman. She was also a small, almost fragile-looking lass. He stared at her for a few moments before speaking.

"Forgive my intrusion, my lady," he said. "I am here at the direction of the Archbishop of Canterbury in response to a tale we heard about Gwenllian of Wales."

Bria was sitting straight, gazing at him curiously. "And you think I am she?" she said. "Liam told me the story. I find it remarkable, to be truthful."

Tyrus glanced at Liam, who was standing behind her, his features like stone. "Aye," he said slowly. "I was wondering if you were the princess. Keep in mind that I have no stake in this situation. I am simply doing an investigation for the archbishop."

Bria shrugged. "I do not think I am her, although I suppose I would truly not know," she said. "My father found me at a church in Wales. I was intended for a foundling home, but he brought me back to England instead. I suppose there was something endearing about me, but you will have to ask him. Is that not correct, Papa?"

Sitting at the far end, Carlton was absolutely stumped. He had no idea who the young woman was because he'd not seen the de Wolfe carriage unloading and the women coming out of it. Therefore, he had no idea where Liam had come up with an imposter for his daughter, but he wasn't going to argue, nor was he going to waste the opportunity. When Liam had gone to retrieve the woman he implied was his bride, there was genuine fear in Carlton's heart that he would, in fact, bring Cambria.

Instead, he'd brought a miracle.

Carlton cleared his throat softly.

"You were the loveliest child I'd ever seen," he said, and that wasn't a lie. Cambria *had* been the loveliest child he'd ever seen. "You were simply a foundling and nothing more. Given that your mother and I had recently lost our son, I thought you might help ease your mother's grief. And there is nothing more to the story than that."

Bria returned her attention to Tyrus. "You see?" she said. "It is that simple. But I could pretend to be the missing princess if that helps your cause. Is there money or jewels involved? Was she rich?"

The conversation had taken an unexpectedly mercenary turn, and Tyrus shook his head. "I do not know, my lady," he said. "My concern is more with the wishes and intentions of the king as it relates to the situation."

"What situation?"

"The missing princess, of course."

Bria cocked her head curiously. "You mean there really is one?" she said. "This is not simply a wild tale?"

"Have you not heard of Gwenllian of Wales?"

Bria nodded. "In my lessons, I have," she said. "I was educated by the priests from St. Andrews. That parish is not far from here. Because Gwenllian is part of local lore, I know about her. She is at Sempringham and everyone knows that. Is that not correct, Papa?"

Carlton nodded. "She was taken there, aye."

Tyrus' focus shifted to Carlton. "And you know this for certain, my lord?"

Carlton nodded. "As certain as I can be, though I did not take her myself," he said. "The Earl of Warenton sent his sons to deliver her. That is all I know."

Tyrus listened carefully before switching his focus to Scott. "You are one of William de Wolfe's sons," he said. "Did you deliver the princess, my lord?"

It was clear that Scott had no patience for the interrogation. He was leaning forward on his elbows, listening to the conversation, but when attention shifted to him, he was clearly displeased.

"As I told you earlier," he said, "this is not an interrogation. I will politely answer your questions and that will be the end of it."

Tyrus nodded his head. "If you would not mind, my lord," he said. "I would like to hear it from you."

Scott cocked an eyebrow at the man, perhaps to emphasize he was not to question him further once he answered. "My brothers delivered the infant we brought from Wales," he said. "I was part of the escort that brought her here. While de Royans and the majority of the escort stopped at Folkingham, my brothers continued on to Sempringham and delivered the infant Gwenllian, as ordered. Now, you said that the woman you interviewed was not the princess based on physical characteristics you were told about. Did it ever occur to you that Sempringham was responsible for that?"

Tyrus' brow furrowed. "How do you mean, my lord?"

"I mean that *they* could have replaced the princess," Scott said. "It makes much more sense than the crime you are trying to accuse honorable men of."

"I still do not understand."

"Think on it this way," Scott said. "If the princess was delivered, yet became ill and died at some point, Sempringham could have replaced her with a child of their own to continue the illusion that she was still alive, still under their protection. Edward was giving them money for her care, and I'm sure it is a goodly amount, so not wanting to lose that money, and not wanting to be blamed for the death of the princess, they found a child to replace her. That makes the most sense to me. And your mystery is solved."

A new pebble of controversy was thrown into a pond that was already rippling with facts and speculation. The waters were being muddied by Scott's statement. Tyrus had come to Folkingham with a firm direction, but now he didn't know at all. He'd met the woman de Royans had allegedly raised and now Warenton was suggesting it wasn't a mystery at all, but a cover-up perpetrated by Sempringham itself. Certainly, he was facing more than just a simple case.

This one was getting out of hand.

Quite honestly, he wasn't sure there was anything more he could do here.

"I suppose anything is possible," he said after a moment. "In any case, please understand it was not my intention to come here and insult legendary men or their sons. I am simply a knight carrying out my orders. I am trying to get to the bottom of things. I will return to Canterbury with my findings and he will decide how to proceed."

"The only way to proceed is to punish Sempringham if the woman said to be the princess is, in fact, an imposter," Scott said. He gestured to Bria. "Just because de Royans brought a child back from Wales and gave her a home, that does not mean he stole a Welsh princess."

Bria smiled at the men at the end of the table. "But what if I *were* a princess in disguise?" she said excitedly. "How romantic! But I should want her money and her jewels. She must be very rich, don't you think? Aren't all princesses?"

Scott held up a hand to her. "Not this princess," he said. "And not this family. Be glad you are a de Royans daughter, my lady. You have had a much better life than a Welsh princess kept as a hostage."

"And you will have a much better life as Lady Herringthorpe," Liam said, taking her by the hand and pulling her up from the chair. "I believe you must continue packing, so I will leave you to it. Thank you for coming and putting le Mon's mind at ease."

Bria smiled prettily for Tyrus. "I hope you find your princess, my lord," she said. "I am sorry it was not me."

Tyrus simply nodded, feeling some disappointment at the course the conversation had taken. Bria skipped over to Carlton and kissed him on the cheek before skipping happily out of the hall. The silence she left in her wake was deafening as all eyes turned toward le Mon.

It was over.

For now.

"Well?" Liam said, leaning forward and bracing himself on the table with his big arms. "Satisfied?"

Tyrus looked at the man, clearly displeased. "I suppose I shall have to be," he said. He stood up and collected his sword, turning from the table. But he paused. "I am satisfied for now, but that does not mean forever. There is something amiss about this situation and I will discover what it is. Thank you for your time, my lords. It was an… interesting discussion."

With that, he headed out of the hall, perhaps not moving very quickly because of his last comment. He was convinced that there was more to the situation, but for now, there was nothing he could do.

That was good enough for Liam.

All he wanted was the bastard out of Folkingham. Let him get back to London and figure out what to do, because that would give Liam and Cambria plenty of time to go north and find a hiding place until the situation blew over. That was all Liam wanted.

Time to get Cambria safe.

As le Mon departed through the hall entry, Liam went over to his father and Carlton and Scott.

"Bloody brilliant," War muttered. "My God, I've raised a clever lad."

Liam perched himself on the edge of the bench, right next to his father. There was a half-full wine cup in front of War and he picked it up, draining it.

"He wanted to see a Welsh princess," he murmured. "I gave him one."

"You told Caria everything?" Scott said softly.

Liam nodded. "I had to," he said. "I needed her help."

Scott understood. He emitted a pent-up sigh, signifying his relief. "She'll keep it to herself forever," he said. "You do not have to worry about her. But for now, I suggest we still go through with our plans. Marriage and then sending Liam and Bria north to Questing."

Carlton nodded his head. The man looked so relieved that he was surely going to slither right to the ground. "We did not have time to summon the priest before le Mon arrived, so let us do so now," he said. "There will be a wedding and a feast tonight and then Liam and Bria can be gone in the morning."

"I would make sure le Mon is well clear of this place first," Scott said. "And make sure he is not lingering somewhere, watching the roads."

That made sense. "Then mayhap we'd better not leave immediately," Liam said. "Mayhap we should stay until we know he is well back to London."

That brought about an entirely new discussion, and they proceeded to finish off the pitcher of wine on the table and called for another because they'd earned it. As the wine flowed, so did the relief.

But that was until the shouting started.

CHAPTER EIGHTEEN

THERE WAS A gentle rapping, rapping on the solar door. Startled, Cambria came off her chair.

The rapping came again, more loudly this time, and she timidly made her way over to the door.

"Who is it?" she whispered.

"Me, my lady! Alwyn!"

Cambria knew the servant. He was from the kitchen yard and helped her watch out for her puppies.

"What is it, Alwyn?" she asked.

"It's one of the puppies, my lady," he said. "A hawk injured him. You must come!"

If anything could make Cambria forget Liam's orders to remain in the solar, it was any mention of her puppies in danger. Quickly, she unbolted the door only to see Alwyn standing there, looking quite upset. Her gaze darted around the keep entry to see if anyone else was present.

"How did you get in here?" she asked.

He turned and pointed to the entry door. "It wasn't locked, my lady," he said. "I thought you might be in here. Hoped you would, anyway, so I knocked on the door. You must come!"

Cambria wasn't sure why the entry door wasn't locked, but she looked around again and didn't see anyone in the entry or on the stairs. She knew that a young de Wolfe knight had been inside, making sure the door was locked, but he was gone and the door hadn't been locked by anyone else. Alwyn had managed to get in with news of an injured puppy, and although she knew she wasn't supposed to leave, she couldn't ignore the distress of one of her dogs.

"How badly is he wounded?" she asked. "What happened?"

Alwyn held up a hand, like a hawk hovering. "He went after the littlest pup," he said. "The others were feeding in the den, but the littlest one hadn't managed to make it in to feed. I was standing just a few feet away and the hawk still swooped. It must have been watching and waiting. Usually, it tries to take a chicken, but this time it went for the pup. The little thing has punctures and is bleeding. Will you not come to him?"

After hearing that, Cambria couldn't stay away.

She hoped Liam would forgive her.

"I am coming," she said, emerging from the solar and shutting the door behind her. "Quickly, now. Show me where the pup is."

Since there was only one way in and out of the keep, they could only go through the keep entry that faced the bailey, and Cambria was close on the heels of the servant as they raced down the stairs. The kitchens were to the south of the keep, with a covered passageway that went from the kitchens to the hall, but in order to get to the yard, they had to go outside of the keep's perimeter. Cambria was practically running by the time she hit the dirt of the bailey, picking up speed as she headed for the kitchen yard. She rushed past the stables and into the yard, which was behind a stone wall and a gate.

Once she was inside, she was able to breathe a little.

She knew she shouldn't be out. Liam had told her to stay in the solar, but she simply couldn't stay there while one of her puppies suffered. She had to keep telling herself that, telling herself that no harm was done. There were so many soldiers in the bailey that surely she was safe for the quick dash into the yard. She ran straight to the series of pens and dens she had for the puppies only to see another young servant boy there, holding the wounded puppy.

Cambria climbed right inside the pen.

"Let me have him," she said.

Reaching out, she scooped the pup off the lap of the servant. The boy laid out a piece of cloth he had, one a kitchen servant had given him to stem the blood, and Cambria put the puppy down on the cloth to inspect him. He was yelping in pain and she could see two distinct puncture marks and a big scrape. The mother dog, lured by the sounds of her injured puppy, came out of her den and began to lick the injured pup as Cambria critically assessed the situation.

"I am going to need wine and honey," she told the servant hovering over her, the one who had fetched her. "I will also need my sewing kit, something to sew up the cut. Hurry!"

The servant fled. Meanwhile, the mother dog was very concerned with the puppy, so Cambria coaxed the dog back into her den and then put the injured puppy against the mother. The puppy began to nurse, and the mother dog licked the wounds, and that was the best they could do until Cambria received the things she'd asked for.

At that point, all she could do was wait.

Tyrus thought he was seeing things.

He was in the stable yard, which was next to the kitchen yard, tightening up his saddle when a woman with coal-black hair and a finely featured face ran past him into the kitchen yard. She had been with a servant, focused on what was ahead of her, so he only saw her in profile. He thought he might have caught more of a broad view of her face, just a flash of it, and it seemed to him that her eyes were light.

Blue eyes.

Black hair.

Suddenly, the cold light of suspicion dawned.

So did a rising anger. He was starting to think that, somehow, there *was* a woman with black hair and blue eyes at Folkingham and he'd been convinced otherwise by those who lived here. Therefore, he was going to do more investigation on the subject that didn't involve the lord or his complicit friends. He looked around for the nearest stable servant and found an old man bent over one of the horses inside, picking stones out of a hoof.

Tyrus was, if nothing else, cunning. He was going to have to be discreet about what he wanted because that usually achieved the desired results. Demands and going straight to the point would only cause fear and, perhaps, even reserve and suspicion. And he didn't want that.

Therefore, he was going to have to be subtler about it.

"I was wondering," he said to the servant, "where's the nearest tavern around here?"

The man paused what he was doing, pointing with the metal pick he had in his hand. "There's a small one in the village," he said. "They don't have rooms, but they'll let you a bed if you pay. You'll just have to sleep in the common room or in the barn."

"Are there better inns within a few hours' ride?"

The man nodded. "Go on the road to the east and you'll run into the village of Billingborough," he said. "They have an inn called The Fish House. You can find a room there and the food isn't bad, so I've heard."

"Thank you," Tyrus said. Then he paused a moment, looking to the bailey beyond the stable. "Everyone seems very excited for the wedding."

The old man grinned and went back to the hoof. "It's been a long time in coming," he said. "I've watched that little lass grow up. It's time she was married. No pretty lass should be left unmarried at her age."

Tyrus smiled weakly. "Pretty, you say?"

The old man snorted. "Don't get any ideas about her," he said. "Liam Herringthorpe will run you through."

"Is that so?"

"'Tis," the old man said. "He's been waiting for this longer than anyone."

Tyrus was still smiling, though it was an act. "I've got a woman of my own," he said, though it was a lie. He was making a calculated statement to get the answer he wanted. "I do not need another one, though I suspect mine is the prettiest. Blonde like an angel."

The old man shook his head. "Then de Royans' daughter is the devil to your angel," he said, chuckling. "Hair as black as night and eyes the color of a summer sky. I hear that people in Wales are dark, you know. She was brought by the master from Wales a long time ago. A foundling, they say. But she's a beauty."

Tyrus had his answer. It had been so easy that it had almost been child's play. Whoever Liam had presented in the hall as

Bria de Royans, if that was even the name of Carlton's daughter, wasn't who Liam said she was.

He'd been lied to.

Damn.

"I think I just saw her walk by," he said, his attention now turning toward the kitchen yard. "What is her name?"

"Lady Cambria."

Cambria. That was why Liam had called the other woman "Bria." Now, things were starting to make a little sense. Tyrus pointed toward the kitchen.

"She went into the yard over there," he said.

The old man snorted again. "It's the dogs."

"The what?"

The old man stood up and began pointing off toward the kitchen yard. "Dogs," he said again. "She raises dogs. Sells the puppies for a tidy sum, so I've heard. That's where she keeps the dogs. Are you looking to buy one?"

Tyrus shrugged. "I hadn't thought about it," he said. "I suppose I could take a look."

The old man came away from the horse, gesturing to the gate in the stone wall. "In through there," he said. "She'll be in there with the dogs if you want to look for one. All men should have a dog. They're fine companions."

Tyrus had his answer. In fact, he had everything he needed. Liam Herringthorpe and the rest of them weren't going to make a fool out of him. He had what he wanted now and he was going to finish it.

"Thank you," he said, gaze on the gate. "I'll see for myself. Mayhap I do need a dog."

He started to head toward the gate as the old man called after him. "Tell her you'll take good care of it," he said. "She'll only sell you a dog if you tell her you'll be kind to it!"

Tyrus waved at him in acknowledgment, but his focus was on that gate. He was in no rush as he made his way to it, peering through the small iron grate in the middle of the panel that gave him a view to the yard beyond. It was a normal kitchen yard, with chickens and goats and a sheep that was gnawing on a fencepost over in the corner. There was a lone female servant over by what looked to be a well, and then closer to him there was a series of small pens, each one with a shelter in it.

And then he saw her.

Huddled on the ground with a servant beside her as she peered into one of the shelters was, in fact, the black-haired woman. Tyrus watched her for a moment, his mind working quickly on the best way to handle the situation. Whatever he did, it was going to have to be fast. He had to get to her, and get her out of Folkingham, before Liam or anyone else showed up. He would have a fight on his hands if he didn't move swiftly enough, and given the fact that Scott de Wolfe and War Herringthorpe were both here, he wasn't entirely sure it was a fight he could win.

Opening the gate, he made his way in her direction.

"My lady," he said evenly. "My apologies for disturbing you, but the man in the stable said that you have puppies to sell. May I trouble you with a question about them?"

She looked at him, startled, and Tyrus was struck by the color of those blue eyes. They were positively glowing, a color he'd never seen before. Along with her black hair, he had to admit that he'd never seen a more beautiful woman. But the moment she saw him, he could see something in her expression that suggested fear. Panic, even.

He had to act fast.

"My deepest apologies if I startled you," he said quickly, holding out both hands to show her that he was not a threat. "I simply wanted to know if you had any puppies for sale. I'm told they are fine dogs."

She stood up to face him. "Who are you?"

He shook his head. "My name is Ty," he said. "I was simply passing through and stopped here because my horse… He seems to be lame. The man in the stable said that you are Lady Cambria."

The servant boy was now standing alongside the woman with the blue eyes, and she leaned over, whispering something to him. He bolted out of the pen area and ran off. When the child was gone, the fear in her expression seemed to ease.

"You're a traveler, then, Sir Ty?" she said.

He nodded. "I am," he said. "A dog would keep me company on the road."

"A dog is for more than simply running alongside your horse," she said. "My dogs are the best in Lincolnshire. They are big, strong, and loyal. Men pay me a great deal for one of my dogs."

"How much do you want for a male?"

"Three pounds."

"Three *pounds*?"

"Five for a female."

His eyebrows lifted. "That is tidy sum, my lady."

"My dogs are worth it," she said. "Do you want one or not?"

He pretended to consider it. "Possibly," he said. "But I'm interested in something far more intriguing."

"What?"

"You."

Her brow rippled in confusion. "Me?" she said. "My lord, if

you think to woo me, know that I have been betrothed for years. I am to be married imminently."

He nodded. "I know," he said. "I heard about the wedding. To Liam Herringthorpe."

"Aye," she said, eyeing him. "Know that I have sent for him, so if you do not wish to buy a dog, you should leave me in peace."

It occurred to him that was why the servant had run off so fast, the one she'd whispered to. Tyrus had an assortment of daggers at his waist, as he always did when he traveled, so it was a simple thing to put his hand on the hilt of a big one that was in a sheath. He wanted to make sure she saw it as he took a couple of steps closer.

"Then we have little time," he said, lowering his voice. "I know who you are, Gwenllian. You are the daughter of Llywelyn the Last, the granddaughter of Simon de Montfort, and the great-granddaughter of King John. I have been sent to bring you to London, and if you scream, I can cut your life short faster than anyone can get to you. They may kill me in the end, but you will still be dead, so unless you want that scenario, you will do as I say. Come to me now."

Her expression was full of anger and fear. "You are from Canterbury," she spat. "You are that knight!"

"I am," he said. "And you are now my captive. Come to me."

"I will *not*!"

"If you do not, I will kill half of these dogs before you can stop me."

That was the only threat that meant anything to her, and she stiffened up. "Do not touch them," she said. "You will leave my dogs alone!"

"Then do as you are told."

"I am not going anywhere with you!"

He began to move, a big and imposing presence, heading straight for the dog pen, and she ran at him, fists flying.

"*Stop!*" she shrieked. "You will not hurt them!"

She was close enough now that he could grab her. He clamped a hand on her soft arm in a grip that was like a vise. "Thank you for complying," he said, which sounded oddly out of place given the situation. "Now, we are going to walk to the stable and you are going to get on my horse."

Cambria wasn't one to go peacefully. She began to struggle against him, trying to hit him, but his grip tightened to a painful point and she was forced to stop purely because he was causing her agony. But she was still trying to pull away, even as they walked. That was her only plan until they passed by the big iron pot used to boil down hides. There were two large iron rods leaning on it, both of them used to either stir the pot or stir the fire, and she grabbed one of them. The next thing Tyrus realized, she was swinging the iron rod at his head.

He was forced to let her go as he dodged the rod. With a scream, Cambria took off running, but he was faster. He threw himself at her, tackling her legs, and they both went down.

That was when Kyle Herringthorpe walked into the yard.

"What is...?"

He couldn't even get the words out before he was throwing himself on top of Tyrus, trying to pull him off Cambria, who managed to get a hand up and poke Tyrus in his right eye. He grunted, grappling with both her and Kyle, so she poked him twice more until he put a big hand on her head and rammed her face right into the ground. By this time, Kyle had him around the neck and was choking him, pulling him off

Cambria, who managed to scoot out from underneath him. Kyle was strong and had a good grip on Tyrus' neck, and the man was starting to feel faint. But he retained his wits enough to grab at one of the daggers around his waist and ram it backward, stabbing Kyle at the base of his neck.

The young knight immediately fell away.

On her feet, Cambria had the iron rod in her hand again and she swung it as hard as she could at Tyrus' head. She was fortunate enough to make contact and Tyrus was knocked sideways as stars danced before his eyes. About this time, Nathaniel burst through the gate because he'd been near the stable and heard the noise. But Tyrus was armed and he unsheathed his broadsword just as Nathaniel rushed in. The young knight barely missed being gored.

"Here!" Cambria cried, tossing Nathaniel her rod.

Fortunately, the knight was able to catch it, bringing it up to block a strike that surely would have cut his left arm off. He wasn't in armor, nor did he have his broadsword with him, so all he was able to do was dodge the sword strikes that were coming at him.

Meanwhile, the entire bailey was running in the direction of the kitchen yard, lured by the shouts. Cambria was trying to get to Kyle, who was in the dirt, bleeding from the knife in his neck. She finally managed to duck around the battling knights and grab Kyle by the arm, pulling him away from the fight. Seeing all of the blood, she grabbed the sleeve of her dress and yanked hard, pulling it free from the bodice.

"I have to take the knife out," she said to Kyle, looking him in the eye as blood ran from his mouth and the wound. "Do you hear me? I must get this out and then I will apply pressure to stop the bleeding. You will heal, I swear it. Be brave, young sir. I will be swift."

Kyle simply nodded. Cambria yanked out the dirk, which was about three inches long, and immediately put the torn sleeve to his neck, applying pressure. He tried to lie back, to put his head on the dirt, but she wouldn't let him.

"Nay," she said, her voice trembling. "Turn on your side and let the blood run to the ground. Better still, can you sit up?"

Kyle nodded. "Aye," he said weakly. "I do not think it is too bad, just bloody."

Cambria helped him into a sitting position, leaning him against the buttery. By this time, the kitchen servants were spilling out, watching the fight in horror, and Cambria had them help Kyle into the kitchen. With his blood on her hands and on the front of her blue dress, she turned to watch Nathaniel hold off Tyrus. The young knight was doing a splendid job of it, but Tyrus was strong. He was gaining ground. Just as she feared she would have to jump in and assist the young warrior, the entire world seemed to explode with knights.

Liam, followed by Scott and War, burst into the kitchen yard and went after Tyrus. For his part, Tyrus saw his life flash before his eyes, so he disengaged with Nathaniel and began to run toward Cambria. His intent was clear—use her for protection against the onslaught. Seeing this, Cambria made a break for the kitchen door, but Tyrus was fast. He was nearly upon her.

Liam, however, was faster.

He reached Tyrus before Tyrus could reach Cambria and grabbed the man by his tunic. It was all he could get his hands on. He yanked hard, pulling him off balance, but Tyrus came around with his broadsword and nearly stabbed Liam with it.

As it was, he caught him in his midsection, tearing his tunic and drawing first blood. As Liam leapt back, out of range of the man's arcing broadsword, Scott charged in and nearly took off Tyrus' head.

After that, the fight was on.

The truth was that Tyrus never had a chance against three seasoned knights. Logan and eventually Jeremy tried to join it, but there was no room for them. The veteran knights were having all of the fun as Jeremy and Logan managed to make it over to Cambria to protect her should Tyrus break free.

But the man wasn't going to break free.

He was on borrowed time.

Truthfully, Scott and War were only involved for the first minute or so. After that, Liam shoved them away. This was his fight and he was going to finish it himself. Therefore, they backed off—far off—and stood by the yard gate, watching Liam thrust and parry, shove and kick, as Tyrus gave nearly as good as he got. It was a brutal fight, with brutal blows being thrown, until Liam managed to disarm Tyrus. The man's sword was knocked from his hand when Liam managed to slice the tips off two of the fingers on his right hand.

Tyrus didn't utter a sound.

The little finger pieces on the ground were stomped on and crushed as they battled across the yard. Mostly, Tyrus was dodging Liam because Liam was coming on like fire, but when they passed by the big iron pot used to boil hides, Tyrus picked up the second iron rod and swung it at Liam. He managed to smash some fingers, knocking the sword out of Liam's hand. But Liam grabbed the rod and they wrestled over it until it finally ended up on the ground.

Then the punches started to fly.

Carlton eventually showed up, watching in horror alongside Scott and War, at the bloodbath happening in his own kitchen yard. He caught sight of his daughter, with a torn and bloodied dress, and tried to go to her, but Scott held him back. They didn't want the man crossing the yard and possibly getting hurt. She was well protected by Logan and Jeremy, but all of them were watching Liam and Tyrus throw monstrous punches at one another. That went on for several long and painful minutes. It seemed like forever. Then a punch to the head from Liam sent Tyrus to the ground.

The battle seemed to be waning.

Both Liam and Tyrus were bloodied, beaten, and exhausted. It was a horrible sight. Cambria was trying her hardest not to weep at the sight because, truthfully, she felt as if this entire situation was her fault. Had she not left the solar, none of this would have happened. Kyle would not have been stabbed and Liam would not be covered in blood and bruises. His left eye was already starting to swell. But she kept her mouth shut, standing with two young knights who would have liked nothing better than to charge in and finish it.

But they would never have the chance.

With Tyrus face-down on the ground, Liam staggered over to him and bent down, grabbing him by the hair with the intention of flipping him onto his back. But just as he did that, Tyrus suddenly came alive and rammed one of those daggers from his belt straight into Liam's torso. It was a big dagger, with a big blade, and Cambria screamed when she saw what he'd done. Life seemed to move in slow motion after that because it seemed as if everything was ending. Time, life, love… everything was ending at the tip of that big knife.

But it wasn't ending for Liam.

Only for Tyrus.

As Liam staggered back, Tyrus lurched to his feet. That brought Scott and War away from the gate, running toward Tyrus, intending to prevent the man from laying the death blow upon Liam, but they never had the opportunity to prevent anything. They were halfway to the battling pair when Tyrus was suddenly struck in the upper torso by not one, but two big bolts, in quick succession. They were like hammer blows against the man. Startled, everyone looked in the direction they'd come from only to see Cassius standing on the wall walk with a wicked-looking double crossbow in his hand.

Both bolts had been released.

Tyrus saw Cassius but could hardly believe his eyes. Eyes that soon closed as he fell backward, onto his back, and lay there as still as stone. Realizing that the fight was finally over, Cambria, along with everyone else, ran toward Liam. Scott and War were already at his side as Logan and Jeremy went to Tyrus to ensure he didn't rise up again.

"My lord," Cambria said, reaching out to grab War's shoulder. "Kyle took a knife to the neck. He's in the kitchens."

War looked at her, horrified, and Scott spoke quickly. "Go to him," he said. "I will tend to Liam. Go to your other son."

War was absolutely devastated. He stumbled to his feet, rushing off toward the kitchens as Cassius made his way off the wall and came running into the yard. He was still holding the crossbow, but he handed it over to the nearest soldier as he rushed to Liam's side.

"Uncle Scott?" he said, gravely concerned. "I'm sorry I wasn't here sooner. I tried!"

Fortunately, Scott was an excellent healer. It was a gift he had and had used many times on the field of battle. He was inspecting the knife and the placement of the blade in Liam's body.

"Thanks to God that you came when you did," he said, glancing up at Cassius. "Where have you been?"

"Hiding in the armory," Cassius said. "But I heard the commotion and armed myself. Tell me what I can do for Liam and I shall do it. What do you need?"

Scott carefully touched the dagger where it was buried in Liam's torso. "We must get him inside so I can remove this," he said. "Find men. Tell them to bring something flat to carry him on, like a door. He must be kept flat so the dagger does not do additional damage."

As the two of them were deciding the best and swiftest way to remove Liam, Cambria crept to Liam's head and gazed down at him. He was simply lying on his back, gazing up at the sky, but when he caught movement in his periphery, he turned his head to look at her.

"Greetings, sweetheart," he said softly, smiling at her. "I will heal. Do not be troubled. Are you well? Did he hurt you?"

Cambria burst into tears. "I am sorry," she wept, trying to put her arms around his neck as she buried her face in the side of his head. "I am so sorry. I did not mean for any of this to happen."

Liam put his hand up, holding her head against his as she wept. "I told you not to be troubled," he said. "All will be well. As long as you are unharmed, that is all that matters to me. How did he find you?"

Cambria didn't want to tell him but had no choice. "I disobeyed you," she said, sniffling. "One of the puppies was injured so I came out to tend it. I am so very sorry."

Liam's eyes closed briefly. He was exhausted, and beaten,

but he didn't want to move too much because of the knife in his gut. He didn't want to create more damage.

"Since it was for your puppies, I forgive you," he said. "What happened to the dog?"

"A hawk."

He grunted, a regretful sound. "When we return to Easington, I will have an entire stable built just for the dogs so they are always protected," he said. "I do not want to chance more hawk attacks. Speaking of dogs, where is Bran?"

Cambria lifted her head, looking around. "I do not see him," she said. "I will go find him."

"Nay," Liam said, gripping her hand. "Do not leave me. Stay."

Cambria did. She wrapped both hands around his, holding it tightly as Cassius ran off to find men to bring Liam inside. Leaning over, she kissed his forehead, his cheek, trying to give him some comfort.

"Tell me about Easington," she said, trying to distract him. "You've not told me much about it, you know. If I am to live there, I would like to know everything about it."

He grunted as he shifted a little and the knife caused him pain. "It is a large castle," he said, his voice faint. "Bran has a lady-friend who lives there."

Cambria nodded. "Is that so?" she said. "What does she look like?"

"Hairy."

Cambria chuckled, stroking his forehead. "So you and I will not be the only couple in love at Easington?"

His eyes opened and he looked at her. "Nay," he said. "But we will be the most important. In the years and centuries to come, long after we're gone, there will be a legend about the

Wolfehound and his mate, and how their love was so strong that it defied death itself. How their love blended into the stars and became one with the beauty of the sky. That's *our* legend, Bria. A legend of love."

There were tears in Cambria's eyes. "Wolfehound," she murmured. "I've not heard you call yourself that before."

He smiled faintly. "That is what the men at Easington call me," he said. "It started because Bran and I were inseparable, but it's come to mean more than that. Loyalty and relentlessness when facing adversity. Like today—I was your faithful companion, your protector in the face of danger. Your Wolfehound. And I always will be, Bria."

Tears popped from Cambria's eyes as she bent over and kissed his lips, tenderly and sweetly. It was a moment they shared, just the two of them, as the yard was swarmed with soldiers. A group of them carried Tyrus out, followed by men with a wide plank for Liam. Cambria was forced to let him go as they put him on the wood and carefully lifted him, removing him from the yard and heading for the keep.

Cambria followed.

But his words stuck with her, something poignant and powerful that she would never forget. Theirs was an old love story, as they'd been part of one another nearly their entire lives. A love that was embedded in them, part of their very bones. Something that could never be removed or separated.

I am your faithful companion, your protector.

He'd left out just one thing.

The love of your life.

And she was the love of his.

CHAPTER NINETEEN

Two Weeks Later

THE CHAMBER WAS dark and warm, with the only light and heat coming from the hearth. The little hearth worked quite well and the fires in it tended to be big and blazing, so much so that the entire wall above the hearth was blackened with soot. Even the bottom of the bed was blackened with soot in spite of the fact that they'd moved it as far away from the hearth as they could without actually moving it out of the room. That meant that the bed was right by the door, so when she walked in, he saw her immediately.

He must have started, or otherwise moved, because she approached the bed with her hand up in a soothing gesture.

"Be at ease, lad," she said in a thick Scots accent. "I'm here tae check her wounds."

He relaxed when he realized who it was. "Lady Warenton," he said. "I am grateful for your attention yet again."

Jordan's gaze lingered on the big knight for a moment before she bent over and began to carefully pull away the bandages. The firelight wasn't enough to really see the wounds in great detail, but at least she didn't smell them anymore. That was something.

"I've tended many battle wounds in my time," she said, peeling back the first bandage. "I've seen worse than yers, though yer wound wasn't nearly so bad as the poison that infected it afterward. Still, it seems tae have gone away."

"Thanks to you," Tyrus said. "Will I recover?"

"I believe ye will," Jordan said, peeling back the second bandage. "But that is why we must talk."

"What about?"

"This life ye lead."

"What about it?"

She stopped with the bandages and looked at him. "I dinna heal ye simply so ye could run back tae Canterbury and tell him what ye know about Cambria," she said. "This ends now or I'll make it so ye'll never rise from this bed again."

Tyrus believed her. This small, old woman had so deftly taken on the wounds he'd received from the double-bolt shot to his torso because she was the only one at Folkingham who would touch him. Everyone else was focused on Liam and Kyle, but she wasn't. She'd spent days and nights with him, tending the wounds, flushing them out with wine when they became infected and forcing him to drink a brew made from rotten bread. Whatever she did had killed the poison in the wounds, which were now healing, and Tyrus was the first one to say that he owed her everything.

He sighed heavily.

"I've never owed a debt of gratitude to anyone in my entire life," he said, turning his head away as she began to poke at the healing wounds. "I am a man with no debts, no loyalties."

"Untrue," she said. "Ye're loyal tae me now for saving yer

life. I could have let ye die, but I dinna. I healed ye."

"Why?" he asked.

She didn't answer right away, focused on the wounds. "Because ye're someone's son," she said softly. "I did this for yer mother, lad. Tell me about her."

He looked at her then. "*My* mother?"

"Aye."

"There is not much to tell except that I had one."

"Is she still alive?"

"Nay."

"Did ye love her?"

He sighed again and averted his gaze. "She simply gave birth to me," he said. "She gave birth and then she died. My father, dedicated to service for the king, gave me over to the servants to raise, only I was passed from one to another to another. I was put into situations that no child should be put in. When I had reached about five years of age, my father sent me to foster at Fotheringhay Castle, where I was educated, beaten, and abused. But I rose above it and became the knight I am today. Why do you ask?"

By that time, Jordan had stopped fussing with the bandages and was looking at him seriously. "I was told about ye," she said quietly. "How ye were an Executioner Knight, only ye were too heartless, even for them. Now I understand why."

He didn't say anything for a moment. He regretted what he'd said already. There were reasons why Tyrus le Mon was the way he was, and that wasn't something he divulged to many. But he'd divulged it to Lady Warenton because she asked. As she'd said, she'd saved his life, so he reasoned that she deserved to know something about the man she'd saved.

Even though he probably wasn't worth the effort.

"I have never failed in a mission," he finally said. "My upbringing has made me who I am. If that sounds harsh, then I suppose it is to you. But not to me."

"It sounds harsh, but it also sounds lonely."

"There is safety in solitude."

"Why do ye say that?"

"Because you cannot be hurt if you are alone."

Jordan collected the dirty bandages and set them aside, picking up a small container of wine that she'd brought. "I'm sorry ye had a difficult upbringing," she said. "I'm sorry ye've resorted tae an outlook on the world tae protect yerself."

"I am not protecting myself," he said. "I simply do not like other people."

She chuckled, but it was not from humor. It was from irony. "Given what ye do, I'm sure there aren't many who are fond of ye," she said. "But it comes tae this—I saved yer life and ye owe me something for it. Would ye agree with that?"

He looked at her. "I would."

"Do ye believe in honor?"

"It may come as a surprise to you that I do."

"Do ye believe that ye have honor?"

"It is all I have. I honor my word, my bonds, my agreements."

"Then if ye believe that ye owe me for yer life, the price ye pay is yer silence in the matter of Gwenllian of Wales," she said quietly. "If ye dunna honor yer word, and ye tell anyone about it, I have more connections than ye'll ever know. I'll make sure ye're discredited from the top of Scotland tae the bottom of England and beyond. I'll make sure everyone who matters knows that ye're not tae be trusted. I'll run yer reputation intae the ground, lad. Believe me when I say this."

His gaze upon her was steady. "Not strangely, I have been lying here wondering what I was going to do from now on," he said. "You may be surprised to know that I have already made the decision not to speak of Lady Cambria."

"Why?"

"Because I knew you were going to use my wounds against me," he said. "I am not naïve, Lady Warenton. I knew this was coming."

She eyed him before she began to use the wine in her hand to cleanse the scabbed-over wounds, which were healing nicely now that the infection was gone. "Then we have a bargain," she said. "And since ye've been wondering how ye're tae make a living after this, I've news for ye on that front."

He frowned. "What news?"

She was concentrating on the scabs as she spoke. "Ye're a good knight," she said. "I saw the fight from the keep, when ye and Liam went tae battle. My son, Scott, thinks ye have an excellent sword. He wants ye for Berwick Castle. Trouble with the clans, lad. I'm going tae send ye tae Berwick Castle tae help."

He just stared at her. "Berwick?" he repeated. "But… I cannot. I have a contract with the Archbishop of Canterbury at the moment. I am going to have to figure out what to tell the man if I cannot tell him what I have discovered."

"I have already taken care of that," Jordan said. "I happen tae know a few priests. My husband and I are patrons of a few churches. I've already sent word tae the priest I'm closest to, a man at Kelso who will do anything I want and not ask questions. I've sent Scott's son, Jeremy, tae ask the priest tae send the archbishop a missive, from ye, stating that yer investigation has taken ye far tae the north. That ye're chasing clues and ye dunna know when ye'll return, but tae have faith that ye will, someday. That will keep the man from sending anyone else if he knows ye're still hunting the truth. He'll simply have tae wait for ye tae return."

"And I never will."

"Nay, ye never will."

That explained quite a bit and, quite honestly, Tyrus wasn't surprised that she was that thorough. A woman like Lady Warenton had been around a very long time and understood the political game. She understood how it all worked and he had to respect that. But there were other things that weren't clear to him at the moment.

"So you want me at Berwick," he said. "That castle belongs to Cassius' father."

"It does."

"And Cassius does not mind if the man he tried to kill serves his father?"

Jordan shrugged. "Another thing ye'll have tae keep silent on is the fact Cassius knew of Cambria's rumor," she said. "Ye saw him at Folkingham. Ye knew he came back tae warn everyone. And he only injured ye so ye'd not kill Liam, not because he had a personal vendetta."

"I assumed," Tyrus said. "Is he still here?"

Jordan shook her head. "He's returned tae Edward now," she said. "He has no objection tae ye serving his father so long as ye do it well and keep the secrets."

That explained Cassius. The man had gone back to serve Edward as if nothing had happened and, frankly, Tyrus didn't particularly care. He wasn't sworn to Edward, nor did he have any real respect for the man. But there was one more thing he was curious over.

"And Herringthorpe?" he said. "*Did* he survive?"

Jordan nodded. "Survived and thrived," she said. "He had a bit of the poison like ye did, but it dinna last for long. He's already up and walking. At least as much as Bria will let him, but he's recovering."

Tyrus was somewhat relieved to hear it. He was convinced he'd killed Liam, but maybe not all that surprised to hear he hadn't. "He was the best man I've ever fought," he said. "You do understand that there was nothing personal against him. It was only because he interfered with what I'd been tasked to do."

Jordan nodded. "I understand it," she said. "After the fight was over and everyone was calm again, they understood, too. Even Cassius, who was the first one tae point it out. No one here is yer enemy, lad, at least not yet. But ye're in possession of knowledge that canna make it tae the archbishop or the king. So we're going tae keep ye close. Ye're going tae Berwick and serve with distinction or ye'll have tae answer tae me."

Tyrus was thinking that the dowager was more intimidating than anyone he'd ever served before. It wasn't her size or strength or skill in battle, because she didn't have any. But the woman had a mere presence that could melt steel.

He found that fascinating.

"Incredible," he finally said. "Your show of mercy is… incredible."

"I know," Jordan said. "And ye'll remember that mercy should the urge tae speak of what ye know comes tae ye. Ye'll never be shown mercy again if ye do."

"I am well aware of that," he said quietly. "It's simply that I've never been one to show mercy. And now it has been shown to me and I am puzzled."

"Then mayhap ye understand it better than ye did before."

"Mayhap," he said. "But this position at Berwick… I haven't

had a legitimate position in years."

"Ye have one now."

Tyrus could only shake his head in awe. The last position he'd had was serving with the Executioner Knights and the House of de Lohr, but when they exiled him from the spy coven, he'd been without any income, anywhere to go, and anyone to answer to. He'd been alone. It was true that he'd found business as an independent, as he had for the Archbishop of Canterbury, but given that he was now indebted to Lady Warenton, the fact that an actual position had come out of this—with the de Wolfe empire, no less—was truly astounding to him. He'd come to the north to get to the bottom of a mystery and wound up being tasked to serve at a powerful castle.

Truth be told, he was up for the challenge.

"If that is what you wish," he said. "I've never battled the clans before. Can I expect them to be as shrewd as you?"

Her lips twitched with a smile. "No one is as shrewd as me."

"I would sincerely believe that."

Before he could reply, another figure entered the chamber and Tyrus found himself looking at the young woman whom Liam had once introduced to him as Bria. He hadn't seen her since the day he met her, but here she was, in the flesh. She flashed him a smile before handing Jordan neat rolls of bandaging.

"Here, Matha," she said. "Do you need more than that?"

Jordan peered at the wounds. "Nay," she said. "That'll be sufficient."

As the woman turned to leave, Tyrus stopped her. "Wait," he said. "You there, lass. You're *not* Bria."

She smiled broadly. "Nay, I am not."

"Who are you, then?"

"A de Wolfe."

She wasn't going to tell him, but she was smirking about it. Things like that usually annoyed him, but he could see that she was being playful, not nasty. Endearing, even. Whatever it was, it was just this side of sweet.

"Fine," he muttered. "Whoever you are, your deception was clever."

"Did you believe it?"

"I did."

She laughed. "Then I am going to make an excellent spy!"

With that, she skipped out, leaving Jordan grinning and Tyrus grunting. "Please do not let her become a spy," he said softly. "Even if she's not entirely serious, discourage her. It is no life for someone like that."

Jordan began unrolling the bandages. "Ye think not?" she said. "I canna agree with ye. She fooled ye. She can fool anyone."

Tyrus sighed heavily. "Are all of the de Wolfe women like this?"

"Like what?"

"Lovely tyrants?"

Jordan snorted. "Aye, lad," she said. "Every one of us. And don't ye forget it."

He wouldn't.

For as long as Tyrus le Mon lived, he wouldn't.

EPILOGUE

Folkingham Castle
Three Months Later

"IT'S CALLED A Welsh diamond," Liam said. "I hope you like it."

Cambria was still staring at it, the enormous clear stone in a gold setting that he'd placed on her finger. It was absolutely magnificent and she couldn't get enough of it. Nor could Caria, who was seated beside her. The woman had practically torn her hand off trying to get a look at that glorious wedding ring.

"Welsh diamonds!" Caria said gleefully. "I've heard of those, but I've never seen one. Liam, it's beautiful!"

He stood over the pair, smiling down at his wife. "Remember the day my family and I came to Folkingham for the wedding?" he said. "The day that le Mon arrived and the world became chaos? You may or may not recall that I'd brought a gift for you that I was unable to retrieve before everything happened. This is it."

Cambria held up the ring, looking at it in the light. "It was worth the wait, my love," she said. "It's absolutely magnificent. I shall wear it proudly."

Liam simply beamed.

In fact, he couldn't seem to stop beaming. He had been beaming steadily for the past three months as he recovered from his injuries resulting from his battle with Tyrus. The knife wound hadn't been too serious, thankfully, and had missed all of his vital organs, which was a stroke of luck. Therefore, all he'd had to do was endure the stitches, the poison that had briefly touched him, and a recovery time that had been longer than he would have liked. Cambria had been by his side through the entire process, and that was what had him beaming so much. He had never spent three solid months with her during the course of their lifetimes and certainly not during the course of their courtship.

Three solid months with her and he couldn't wait to marry her.

No one had tried to discourage them from being married immediately except for War. He was the one who was reluctant this time because he wanted his son to fully recover before taking on something as taxing as a new marriage. The last thing he needed was for his son to exert himself and end up setting back his recovery. He had tried to explain that to Carlton, who didn't want to hear it because Cambria was weeping daily about not being married. At the ten-week mark since Liam's injury, War finally gave consent for the wedding to take place.

And it had.

Today.

It had been a small ceremony involving the couple and their parents and a priest who blessed the union. All of this took place right outside of the great hall because inside the hall, the festivities had already begun. Brothers and cousins had all taken to drinking the expensive wine that Carlton had provided for the occasion, so by the time the happy couple arrived, everyone was fairly drunk. The attempt to actually make it to the dais had been interrupted by many brotherly hugs, and slugs, and drunken kisses to the bride's cheek. After they suffered through all of that and made it to the table, they were plied with plenty of food and drink and the wedding feast began in earnest.

And what a feast it was.

Scott and his family were in attendance with the exception of Jordan, who'd chosen not to make the long trip back to Folkingham. She was missed, of course, but her presence was felt in the silken veil she'd sent Cambria to wear during the wedding ceremony. Even now, Cambria wore it pinned to the back of her head, proud to wear it, as Caria continued to admire the Welsh diamond ring. Truthfully, she was trying to tug it off, and it was Scott who reached over and pulled her hand away.

"Enough, Cari," he told her. "You are going to break Bria's finger."

Caria grinned up at her adoptive brother. "I just wanted to get a better look at it," she said. "It sparkles so."

He cocked an eyebrow. "You were going to run off with it, you little thief," he said. Then he pointed to the center of the hall, where people were dancing to the music of a man with a lute. "Go and dance. Take the others with you."

He meant his children, sitting at the table and bored because they didn't yet appreciate a good wedding feast. But they did appreciate a good dance. Caria leapt up and ran down the table, collecting Seraphina and then Scott and Avrielle's youngest daughter, Jordan. The little girls rushed out to those dancing, pulling on the hands of Kyle, now fully recovered, and Logan, who viewed young girls as one would view the plague—

uninteresting, disgusting, and not to be danced with. He preferred a lass his own age, of which there were none, so in the end, he was forced to dance with little Jordan.

The sight made Scott grin.

"The lad needs to learn to be tolerant," he said. But then he turned to the couple. "As for you two, now might be the time to slip away. Everyone is either drunk or dancing and not paying attention to you."

Carlton, on his daughter's other side, heartily agreed. "Aye," he said. "Go, now. Your mother is already in your chamber, making sure it is warm and well prepared. You can bid her a good night and send her back to me."

Liam was already on his feet, looking to his father down the table. "Papa?" he said. "We are retiring. If you wish to kiss the bride, now is the time."

War, who had been trying to convince Annaleigh to dance with him, got out of his chair at his son's statement. Annaleigh stood up also, and together, the pair of them moved for the happy couple. Annaleigh hugged her son, but she was more interested in Cambria. In fact, she took the woman affectionately by the arm and began to walk away with her.

Frowning, Liam watched them go.

"She's running off with my wife," he said, pointing. "Where is she going?"

As Scott and Carlton chuckled, War fought off a grin. "Probably telling her what to avoid in the marital bed," he muttered. "Telling her that she should not do anything involving whips or ropes."

Scott, and even Carlton, burst out laughing as Liam scowled at his father. "Christ, Papa," he hissed. "Why do you do it? You are a terrible, terrible man to say such things."

War broke down in soft laughter, putting his arm around his son's shoulders and kissing him on the side of the head. "You make an easy target," he said. But quickly, he sobered. "In truth, I wish you nothing but the best. Bria is a wonderful woman, Liam. You are blessed."

Liam softened. "I am," he said. "Thank you, Papa."

War simply nodded, feeling emotional. He honestly didn't trust himself to speak more than he already had, but there was something else he needed to say before his emotions overwhelmed him completely.

"Your mother has something to give you and Bria," he said, gesturing to the women heading out of the hall. "Go with them."

Liam didn't hesitate. He made his way out of the hall, with his father following behind him, before catching up to his mother and wife as they stepped out into the sunset. But just as he reached them, he noticed a shadow by his side and turned to see Bran strolling next to him. Smiling, he paused long enough to bend over and give his dog an affectionate pat.

"Not tonight, old man," he said. "Go back and sit with Papa. Go on, now."

He was pointing to the hall, where War was standing in the entry. War whistled to the dog, who ran happily to the man who would feed him scraps from his plate. As War and Bran headed back into the hall, Liam bolted after his mother and his wife. By the time he caught them again, his mother had her arm around Cambria's shoulders, so Liam took her hand as they headed for the keep.

"I must say, that was one of the tamest weddings I've attended with a de Wolfe involved," Annaleigh said. "The de Wolfe weddings are legendary for their debauchery."

Cambria looked at her in disbelief. "Lady Jordan would permit such a thing?" she said. "I do not believe it."

Annaleigh chuckled. "I'm not saying she permits it," she said. "But her lads do it anyway. They sing terrible songs, jump on tables, and become ragingly drunk."

"Sounds like a good time," Liam said. "Scott was here. He's her lad. Why did he not jump on the table and sing?"

Annaleigh laughed. "Because Scott couldna carry a tune in a bucket," she said. "Moreover, he's the Earl of Warenton, so some decorum must be maintained."

They were all grinning by the time they passed into the keep and up the stairs. Cambria was wearing the magnificent scarlet wedding dress, and it took both Liam and Annaleigh to help her up the steps with it. By the time they reached her chamber, everyone was carrying some part of the skirt. Liam let his portion fall to the floor as he escorted his bride into her chamber.

Fair Lydia greeted them.

"Ah," she said, moving away from the table she'd just set, laden with food and drink. "Are the festivities over now?"

Cambria shook her head as Liam inspected the offerings on the table. "Nay," she said. "There is dancing and music happening now. Papa wants you to come to him and enjoy it."

"I will," Fair Lydia said. "I simply wanted to make sure your chamber was perfect. And my thanks to Lady Warenton for escorting you."

She smiled at Annaleigh, who smiled in return. The women had developed a fond friendship with one another, which was lovely to see.

"Thank you, Mama," Cambria said sincerely. "For everything you've done… thank you."

Fair Lydia hugged her daughter before gently kissing her on the cheek. "You have been worth every joy, every tear," she said, gazing at her sweetly. "Some women have daughters by blood, but I had a daughter by heart. You *are* my heart, Bria. And this life we have led at Folkingham is the life you were meant for. Sometimes destiny is not always what is expected. It is what is chosen. I chose your destiny the day I met you."

Cambria hugged her mother tightly. "Thank you," she whispered. "I love you very much."

Fair Lydia kissed her daughter once more and released her, heading out of the chamber. Annaleigh paused before following.

"I have something for ye two," she said. "Liam, I want tae give ye something that William de Wolfe gave tae me on the day I married yer father. As ye can imagine, the subject of yer father was a difficult one with Jordan, though she never let on. She's been nothing but accepting of War since the beginning. Even though he dinna carry the de Wolfe name, William wanted yer father and me tae have something from his family that meant something tae him."

That had Liam's interest. "What is it, Mama?"

Reaching into a pocket on her surcoat, she pulled forth a small, silken pouch. Taking Cambria's hand, she opened the pouch and poured the contents into Cambria's palm. A golden brooch suddenly came into focus, gleaming in the weak light of the chamber. It was of a flower design, with yellow stones in it, and Cambria gasped in delight.

"It's beautiful," she said, holding it up for Liam to see. "Where did it come from?"

Annaleigh watched Liam carefully grasp it and hold it up to the light. "It belonged tae William's mother, Adalira," she said.

"She wasna born in England, but in a faraway country where a flower like this grows. William told me that the brooch is hundreds of years old and has been in his mother's family all that time. All the way back tae the beginning of the world, she told him."

"It's beautiful," Liam said, turning it over and seeing something on the back. "What's this writing?"

Annaleigh smiled at him. "It's not from this land," she said. "It says 'love is the beginning of forever' in the Saracen language. William's mother was half Saracen, ye see. From an ancient family with ancient bloodlines. He told me that she died when he was quite young and this was the only thing he had of her, so guard it well. It is meant tae be cherished."

Cambria had it back in her hands now, inspecting it. When she looked up again, there were tears in her eyes.

"I have nothing from my ancient bloodlines," she said. "Royal bloodlines that go back for centuries, yet all I have of that is who I am. I cannot even be called by my real name. All of that was taken from me, and although I do not regret the life I have or the people I love, I do regret having nothing that was part of my past. But this… this is part of Liam's past, from a woman who passed it to her son because it was precious to her. It represented those who went before her. I shall always treasure it as a representative of those who lived and loved."

Annaleigh smiled, giving her a hug and kissing her on the cheek. "It has been a beautiful day," she murmured, blowing her son a kiss. "Make tonight the beginning of yer forever."

With that, she was gone, shutting the door quietly behind her. Liam went to the panel and threw the bolt before turning to his wife.

"Well?" he said. "Do you want to eat something? I do not

think you have eaten very much today."

Cambria shook her head. "I haven't," she said. "But I am not terribly hungry."

She was still clutching the gold brooch, looking at it as she wandered toward the hearth. He was just picking up a cup of wine, but when he noticed how close she was to the flame in her voluminous dress, he stopped her.

"Wait," he said, setting the cup down and going to her. "Back up from that fire. It would not be conducive to a glorious wedding night if your dress went up in flames, so let's get you out of it and then you can wander as you like."

Cambria snorted. "That is an original excuse."

He was already going to work on unfastening the stays on her back. "Excuse for what?"

"Getting me out of this dress."

He started to laugh. "It is working, is it not?" he said. "Worse still, you fell for it. You carry the blame for shedding your wedding dress, not I."

She giggled as he finished with the stays in the back, buffeting her around as he went for the ones on her right side. With everything loosened, she was able to step out of the dress without a problem. He picked it up and laid it on a chair near the wardrobe as she went to her dressing table and put the brooch in a small box that contained her jewelry.

"There," she said. "The brooch is safe."

He smiled at her, hands on hips as he looked her over in her shift. "It was sweet of my mother to give that to us," he said. "Not that I need a brooch to tell me that our love will last forever, because I know that already. But the sentimental value of the piece is priceless."

Cambria went to sit down to remove her shoes. "I must say

that it is quite generous of the dowager Lady Warenton to embrace your father and your family as she has," she said. "Honestly, Liam, if a woman came to me in twenty years and told me that she had your child before we knew one another, I'm not entirely sure how I would react."

He suddenly bolted for the door, startling her. When she saw him reaching for the latch, she called after him.

"Wait!" she said. "Where are you going?"

He still had his hand on the latch. "I have to find all of those women I had children with and tell them not to come!" he said. "I do not want you to box my ears!"

Cambria shrieked and threw both of her shoes at him, one at a time. He began laughing, fending them off easily, picking up one of them and throwing it back at her. The shoes went back and forth, and so did a pillow until Liam grabbed it and ran at her, trying to smack her with it. Cambria screamed and climbed up on the bed, but he threw himself on top of her to prevent her from escaping.

"Now what are you going to do?" he said, trapping her wrists with one hand and letting his free hand tickle her ribs. "You're brave when I'm across the room, but you are a coward when I'm next to you. Go ahead—tell me how you would react to news of my bastard children."

Cambria was giggling and screaming at the same time. "Stop!" she commanded. "Stop or you'll be sorry!"

"I do not think so."

He continued to tickle her, only to pause so she could catch her breath, and then he'd start again. That went on a few times until the final pause. Instead of trying to catch her breath, Cambria craned her neck up and kissed him on the mouth.

That was all it took for the mood to shift.

And it shifted very quickly.

The bed they were upon was big, commensurate with the size of the chamber, with four posters and a great curtain strung around it. As the flames burned in the hearth, sending rippling, golden light into the room, Liam stopped his tickling, his playing, and fused his mouth to Cambria's. It was a deep, lusty kiss. But the problem was that he was still clothed, so, keeping his mouth on hers, he began to remove anything he could get his hands on.

Cambria's arms were around his neck as he kissed her and she could feel him moving about, removing his belt. As that fell away, he pulled his mouth away from hers and silently stood up, bending over and yanking his tunic over his head. He tossed it aside, barely missing the fireplace, and they both laughed. Naked from the waist up, he quickly returned his attention to his wife.

She was sitting up on the bed now. Without a word, he sat down beside her, his eyes drifting over the white shift she was wearing. Her shoes were off, but the hose were still on. Pale cleavage swelled from the neckline of the shift and Liam's gaze was drawn to it. God, he'd dreamt of this moment. He simply couldn't wait any longer. One arm went around her shoulders as the other went to her torso, and he pulled her close again, his mouth on her neck as the hand on her torso began to gently stroke the curve of her hip.

"My Bria," he murmured, kissing her tender flesh. "I cannot tell you how long I have waited for this moment, and now that it is here, all I want to do is touch you. You are the most beautiful creature in the world."

Cambria's eyes were closed as he kissed her neck, the hand on her hip moving gently to her ribs. She was so overwhelmed with his heated lips against her skin that she threw her arms around his neck again, falling back onto the bed and pulling him down with her. Liam gladly let her take the lead, his enormous body covering her own. Flesh to flesh, touch to touch, it was a magical moment.

His seeking lips found her mouth again and he resumed kissing her with more passion than he could express. The hand on her ribs moved to her left breast and she emitted a soft groan as she felt his hand against her bosom. Like the most natural of actions, his hand enclosed her breast and he squeezed gently, fondling her. Cambria groaned again when she realized how good it felt.

The sounds coming out of her mouth were setting Liam on fire. He couldn't seem to kiss her enough, taste her enough, and the hand on her breast grew bolder. He slipped his fingers along the neckline, trying to pull it away somehow, but the shift didn't have much give and he had no patience for it. As their kisses increased in intensity, he took hold of the top of her neckline and ripped it in half in one swift, clean motion.

Cambria gasped with surprise as the shift fell away and her naked torso was exposed underneath. Liam's mouth was on her cleavage before she could take another breath, and before she realized what he was doing, he took a pink nipple in his mouth and latched on furiously.

That nearly brought Cambria off the bed.

Clutching the coverlet beneath her as if that could keep her sane, she cried out softly as his hot, wet mouth pulled her nipple into a hard little pellet. He had somehow managed to wedge himself in between her legs at that point, his heated body overwhelming her, and Cambria was consumed with him. He was finally touching her, as a husband touches a wife, and she was enjoying every second of it.

She wanted more.

Liam paused long enough to yank his breeches off before collapsing back against her, his mouth returning to her breasts. Her flesh was sweet and delicious and he nursed hungrily, first one and then the other, leaving her flesh wet with his saliva. Her entire chest area was wet with his saliva, and it further inflamed him as he feasted on her flesh.

He'd never been so wildly aroused in his entire life.

But there was more.

He wanted to taste everything.

From where he was, he could smell the delicious, musky scent of her woman's center, and his mouth left her breasts, trailing down her torso until he came to the thatch of dark hair between her legs. Grasping her buttocks with both hands, he descended on the sweet pink folds with gusto.

He feasted.

Cambria had to shove her hands into her mouth, stifling a cry of passion that would have surely raised the roof, as Liam put his face between her legs. If there had been any words of protest, they died on her lips when she quickly realized how marvelous it felt. His tongue was stroking her, and he was grunting softly with every lap of the tongue as he became acquainted with her in the most intimate way possible. He thought it would be enough to satisfy him, at least for a little while, but it wasn't.

He needed all of her.

All he could think of was joining his body to hers at that point. He'd shown her what pleasure was like. Now he was going to show her what ecstasy was like. When he realized she had opened her legs wide to him, waiting for that innate act of mating to take place, he knew that the time had come.

He wasn't going to make either one of them wait any longer.

Lifting himself up, Liam found Cambria's lips once again as he carefully guided his manhood into her tender, virginal walls. Thrusting gently with his hips, he seated himself halfway on the first thrust, giving her a little time to adjust, before thrusting a second time that saw him nearly completely buried in her. Beneath him, Cambria cried out softly at the sensation of his enormous member inside her, but she was so consumed by his delicious kisses and heated body that all she could do was encourage him as he thrust into her. It seemed like the most natural state of being, his body buried deep within hers as it was always meant to be.

It was bliss.

They were so highly aroused that on the fourth or fifth thrust, Cambria cried out softly at the thrill of her first climax. Liam could feel her wet heat throbbing around him, milking him for his seed, and he didn't want to answer her. Not now. Not yet. He wanted to enjoy this moment he'd waited so long for, but already, he knew it was the best moment of his life. It wasn't long before he could feel his own release approaching, and he embraced it, thrusting into her with one hard, final movement before releasing himself, filling her womb with his essence. But even after he released himself, he continued to grind his pelvis against her, feeling her shake with another climax.

And another.

Liam wasn't entirely sure when he stopped thrusting into her. Maybe he hadn't. Maybe he still was. He was dazed from it all, lingering in a world where only Cambria's body mattered to him. The feel of her, the touch of her, the smell of her. Her legs were wrapped around his hips, her arms around his neck, and her soft breasts pressed against his chest. Wasn't this what pure perfection was supposed to be? Pure delight?

Pure love?

He considered himself the most fortunate man who had ever lived.

In fact, he knew he was.

Nine months and two days later, a fat baby boy was born to Cambria and Liam after an entire day of labor. The wait was excruciating for Liam, but he didn't have to endure it alone because his parents had come to Easington Castle for the birth. Therefore, he sat with his father and all but two of his brothers, drinking and talking, waiting out the birth while Cambria struggled to bring forth their son. When the baby finally came, big and healthy, the first thing Liam noticed about his son was that he had black hair like his mother.

It was the most beautiful sight he'd ever seen.

Little William Cai Herringthorpe, who was to go by his Welsh name of Cai, had a hell of a heritage to live up to as the grandson of Llywelyn the Last. Although his creation had originally been the result of an act of vengeance, and one of political rebellion, the fates had been kind. What had started out as something harsh and punishing had turned into a love story for the ages.

A romance of legend.

An English knight, a Welsh princess, and a love that would last for eternity. Eventually, Liam and Cambria's youngest daughter was named Gwenllian in tribute to Cambria's birth origins and her royal heritage, and when Gwen Herringthorpe married, it was also for love.

But that's another story altogether.

Cariad yw dechrau am byth.
Love is the beginning of forever.
For Liam and Cambria, it was.

☙ THE END ☙

Children of Liam and Cambria
Cai
Rhys
Theo
Ophelia
Morgana
Adalira
Gerallt
Roan
Gwenllian

De Wolfe Pack Generations:
WolfeHeart
WolfeStrike
WolfeSword
WolfeBlade
WolfeLord
WolfeShield
Nevermore
WolfeAx
WolfeBorn
WolfeBite
WolfeHound

Author's Afterword

I truly hoped you enjoyed Liam and Cambria's story.

Quite a wild ride, wasn't it? But what a joy it was to write about those two. Every story I write is different, and while conflict between the main characters can make it fun sometimes, I really enjoy the stories where the hero and heroine really get along. That just makes it so sweet. And that's what we're all here for—romance!

Now, here's where fact and fiction are seamlessly blended in this tale. I had so much fun using a real historical figure in this novel. As I mentioned in the note, I don't ever do that. I can't recall when I have. So it was a challenge keeping what we know about Gwenllian of Wales accurate while also writing a fictional, alternative-reality story about her.

Here's where it gets interesting:

It was true that, whilst in captivity at Sempringham Priory, Gwenllian called herself "Wentliane." Speculation was that she either didn't know her real name or simply didn't remember it, but she signed documents "Wentliane." That being the case, wouldn't it make sense that if she had truly been a farmer's daughter, a toddler who went by the name Wentliane, then she would know her name and continue to use it even as she grew into adulthood even though others told her that she was someone else? Even the priory recorded her name as "Wentcilian."

So… maybe it wasn't Gwenllian, after all. At least, in my

story it wasn't. I think an ending like this for her is much more satisfying than living a life of isolation in a convent.

You may be asking what actually happened to Wentliane/Gwenllian—in real life, she lived into her fifties and died a nun. No fanfare. No revolts or rebellions. She simply died relatively young and faded in the annals of history. A rather sad ending, I think, for so important a historical figure.

In our story, it's the same thing—the decoy Gwenllian/Wentliane died and that was the end of it. In real life, Edward II had no interest in the Welsh princess, certainly not the interest that his father or even his grandfather had in the Welsh, so we'll have to assume in our story that that's what happened, too. No pursuit of the rumor of the de Royans' daughter. Edward II really didn't care. He had bigger fish to fry, so to speak. We can rightly assume that there was never the threat against Cambria again after Tyrus was so ably controlled by Lady Warenton. Gotta love Jordan.

Speaking of Tyrus, he's the wild card in all of this. I will admit that I was going to kill him off. That was always the plan. But the more I wrote about him, the more I liked him and thought he'd be a great addition to the Executioner Knights series. What better antihero than a guy who got himself kicked out of the Executioner Knights because of his inability to show emotion? And what if it takes the right woman for him to finally fall in love? What Jordan did for him when he was wounded already started that ball rolling—he experienced genuine mercy and compassion. Does he remain at Berwick? We may find that out. Look for a future EK novel with Tyrus as the hero. What fun that one will be!

And how much fun was a brief appearance by Caria de Wolfe? I had TWO Welsh princesses in this book. Caria is slightly younger than Cambria (about a year) and remember that she and Atlas Abril fell in love (from WOLFEHEART), so there's no way I can pair her up with Tyrus if you were hoping for that. But, then again, never say never. It would be a lot of fun—and so ironic—if she ended up as Tyrus' love interest. We'll just have to wait and see if that pans out.

For those of you who read BATTLEWOLFE, did you realize the brooch Annaleigh gave to Cambria was, indeed, the same one William de Wolfe had given to her? I love being able to pass that down to the next generation.

Now, a few things to note also.

The poem spoken to Cassius in the tavern when he was toasting his grandfather and Paris and Kieran is, indeed, a very old Nordic poem about Valhalla:

Wine to carry,

as for a king's coming,

here to me I expect

heroes' coming from the world,

certain great ones,

so glad is my heart.

The entire poem is quite long, so this was just a snippet of it.

Lastly, Welsh diamonds really are a thing. Google them!

With lasting appreciation and affection,

Kathryn

The Parents, Children, and Grandchildren of de Wolfe

(Note: Don't be intimidated by these family trees—skip over them if you wish and then refer back to them if you need clarification on a relationship)

William (deceased 1296 A.D.) and Jordan Scott de Wolfe
Total children: 10
Total grandchildren: 75 (including 4 deceased, 7 adopted, 3 step grandchildren)

Scott (Troy's twin)—(Wife #1 Lady Athena de Norville, has issue. Wife #2 Lady Avrielle Huntley du Rennic, has issue)

With Athena
- William (married Lily de Lohr, has issue.)
- Thomas "Tor"
- Andrew (deceased)
- Beatrice (deceased)

With Avrielle
- Sophia (with Nathaniel du Rennic)
- Stephen (with Nathaniel du Rennic)
- Sorcha (with Nathaniel du Rennic)
- Jeremy
- Nathaniel

- Alexander
- Seraphina
- Jordan

Troy (Scott's twin)—(Wife #1 Lady Helene de Norville, has issue. Wife #2 Lady Rhoswyn Kerr, has issue)

With Helene
- Andreas
- Acacia (deceased)
- Arista (deceased)

With Rhoswyn
- Gareth
- Corey
- Reed
- Tavin
- Tristan
- Elsbeth
- Madeleine

Patrick—(Married to Lady Brighton de Favereux, has issue)
- Markus
- Cassius
- Magnus
- Titus
- Thora
- Kristiana

James—(Wife #1 Lady Rose Hage, has issue. Wife #2 Asmara ap Cader, has issue)

With Rose
- Ronan
- Isabella

With Asmara (as Blayth)
- Maddoc
- Bowen
- Caius
- Garreth (known as Garr)

Katheryn (James' twin)—(Married to Sir Alec Hage, has issue)
- Edward
- Axel
- Christoph
- Kieran
- Christian

Evelyn—(Married to Sir Hector de Norville, has issue)
- Atreus
- Hermes
- Lisbet
- Adele
- Aline
- Lesander (goes by Zander)

Baby de Wolfe—(Died same day. Christened Madeleine)

Edward—(Married to Lady Cassiopeia de Norville, has issue)
- Helene
- Phoebe
- Hestia
- Asteria
- Leonidas
- Dorian
- Dayne
- Stephan
- Pallas

Thomas—(Married to Lady Maitland "Mae" de Ryes Bowlin, has issue)
- Artus (adopted)
- Nora (adopted)
- Phin (adopted)
- Marybelle (adopted)
- Renard & Roland (adopted)
- Dyana (adopted)
- Alexander
- Cabot
- Matthew
- Wade
- Tacey
- Morgan

Penelope—(Married to Bhrodi de Shera, Earl of Coventry, hereditary King of Anglesey)
- William
- Perri
- Bowen
- Dai
- Catrin
- Morgana
- Maddock
- Anthea
- Talan

Warrick "War" Herringthorpe (William's illegitimate son with Jane de Percy, born before Scott/Troy)
- Liam "Wolfehound"
- Kyle
- Taggart "Tag"
- Logan
- Brody
- Jane
- Mary
- McCall "Mac"
- Edmund "Teddy"

Holdings and Titles of the House of de Wolfe and close allies as of 1300 a.d.

Scott de Wolfe—Earl of Warenton (Heir: William "Will" de Wolfe, Lord Killham)

Troy de Wolfe—Lord Braemoor (Heir: Andreas de Wolfe)

Patrick de Wolfe—Earl of Berwick (Heir: Markus de Wolfe, Lord Ravensdowne)

Blayth (James) de Wolfe—Baron Sydenham (Heir: Ronan de Wolfe)

Edward de Wolfe—Baron Kentmere (Heir: Leonidas de Wolfe)

Thomas de Wolfe—Earl of Northumbria (Heir: Alexander de Wolfe, Lord Easington)

Wark Castle (Wolfe's Eye):
Larger outpost for the Earl of Warenton. Literally sits on the border between England and Scotland.
- Titus de Wolfe (son of Patrick de Wolfe), commander
- Ronan de Wolfe (son of Blayth/James de Wolfe)

Berwick Castle (Wolfe's Teeth):
Massive border castle, strategically important, de Wolfe holding and seat of the Earl of Berwick, Patrick de Wolfe
- Alec Hage, commander
- Edward "Eddie" Hage, commander
- Hermes de Norville, second

Castle Questing (Wolfe's Heart):
Massive fortress, seat of the Earl of Warenton, Scott de Wolfe.
- Apollo de Norville, second
- Nathaniel Hage
- Owen le Mon

Rule Water Castle (Wolfe's Lair):
The largest outpost in the de Wolfe empire, known as The Lair. Seat of William "Will" de Wolfe, Viscount Kilham, heir apparent to the Earldom of Warenton.
- Magnus de Wolfe, second
- Adonis de Norville, second
- Perri de Shera, son of the Earl of Coventry and Penelope de Wolfe de Shera (squire)

Monteviot Tower (Wolfe's Shield):
Smaller outpost in Scotland, strategic. Holding of Troy de Wolfe.
- Andreas de Wolfe, commander

Kale Water Castle (Wolfe's Den):
Larger outpost on the England side of the border, strategic.
- Troy de Wolfe, Lord Braemoor, commander
- Troy also commands Sibbald's Hold, former home of Red Keith Kerr (his wife's father). A minor property commanded by son Garreth de Wolfe.

Kyloe Castle (Wolfe's Howl):
Seat of the Earl of Northumbria, Thomas de Wolfe
- Christoph Hage, second

Roxburgh Castle (Wolfe's Claw—unofficially)*

Large royal-held castle near Kelso, formerly manned by knights from Northwood, but awarded to the House of de Wolfe by royal decree for meritorious service to the Crown. Volatile location, often attacked by Scots, and is manned by both royal and de Wolfe troops.

- Blayth (James) de Wolfe, Lord Sydenham, commander
- Axel Hage, second

* Note: Because of the extreme volatile location and nature of this garrison, Blayth (James) de Wolfe was given the title Lord Sydenham and the Sydenham Barony, a small but strategic barony between Wark Castle and the town of Kelso.

Blackpool Castle (acquired by Scott de Wolfe around 1300 A.D.) known as Wolfe's Strike:

- Thomas "Tor" de Wolfe, commander
- Christian Hage, second

Northwood Castle:

Massive border castle, very important and strategic. Belonging to the Earls of Teviot. Not part of the de Wolfe empire, but strongly allied to de Wolfe by marriage and blood. The Earl of Teviot is John Adrian de Longley, Adam de Longley's eldest son. Adrian's mother is Cayetana Fernanda Teresita Silva y Fausto de Longley, Princess of Aragon.

- Hector de Norville, captain of the guard (also Lord Bowmont)
- Atreus de Norville, second
- Tobias de Bocage, second

Edenburn Tower (House of de Norville):

Smaller tower on the southern end of de Wolfe properties

belonging to the House of de Norville. Owned and commanded by Alec Hage

Castle Canaan (Kendal) Wolfe's Bite:
The Earl of Warenton's southernmost holding, not directly related to the Scottish border but a source of additional troops if needed. Inherited the property when he married the widow of Castle Canaan.
- Stephan du Rennic, commander

Seven Gates Castle (Kendal):
- Seat of Edward de Wolfe's Barony—Kentmere in Kendal that adjoins brother Scott's lands at Castle Canaan
- Isleworth House, Surrey

Cheswick Castle (Northumberland) Wolfe's Roar:
- Seat of Markus de Wolfe, Lord Ravensdowne, heir to Berwick earldom
- Also included in this alliance is Trastamara Castle, home of Markus' stepson, Atlas de Abril (formerly Atlas de Sauque) and wife Caria de Wolfe de Abril.

Easington Castle (garrison to Bamburgh)
- Liam Herringthorpe, commander

(not genuinely considered a de Wolfe property, but Liam bears the de Wolfe tattoo because of his de Wolfe blood and is accepted by the family as such)

Kathryn Le Veque Novels

Medieval Romance:

De Wolfe Pack Series:
Warwolfe
The Wolfe
Nighthawk
ShadowWolfe
DarkWolfe
A Joyous de Wolfe Christmas
BlackWolfe
Serpent
A Wolfe Among Dragons
Scorpion
StormWolfe
Dark Destroyer
The Lion of the North
Walls of Babylon
The Best Is Yet To Be
BattleWolfe
Castle of Bones

De Wolfe Pack Generations:
WolfeHeart
WolfeStrike
WolfeSword
WolfeBlade
WolfeLord
WolfeShield
Nevermore
WolfeAx
WolfeBorn
WolfeBite
WolfeHound

The Executioner Knights:
By the Unholy Hand
The Mountain Dark
Starless
A Time of End
Winter of Solace
Lord of the Sky
The Splendid Hour
The Whispering Night
Netherworld
Lord of the Shadows
Of Mortal Fury
'Twas the Executioner Knight
Before Christmas
Crimson Shield
The Black Dragon

The de Russe Legacy:
The Falls of Erith
Lord of War: Black Angel
The Iron Knight
Beast
The Dark One: Dark Knight
The White Lord of Wellesbourne
Dark Moon
Dark Steel
A de Russe Christmas Miracle
Dark Warrior

The de Lohr Dynasty:
While Angels Slept
Rise of the Defender
Steelheart

Shadowmoor
Silversword
Spectre of the Sword
Unending Love
Archangel
A Blessed de Lohr Christmas
Lion of Twilight
Lion of War
Lion of Hearts
Lion of Steel
Lion of Thunder

The Brothers de Lohr:
The Earl in Winter

Lords of East Anglia:
While Angels Slept
Godspeed
Age of Gods and Mortals

Great Lords of le Bec:
Great Protector

House of de Royans:
Lord of Winter
To the Lady Born
The Centurion

Lords of Eire:
Echoes of Ancient Dreams
Lord of Black Castle
The Darkland

Ancient Kings of Anglecynn:
The Whispering Night
Netherworld

Battle Lords of de Velt:
The Dark Lord
Devil's Dominion
Bay of Fear

The Dark Lord's First Christmas
The Dark Spawn
The Dark Conqueror
The Dark Angel

Reign of the House of de Winter:
Lespada
Swords and Shields

De Reyne Domination:
Guardian of Darkness
The Black Storm
A Cold Wynter's Knight
With Dreams
Master of the Dawn
One Wylde Knight

House of d'Vant:
Tender is the Knight (House of d'Vant)
The Red Fury (House of d'Vant)

The Dragonblade Series:
Fragments of Grace
Dragonblade
Island of Glass
The Savage Curtain
The Fallen One
The Phantom Bride

Great Marcher Lords of de Lara
Lord of the Shadows
Dragonblade

House of St. Hever
Fragments of Grace
Island of Glass
Queen of Lost Stars

Lords of Pembury:
The Savage Curtain

Lords of Thunder: The de Shera Brotherhood Trilogy
The Thunder Lord
The Thunder Warrior
The Thunder Knight

The Great Knights of de Moray:
Shield of Kronos
The Gorgon

The House of De Nerra:
The Promise
The Falls of Erith
Vestiges of Valor
Realm of Angels

Highland Legion:
Highland Born
Highland Destroyer

Highland Warriors of Munro:
The Red Lion
Deep Into Darkness

The House of de Garr:
Lord of Light
Realm of Angels

Saxon Lords of Hage:
The Crusader
Kingdom Come

High Warriors of Rohan:
High Warrior
High King

The House of Ashbourne:
Upon a Midnight Dream

The House of D'Aurilliac:
Valiant Chaos

The House of De Dere:
Of Love and Legend

St. John and de Gare Clans:
The Warrior Poet

The House of de Bretagne:
The Questing

The House of Summerlin:
The Legend

The Kingdom of Hendocia:
Kingdom by the Sea

The BlackChurch Guild: Shadow Knights:
The Leviathan
The Protector
The Swordsman
The Tempest

Guard of Six:
Absolution
Insurrection

Regency Historical Romance:
Sin Like Flynn: A Regency Historical Romance Duet
The Sin Commandments
Georgina and the Red Charger

Gothic Regency Romance:
Emma

Historical Fiction:
The Girl Made Of Stars

Contemporary Romance:

Kathlyn Trent/Marcus Burton Series:

Valley of the Shadow
The Eden Factor
Canyon of the Sphinx

The Eagle Brotherhood (under the pen name Kat Le Veque):
The Sunset Hour
The Killing Hour
The Secret Hour
The Unholy Hour
The Burning Hour
The Ancient Hour
The Devil's Hour

Sons of Poseidon:
The Immortal Sea

Pirates of Britannia Series (with Eliza Knight):
Savage of the Sea by Eliza Knight
Leader of Titans by Kathryn Le Veque
The Sea Devil by Eliza Knight
Sea Wolfe by Kathryn Le Veque

Note: All Kathryn's novels are designed to be read as stand-alones, although many have cross-over characters or cross-over family groups. Novels that are grouped together have related characters or family groups. You will notice that some series have the same books; that is because they are cross-overs. A hero in one book may be the secondary character in another.

There is NO reading order except by chronology, but even in that case, you can still read the books as stand-alones. No novel is connected to another by a cliff hanger, and every book has an HEA.

Series are clearly marked. All series contain the same characters or family groups except the American Heroes Series, which is an anthology with unrelated characters.

For more information, find it in **A Reader's Guide to the Medieval World of Le Veque.**

About Kathryn Le Veque

Bringing the Medieval to Romance

KATHRYN LE VEQUE is a critically acclaimed, multiple USA TODAY Bestselling author, an Indie Reader bestseller, a charter Amazon All-Star author, and a #1 bestselling, award-winning, multi-published author in Medieval Historical Romance with over 100 published novels.

Kathryn is a multiple award nominee and winner, including the winner of Uncaged Book Reviews Magazine 2017 and 2018 "Raven Award" for Favorite Medieval Romance. Kathryn is also a multiple RONE nominee (InD'Tale Magazine), holding a record for the number of nominations. In 2018, her novel WARWOLFE was the winner in the Romance category of the Book Excellence Award and in 2019, her novel A WOLFE AMONG DRAGONS won the prestigious RONE award for best pre-16th century romance.

Kathryn is considered one of the top Indie authors in the world with over 2M copies in circulation, and her novels have been translated into several languages. Kathryn recently signed with Sourcebooks Casablanca for a Medieval Fight Club series, first published in 2020.

In addition to her own published works, Kathryn is also the President/CEO of Dragonblade Publishing, a boutique publishing house specializing in Historical Romance. Dragonblade's success has seen it rise in the ranks to become Amazon's #1 e-book publisher of Historical Romance (K-Lytics report July 2020).

Kathryn loves to hear from her readers. Please find Kathryn on Facebook at Kathryn Le Veque, Author, or join her on Twitter @kathrynleveque. Sign up for Kathryn's blog at www.kathrynleveque.com for the latest news and sales.

www.ingramcontent.com/pod-product-compliance
Ingram Content Group UK Ltd.
Pitfield, Milton Keynes, MK11 3LW, UK
UKHW021302210825
7514UKWH00031B/349